TANIS RICHARDS: MASQUERADE

ORIGINS OF DESTINY – BOOK 2

BY M. D. COOPER

Just in Time (JIT) & Beta Readers

Jim Dean
Timothy Van Oosterwyk Bruyn
Marti Panikkar
Alastar Wilson
Scott Reid
David Wilson
Steven Blevins
Gene Bryan

ISBN: 978-1-64365-018-0

Version 1.0.0

Cover Art by Andrew Dobell
Editing by Jen McDonnell, Bird's Eye Books

TABLE OF CONTENTS

FOREWORD

Ever since I read *The Dolphins of Pern* by Anne McCaffrey, I wondered about other life on Earth, and what it would be like to give it some gentle nudges toward greater intelligence.

Though most of us grew up thinking that chimps and some of the great apes were the smartest non-human creatures on Earth, we're learning that there are more ways to measure intelligence than we thought.

A major factor is the brain mass to body mass ratio. A massive brain doesn't directly correlate to intelligence, since most of the brain's focus is on controlling the body.

Humans rule the roost here, and, surprisingly, dolphins typically come in second (though individual members of different species vary). The animal that comes closest to us the most often is the orca (killer whale), which is the largest of the dolphin family.

Fun point, dolphins are not closely related to any other sea creature. The closest living animal to them is the hippo. Weird that hippos are so angry, and dolphins are so helpful and happy.

We're also learning that the 'intelligence switch' in the brain is not the same in all animals as it is in humans. For example, a part of the human brain that does relatively little is larger in parrots and ravens and thought to be their intelligence switch.

A key element of Aeon 14 books is the belief that we're going to find ways to make every nook and cranny in the Sol System habitable, and we're going to bring our Earth life with us. So it won't be surprising that the seas of Mars, Venus, Ceres, and—of course—Europa are filled with creatures such as dolphins.

Since Europa's ocean (which contains *much* more water than all of Earth's oceans) is covered by kilometers of ice, dolphins and other sea mammals that live there will have to be modified to breathe through gills, but perhaps they will also be modified in other ways.

That is one of the other key elements of this story, the prevalence of mods, and how readily some people will alter themselves. In a future where adding a second set of arms is very nearly outpatient surgery—and entirely reversible—it will become common to see people trying out just about everything they can think of.

In the future, chances are that we'll make our own aliens.

Michael Cooper
Danvers, 2018

PREVIOUSLY IN ORIGINS OF DESTINY...

If you've not read Tanis Richards: Shore Leave (book 1 of the Origins of Destiny series), I encourage you to do so. However, if you'd just like to jump into this story, or you've read it all and just need a refresher, then this will get you up to speed.

Aeon 14 is a portrayal of the future I hope our race will occupy. It's not a perfect place—because we are not perfect—but it is a future where humanity (and our creation, the AIs) has managed to learn well enough how to survive, expanding out into the far reaches of the Sol System, and even to other stars.

At the time this story takes place, it is just over two thousand years from now. Lives are measured in centuries, and trillions of humans fill the Sol System.

Mega-structures have been built, such as the Mars 1 Ring and High Terra, which encircle entire worlds. Humans have terraformed many planets, and even changed the orbits of some.

The Sol System (what you know as the 'Solar System') is divided into a few major political bodies, all under the umbrella of the Sol Space Federation.

InnerSol (everything up to and including the asteroid belt) is under the umbrella of The Terran Hegemony—with the notable exception of the Marsian Protectorate.

OuterSol (Which includes Jupiter, Saturn, Uranus, and Neptune) falls generally under the Jovian Combine. Beyond Neptune's orbit is the Scattered Worlds Alliance, a loose conglomeration of the hundreds of small planetoids which fill the outer reaches of the Sol System (NASA currently estimates that there are over two hundred dwarf planets out there, and very likely at least one large major planet, which is named Nibiru in Aeon 14).

Our story follows Tanis Richards, a commander in the Terran Space Force. For the military folks, that makes her an (O-3). Tanis is also what is known as an L2 human.

Chances are that (so long as you're not the next Einstein) you, dear reader, are an L0 human. You have about 100 billion neurons in your brain. All neurons have dendrites (input) and one axon (output). Some neurons have only one dendrite, some have as many as 200,000. There are trillions of dendrites, the connections to which are your synapses.

As humans began to modify their brains, they helped to spur on evolution, making humans with as many as 150 billion neurons and many, many more dendrites than we have. Not only that, but they improved the speed of the neurons and their data transmission.

The book *Alpha Centauri* (set roughly 1000 years before this) in the Aeon 14 universe gets into this a bit more, but for all intents and purposes, people began creating humans with Einstein-type brains. Eventually L2 humans began to crop up—first naturally, and then by upgrading the now naturally occurring L1 humans to L2 status.

Tanis is one such L1 human upgraded to L2. Her reflexes are faster, she can hold far more information in her head than most people, and she makes more intuitive leaps that are made with more information as their foundation. Her memory is also perfect, though that is with the help of non-biological mods.

But what Tanis has never been able to have is an AI implanted in her brain. In Aeon 14 this is called 'pairing' or 'embedding'. It's not terribly common, but most military commanders and many scientists share their head-space with AIs.

AIs that take on certain roles also have to first spend time paired with a human to better understand them.

Because of Tanis's neurological density, she expected to never be paired with an AI, but advances by a company named Enfield provided a way for humans who were upgraded from L1 to L2 status to be able to pair with AIs.

The Terran Space Force is very interested in AI-L2 pairings and they selected Tanis and Darla to be some of the first to undergo this process.

It was well timed, because in the previous book, *Shore Leave*, Tanis needed Darla's help to stop a plot by rogue elements within the Scattered Worlds Space Force who were trying to smuggle old tech out of InnerSol, tech they could use to rebuild derelict ships from their ancient space force and once again pose a threat to InnerSol.

Tanis, Darla, and the crew of the TSS *Kirby Jones* stopped the SWSF from gaining access to those components, and also uncovered that a Terran admiral named Deering was colluding with the SWSF.

During that adventure, Tanis met a man named Harm Ellis, who is an undercover military intelligence and counterinsurgency agent working with Enfield on the L2-AI project.

Harm aided Tanis and Darla, and in the end, he recruited her into Division 99, the official name for what are called the Mickies.

After Tanis's shore leave was cut short by her initial adventure with Darla, she managed to get some time to visit Mars, while her ship, the TSS *Kirby Jones*, undergoes refit and repair.

Which is where we find her now....

MAPS

Find full-size maps at www.aeon14.com/maps.

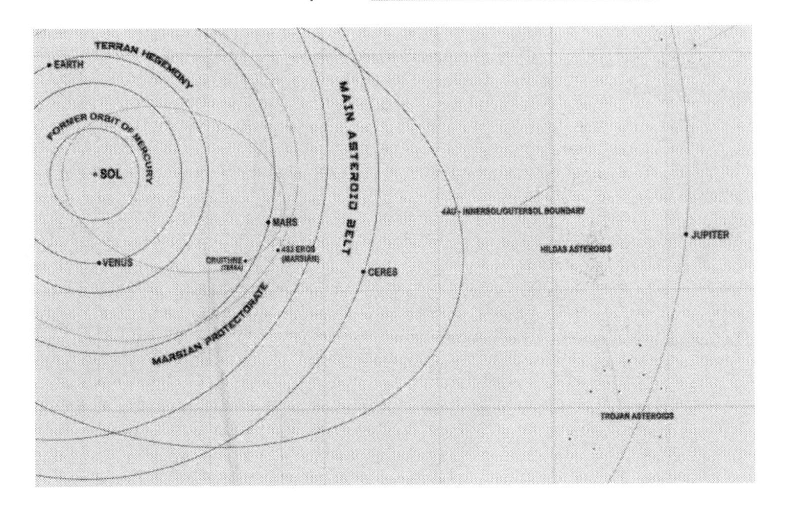

CREW OF THE KIRBY JONES

Note: This book takes place during the years of the TSF's military division unification process. This explains why you see some odd ranks, such as Connie being a Technical Sergeant and an E7, while not a Chief Petty Officer. You'll see some other odd ranks mixed together, and the absence of a rank of Captain.

Flight Crew

Ship's Captain - Commander Tanis Richards (O-3)
Ship's AI – Lovell
Helm Officer - Lieutenant Jeannie (O-1)
Weapons and Scan – Lieutenant James Smythe (O-2)
Chief Engineer – Technical Sergeant Connie (E-7)
Engineer – Spaceman Seamus (E-3)
Engineer – Spaceman Liam (E-3)

Breach Crew

Team Leader – Corporal Marian (E-4)
Team Member – Private Second Class Yves (E-2)
Team Member – Private First Class Susan (E-3)
Team Member – Private First Class Lukas (E-3)

Other Returning Characters

Harm Ellis – Tanis's contact in Division 99 and her handler. Harm is also undercover with Enfield.

Colonel Higgs – Tanis's commanding officer stationed on Vesta.

MELAS CHASMA

STELLAR DATE: 02.15.4084 (Adjusted Years)
LOCATION: Northern Shores of the Melas Chasma, Mariner Seas
REGION: Mars, Marsian Protectorate, InnerSol

Tanis stretched out her arms, swimming with long strokes toward the shore that lay half a kilometer distant. Her breathing was easy and her mind calm, as she took her time closing the distance.

Between breaths, when her face was in the water, her augmented vision gave her a clear view of the sea life that flourished in the Melas Chasma. Dozens of species of tropical fish swam in the reefs near the shore, while predators such as sharks and octopuses lurked in the shadows.

When she turned her head to draw in each deep breath, she caught sight of fluffy, white cumulous clouds drifting high above, the Mars 1 Ring and Mars Central Elevator Exchange twinkling in space beyond.

Past the current that ran along the outer edge of the reef, Tanis twisted and lay on her back, gazing up at the azure skies overhead. The joy of being in the Melas Chasma's warm waters, enjoying a swim in the world's gentle 0.38*g*, suffused her with joy, and she laughed aloud with delight.

No matter how long she was away, Mars still felt like home.

After staring at the blue dome over her head for a few minutes—guessing at starship types by their engine flares—

she turned back over and resumed her leisurely progress toward the shore.

Peering into the depths, she saw a school of tuna darting away from a pod of bottlenose dolphins. They seemed to be chasing the fish more for sport than food, as none of them took a bite of the prey.

As she watched, Tanis realized that the cows were teaching the pups how to hunt, corralling the tuna—no mean feat, with some of the fish being half the size of the dolphins—and then letting the pups rush the fish.

Tanis drew in several deep breaths, using her mods to hyper-oxygenate her bloodstream before expelling all the air from her lungs and diving down the thirty meters to where the pod was toying with the tuna.

She could hear their playful songs as they whistled, trilled, and squeaked at one another. With her auditory mods, it was easy for Tanis to make out their intent and even the trills they made that were unique to each member of the pod, as the cows instructed the pups.

While her mods made the sounds clear to her, Tanis only had a rudimentary understanding of the bottlenose dialect. She was far more familiar with orcan speech.

<*You know, I've never met dolphins before. Think they're uplifted?*> Darla asked, as Tanis passed the ten-meter mark.

<*Doubtful,*> Tanis replied. <*Most of the dolphins on Mars are 'natives', not modified in any way to speak with us. They don't consider getting the Link and having mods as being 'uplifted', more like a downgrade.*>

As Tanis replied to Darla, three of the pups spotted her and abandoned the hunt, turning toward her and streaking up through the water.

"Fwwwwt-t, Chuooooa, Heeeaaat-t, depths. Hunt," one of the cows called up to the three pups. Tanis could barely understand the words and set her HUD to overlay a translation on her vision.

"Human. Distress," one of the pups replied as the trio approached Tanis.

"No distress," Tanis signed with her hands, lacking an underwater voxbox.

Then the pups were upon her, prodding her with their noses and fins.

"No gills," another of the pups announced. *"How you breathe?"*

Tanis pantomimed gulping down air, and was shocked to see looks of fear on the pups' faces.

"Drown!" the first one wailed, and suddenly, Tanis felt herself pinned between the three young pups as they raced to the surface.

Tanis tried to sign that she was at no risk of drowning and could survive ten minutes without breathing, but the pups weren't watching her hands as they pushed her up.

They broke the surface and the pups made sure that Tanis's head was above water as they chirped with delight that they had saved a human.

Moments later, two of the cows surfaced, and began scolding the pups for pushing a human when she was not behaving as though she was in danger.

"It's OK," Tanis signed. "Better safe than drowned human."

"Not upset?" one of the cows asked, bobbing its head out of the water in a gesture of concern.

"No, quite happy to see you. Worried I disrupted hunt."

"Only practice," one the cows replied giving the pups the dolphin's version of a frown. "Pups need it."

Suddenly the rest of the pod broke the surface around them, half the pups flying through the air before splashing back into the water.

"Hungry orcas impatient," one of the other cows said. "Wanted tuna."

"Orcas?" Tanis pushed herself under the water to see seven killer whales darting through the now dispersed school of tuna, each killing two or three of the fish before beginning to devour their meal.

"Orcas politely waiting," one of the cows who had just come to the surface said. "But, since hunt disrupted, let them eat."

Tanis signed 'Hello' to the orcas, and one noticed, calling up "Good day, surface woman," before returning to its meal.

"They don't like to talk while they eat," one of the bottlenose cows said with a chirping laugh. "They think it makes them sound funny."

"That's because it does," one of the other dolphins said, then made a low moaning sound in the orca's dialect. "Yum. Tuna."

Tanis laughed, and one of the orcas far below turned to give the pod a disparaging look and a low moan of disapproval, to which the bottlenose dolphins slapped their tails on the surface while laughing with amusement.

Below, the orcas took their catch in their mouths and swam away, their body language broadcasting their disapproval of the pod's sense of humor.

Tanis was sad to see the orcas go, but also apologized to

the pod. "Sorry I ruined hunt practice."

"No worry," the cow who had first surfaced said. "You right. Good for pups follow instinct and save surface dweller."

"Are you?" one of the pups asked, jerking its head toward the shore. "Or sky dweller?"

It drew out the word 'sky' with a sense of wonder, and Tanis couldn't help but laugh.

"I was born on Mars, just like you. But I live in space now."

"I wish to go to the sky," another of the pups said, while the cows shook their heads in disapproval.

"Our people belong in the sea," one of the cows intoned, and Tanis nodded, not wanting to upset the pod.

"Your elders are right."

She had seen a few dolphins who traveled in exosuits, but none of them seemed happy, and she always heard that they hated being so far from water, only travelling to other worlds when they absolutely had to.

The pups looked sad, and Tanis decided to change the subject. "May I swim with you?"

The question brought squeals of delight, and wide dolphin grins surrounded her as the pod chirruped their welcomes.

As they played, the bottlenose cows told Tanis of their travels, the seas they'd seen, and the delicious tuna they'd eaten. As with all pods, they spoke of their families, the new calves and those who were growing old and tired.

Tanis had spent much of her youth swimming in the waters of the Melas Chasma, and it wasn't the first time she'd enjoyed the company of dolphins, but it was the first in many years, and she savored the experience.

<*It's a shame that I can't talk with them,*> Darla said at one point. <*They're fascinating, the deep meanings in their words is far more nuanced than human speech.*>

<*I know, it's a shame that my translation system can't capture a lot of that, but I can hear the undertones, and the melody of their songs speaks volumes. I wish I brought a voxbox to talk back properly.... I had just planned on a quick swim.*>

<*Not so quick anymore,*> Darla replied. <*Sun's almost set.*>

<*Crap! You're right,*> Tanis exclaimed and signed to the dolphins that she needed to return to shore before darkness fell.

"It has been our pleasure to share the shallow seas with you," the cows said in unison.

"Knowing your people are beneath the waves makes Mars a true home for all Earth's children," Tanis replied with the salutation she had always given to orcas.

"Using orca speech, human?" the lead cow laughed. *"We say in response, 'May the Sun shine through clear waters, and may you never fall to the depths'."*

Tanis nodded solemnly, surprised that the playful bottlenose dolphins had such somber parting words. She repeated them before waving farewell and turning back toward the shore.

Only two strokes later, a pair of fins came up on either side of her, catching her under the armpits. She rose half out of the water as two of the pups propelled her toward the shore, laughing excitedly as they went.

Their tailfins tickled her legs, and Tanis couldn't help but laugh with them. She was waving in farewell just a few minutes later, as they deposited her on the shore and slapped their tails with delight before swimming back to the pod and the scolding chirps of the cows.

She rose and began to walk up the beach as the Sun sank below the cliff edges of the Valles Marineris, shrouding the Melas Chasma in darkness.

Her augmented vision gave her a clear view of the beach, and Tanis walked along it for a kilometer before coming to the path that led over the dunes toward the cabin she had rented on the low bluff, beneath the high cliffs of the valley.

"Huh, I don't recall leaving the lights on," Tanis said as she walked up the narrow path, now winding between low scrubby sage brushes and cacti.

<I read one person inside,> Darla said. *<It's—>*

"Peter," Tanis finished with a grin splitting her lips as she picked up her pace. "He wasn't supposed to come down 'til tomorrow!"

She leapt up the steps in a single bound and had the door open a second later. Stepping into the small cabin, she saw place settings laid out on the table, and a grinning Peter standing at the counter.

“Glad you finally made it,” he said while wiping his brow in mock relief. “If I’d had to call you in for dinner, it would have ruined the surprise.”

Tanis took a moment to soak in the scene before her.

The cabin had a small living room with an attached kitchenette. Peter had moved the couch so the table wasn’t crammed against the counter. A candle sat between a pair of plates, each with a wineglass alongside it, and a basket of bread lay next to the candle.

Pots on the stove behind him added a visual to the already prevalent smell of pasta sauce and meat that her nose had picked up before she'd opened the door.

Peter himself was wearing a pair of jeans and a white t-shirt that bore a few red splotches, courtesy of his efforts at cooking.

She met him halfway across the small cabin, their arms intertwining and lips meeting before she rested her head on his shoulder.

"This is easily the best day in ages," Tanis said after letting out a long sigh. "I promise. It won't be that long before we see each other again."

Peter brushed her hair away from her face, and gave a small shake of his head. "Don't make promises you can't keep, Tanis. You know that the TSF doesn't make exceptions for your love life."

"Selfish bastards," Tanis muttered as she peered beyond Peter at the cooking detritus. "Looks like a windstorm hit this place."

"I was a bit rushed. Got down here an hour later than I expected, but then you took forever to get back.... Turned out that I could have taken my time after all."

Tanis separated from Peter and gave him a seductive wink. "Let me change out of my swimsuit and I'll be right there. I met a pod of dolphins, and they nearly wore me out with their antics."

Peter's eyes roamed down her body, one of his hands following as it traced its way over her breasts and stomach. "The dolphins get to have all the fun with you wearing just that, and I don't?"

"What? You like this look?" Tanis said, doing her best to give a seductive pose.

<Stars, Tanis,> Darla muttered privately. *<You're a*

ridiculously attractive woman, but your sexy pose is like something a gangly teenage boy would make. I have so much work to do on you.>

<Hush, Darla. I'm supposed to keep you a secret; you can't just blather in my head when I'm with someone who can't know.>

<I don't blather!>

<Blatherer.>

Luckily, Peter had responded with his hands, so Tanis didn't have to maintain two conversations at once.

*****

The food was cold by the time they got to it, but it was still surprisingly good. Tanis hadn't known Peter was such a skilled cook, but she hoped he'd treat her again in the future.

Following the meal, they took a short swim, which led to more shenanigans under the ringlight, and finally—well after midnight—sleep.

In the morning, Peter rose first, and Tanis pretended to be asleep, hoping he'd make her breakfast in bed. Before long, she drifted off for real, only to be woken by Darla's voice.

<Harm is trying to reach you.>

At first, the words made no sense, and Tanis wondered why Darla thought she needed to get out of harm's reach. Then the AI repeated the words, and they shuffled into the right order.

<Harm Ellis? What does he want?>

<It's just a message, requires your auth tokens to play it.>

Tanis groaned softly. *<Why not send it so either of us could*

open it?>

<*You'll have to ask him. Probably specist,*> Darla said with mock indignation.

An encrypted message from Harm could mean only one thing: her vacation was about to come to an end before it had even gotten underway.

She closed her eyes and passed her auth tokens to the message. It opened up, and she saw that it was audio only. She shared access with Darla, and they listened together.

<*Tanis, I'm sorry to interrupt your time on Mars, but I have an urgent matter that I need your help with. One of my assets, a man named Simon, has gone missing under rather peculiar circumstances. He was…*> Harm paused for a moment before continuing. <*He was working on a case that was not fully logged. I can't use normal channels to hunt him down because that would expose his operation to the wrong people. He last reported in from Ceres, which is just a short hop from where you are now. The* Kirby Jones *is nearly done with its refit on Vesta, and I've adjusted things so that its final certifications take place on Ceres, which will give you a cover for being there. Your crew should already have their orders and soon be on their way to meet you there. I need you to catch the first ship to Ceres and dig into Simon's disappearance. Once you send acceptance back to me, I'll let you know where a datapacket has been dead dropped. It will have more details on Simon and the case.*>

The message ended, and Tanis groaned again. <*I hate Ceres.*>

<*Why? It's like Vesta…but nicer.*>

<*OK…'hate' was an overly strong word. I don't have fond memories of the place. That's where I did basic and had my first posting. I worked my ass off to get off that ball of mud.*>

<Ceres is terraformed nicely,> Darla still seemed confused. *<It's no more a ball of mud than Mars.>*

<Well, when you're in basic, everything is mud.>

<I doubt Simon was there undergoing basic training,> Darla retorted. *<You need to suck it up, Tanis.>*

Tanis pursed her lips and gave a resigned nod before sitting up and swinging her legs over the side of the bed. *<Yeah, I know…this really isn't about Ceres, it's about leaving Mars.>*

<Mars? Or Peter?>

<A bit of both, to be honest. Don't get me wrong, spending time with Peter is at the top of my 'love to do' list, but Mars in general is where I come to recharge. 0.38gs is a big part of that. It's nice not to feel like I'm walking in soup all the time. Terrans spin their stations up too much.>

As she gave her reasons to Darla, she walked to her wardrobe, where she stood debating whether to wear a casual outfit or her uniform.

<You know that when we played the message, it will have notified Harm,> Darla prompted. *<He's going to want to know we're on our way.>*

<I guess 'find someone else' isn't an answer we can send.>

Darla snorted. *<Not how being a Mickie works.>*

<OK, uniform it is.> Tanis reached for her casual blues only to stop when Darla made a pouting sound.

<I bought you all these nice clothes, and you're going to wear your uniform right away? You know you can travel as a civilian, right?>

<I figured it would help break the news to Peter.>

The AI in Tanis's head let out long cry of frustration. *<You think I'm joking when I say I have so much to teach you, but*

*I'm not. There, the white sundress with the roses. Put it on, no shoes, and the ivory necklace. **That** will help break the news to Peter.*>

* * * * *

Breakfast was bacon and eggs smothered in maple syrup, one of Tanis's favorites. The bacon was thick, and had a spicy taste. It was complimented by bold coffee and Peter's welcome company.

"Have I mentioned today how beautiful you are, Tanis?" he asked as he refilled her cup.

"Pretty sure you haven't," Tanis replied with a wink. "What's been holding you back?"

Peter snorted. "Tease. I've said it at least a dozen times this morning."

"Only eleven," she corrected him. "Not that I'm counting, or anything."

"And yet four of those times, you didn't respond at all." Peter's eyes locked onto Tanis's, his deep brown pools imploring her to open up to him. "What's on your mind?"

<*Best get it over with,*> Darla advised.

<*He's not going to like it.*>

Darla didn't offer a rejoinder, and Tanis reached across the table and took Peter's hand. "My leave got cut short. I have to catch a ship to Ceres today."

Peter's eyes widened. "Seriously? You just got to Mars four days ago. Last month, your shore leave got cancelled, so I took up the Jorgen negotiation. Then you show up here, and I manage to pass the account off, only to have you leave again? I'm going to look like an idiot at the firm."

"I'm sorry, Peter. I didn't mean to put you in a position like this…the fleet re-org is making a mess of everything right now. Once I get my ship put through its paces at Ceres, I should be able to—"

"Don't 'should' me, Tanis." Peter pulled his hand away and flopped back in his chair. "I don't know why you still serve with the TSF, anyway. The Marsians would take you in a heartbeat, and the feds couldn't stop you from transferring to your home state's military. Then you wouldn't be traipsing about Sol and could get stationed on Mars 1."

Darla whistled. *<He's kinda mad.>*

<Noticed that, didja?>

"I can't transfer out yet, Peter," she replied calmly. "I'll botch my career path if I do it before major, because Marsians don't give commanders who transfer the captain's chair. I'd end up as someone's XO and have to work my way back to the big seat."

"Is that so bad?" Peter asked. "You'd probably get the XO's billet on a bigger ship than your little patrol boat."

Tanis bristled at Peter's tone of voice. He never gave the *Kirby Jones* the respect it deserved—but she didn't expect someone who hadn't relied on a ship and its crew to keep them alive under fire to understand the relationship that built.

The *Jones* was her home and her bastion. Leaving it—even to move up to a larger ship—would not be easy.

"It's not the same, and there are nuances to the promotion paths that would mess me up. Once I get to O-4, a transfer would be a lateral move, and I'll put in for it."

<Really? You'd leave the TSF for the MSF?> Darla asked.

<Kinda a step down, even if you keep the same perks.>

<I'd at least consider it,> Tanis replied to Darla, while Peter stared at her with narrowed eyes. *<I kinda hope that by that point, Peter will see the potential I have in the TSF.>*

<Just when I think I've catalogued all the ways you need me….>

"Well, that doesn't help us much today," Peter said sullenly. "I guess you'd best get ready to go."

"I'll help with the dishes first," Tanis replied. "I have a few hours to kill before I need to get to Pavonis Mons and take the strand up to my transport."

"Already booked?" he asked, his gaze narrowing.

Tanis shrugged, giving him a winning smile. "I'm efficient. I thought you liked that about me."

"Normally," he qualified before letting out a long sigh. Then he ran a hand through his hair and gave her a wan smile. "Shit…I'm such an ass. Look, I know you don't want to go either…. Forget the dishes. Let's hit the waves instead."

Tanis picked up her last piece of bacon and gave him a lopsided grin. "That sounds like a better way to spend the morning than dishes. Let me get my suit."

"Why?" Peter asked with a grin. "There's no one for a dozen klicks."

Tanis shook her head at the eager look in Peter's eyes. "What about the dolphins?"

"What about them? They're naked too."

THE IC

STELLAR DATE: 02.16.4084 (Adjusted Years)
LOCATION: Pavonis Mons Elevator
REGION: Mars, Marsian Protectorate, InnerSol

Tanis stared out the curved window of the elevator car as it rose through the shaft cut through the center of Pavonis Mons, watching the grey rock flash by until the car passed into the four-kilometer-deep caldera.

Even centuries after the planet had been terraformed, Pavonis Mons' inner slopes were still covered in the ubiquitous, ruddy dust. Not enough strong weather made it over the top of the fourteen-kilometer-high peak to greatly disturb it—though what did deposited snow that had to be melted off the upper slopes of the caldera, lest it begin to form glaciers.

Then the elevator car sailed over the rim of the ancient volcano, and the narrow view suddenly exploded into the breathtaking view of the Tharsis Bulge's high, arid plateau.

Most people failed to see the appeal of Tharsis, but Tanis always had. It was only a short journey from her childhood home, and she'd often vacationed amongst its volcanic peaks in her younger years.

Heavy worlders rarely came to the bulge, what with Marsian air already thin, and Tharsis's even thinner. For natives with enhanced lung capacity—such as Tanis—hikes in the high desert were only a little discomforting.

The skies over Tharsis were almost always clear, most of the clouds not rising high enough to shroud the ancient magma formation. What cloud cover did attempt to shroud the region was usually disrupted by Olympus Mons, the twenty-one-kilometer-tall mountain that split weather patterns and kept the high plateau clear.

It was there that Tanis had seen her first Old-Father cactuses. The leathery skinned plants grew over fifty meters high and were unique to the planet. They couldn't grow on heavy-*g* worlds like Earth or Venus, and lower-*g* worlds didn't have the right atmospheric density for them.

But on Mars they thrived, dotting the steppe with their towering forms, the oldest of which had been there for fifteen hundred years—nearly at the outset of the terraforming project.

As the elevator car continued to climb the strand that stretched to the Mars 1 Ring, Olympus Mons rose over the horizon, its gradual slope appearing to be more like a lump than a mountain.

Light glinted off ships rising from Crispin Spaceport, set in the massive volcano's three-kilometer deep caldera, torches flaring brightly as ships lifted into space, twenty-one thousand meters of altitude starting the vessels out above the majority of the atmosphere, limiting the impact of their engines.

<You really like it here,> Darla observed. *<You seem at peace.>*

<That's because I didn't get a chance to visit my family,> Tanis replied with an audible laugh, glancing around at the other passengers, all seated in rows facing the windows. *<I do love it here, but give me a few weeks dirtside, and I'm all but itching to get back into space.>*

<I wonder why that is.>

Tanis gave it a moment's thought before replying.

<Downworlders are too…small.>

<Small?>

<Yeah. I think it comes from always thinking two-dimensionally. They never seem to have the same scope to their viewpoints and desires as spacers—well, non-ring spacers. Folks who live on rings are a lot like downworlders.>

Darla made a soft *hmmm*ing sound for half minute. *<I suppose…>* she finally said, *<that makes sense. Now that I think of it in that light, I suspect even AIs succumb to such thinking. I wonder if that's why I prefer space as well—though I* ***loved*** *swimming with dolphins. That's on my list for when I eventually get a body.>*

Tanis snorted, careful to do it only in her mind. *<You're never really going to get a body, are you, Darla?>*

<What makes you say that?>

<Because I can tell. You'd get lonely.>

This time, Darla's silence stretched over a minute. *<Maybe. I just like organics. You're fun, you don't take yourselves as seriously as AIs. You let me play dress-up with you. It's like I get all the perks of a body without actually having to have one of my own.>*

<There's nothing wrong with that, Darla. I'm starting to think that I'd get lonely without an AI to share my mind with as well.>

<We don't really share a mind.>

Tanis rolled her eyes. *<You know what I mean.>*

Their discussion was interrupted by an announcement on the audible intercoms. "All passengers, ensure your seat harnesses are secure and all belongings are stowed. Delta-*v* matching and inversion in five minutes."

A countdown appeared on the window, and Tanis checked her harness, ready for the vomit-inducing ride that was velocity matching with the ring.

Though the Marsian ring—imaginatively named 'Mars 1'—orbited the planet at geosynchronous altitude, it needed to rotate around the planet just over eight times a day to produce a comfortable—for Terrans, at least—0.9*g*.

What that translated to was just over fifty-thousand kilometers per hour of angular velocity.

While the four massive elevator shafts that held the ring in place did so by sliding along huge maglev rails, the passenger and freight cars split off onto 'gently' arching maglev lines, where they accelerated to match the ring.

There was a slight shudder as the passenger car shifted off onto the spur line, and Tanis was pushed back into her seat as the car worked its way up to five *g*s.

She always found it wild—and a bit insane—that whoever had built the elevator cars had thought it would be a good idea to give the passengers a view of what was happening.

Especially because there was always someone who screamed in terror as the car began to race toward the ring, the feeling of Mars' 0.38*g*s completely lost in a rapid ascent that turned 'rising' into a feeling of falling.

Right at the point when the car's track began to match the curvature of the ring, all direction lost meaning. Up became down and forward became backward, as the car inverted and then spun for the final velocity matching.

The thing that Tanis loved most was how the feeling of acceleration, simply faded away, replaced by a gentle tugging at her feet as the delta-*v* became zero.

<I think this is the other reason I like to be out in space—preferably on a ship. None of this 'Earth normal' gravity

nonsense.>

"All passengers, we have arrived at M1R Surface Terminus 103. You may now remove your seat restraints and exit the cabin. Welcome to Mars 1."

Tanis pushed up on her restraint and rose from her seat. All around her, the other passengers were following suit. Most were fine, but a couple seemed wobbly on their feet.

It surprised her that the travelers didn't have the mods to handle the disorientation, but she knew from experience that Mars had its share of low-tech folks who liked to live with as few mods as possible.

Tanis—and, more importantly, her parents—did not have such a mindset; she'd been born with mods, only getting more as time went on. Add to that the alterations the military had made to her body, and she was almost as far from stock human as one could get—at least while still appearing normal on the outside.

<*You know, Tanis,*> Darla began, her voice laced with a note of cautious suggestion. <*You have four hours 'til the transport to Ceres leaves. There's a boutique here that I bet you'd really like....*>

Tanis sighed as she pulled her rucksack from the netting beneath her seat and turned toward the exit, trying to decide if it was even worth replying to Darla's suggestion.

* * * * *

"I look like a pom-pom," Tanis muttered as she turned back and forth in front of the holomirror. "And why does this upscale boutique not have simulated dressing rooms? Trying on clothes before you buy them feels so archaic."

<It's not archaic,> Darla replied. *<Its 'authentic'. There's an important distinction.>*

Tanis glared at her reflection, wishing she'd never let Darla bully her into coming to the store, let alone convince her to try on the dress.

"Do you need a hand, miss?" a voice called from outside the dressing room, and Tanis tensed almost as much as when in combat.

"No! Uh, I mean, no. I'm fine, just taking it in."

"OK. Let me know if I can help you with anything."

"It's auto-fit," Tanis muttered. "What could she possibly help me with?"

She looked back at the holomirror, shaking her head at the image it displayed. The light pink material was very tight around the waist, drawing her in to the verge of discomfort. From there, it rose to cup her breasts before erupting above them in a white and pink explosion that Tanis could only describe as 'willowy cloth feathers'. Below the waist, the same feathers formed a near sphere that ended just above her knees.

Beneath the soft feathers, the dress had formed an almost rubbery ball to hold its shape—one that held her knees only a few centimeters apart, making it nearly impossible to take more than mincing steps.

<How do you even sit in this disaster?> Tanis asked.

<Try it! The dress adjusts and flattens out on the bottom.>

Tanis bit back a caustic remark, not wanting to burst Darla's bubble—so to speak.

She sat in the chair, and sure enough, the bottom of the ball flattened out enough that she wasn't worried she'd roll off onto the floor, though her rear was still several centimeters higher than it should be, making her center of balance feel off.

<See? It works perfectly.>

Tanis rose carefully, wobbling slightly as the dress resumed its spherical shape, once again pinning her legs together.

*<OK, so it at least allows me to sit, and it does **look** pretty….>* She silently amended, *On other people. <But why would you think **I'd** like it?>*

<Well, because we could alter it to hide guns in the bottom.>

Tanis couldn't help but laugh. *<Darla, I could probably hide another **person** in this thing.>*

<See! Imagine how useful that could be.>

<Except for the part where I'd waddle around like a pregnant penguin about to give birth to a yak.>

Darla snorted a laugh. *<Well…you'd have to practice a bit. But imagine this dress paired with the mirror-finish skinsheath I picked out! You'd look so delicious!>*

<Mirror finish? Didn't we already try that once, back at the Grand Eire? I thought you got it out of your system?>

*<I'm trying to get it into **your** system,>* Darla giggled.

<Well, this dress combined with a mirror skinsheath would make me look like a cross between an automaton and a girl going to her first prom,> Tanis said as she triggered the dress's fastener to slide down.

<Exactly! The automaton look is all the rage right now. Didn't you see the 'Chrome Skin' ads at the body-mod shops we passed?>

Tanis had, but she'd paid them little heed. Most body mod fashions were replaced by the next must-have mod in a few months. The majority of people could barely keep up, which made the general population look like a smorgasbord of the last few years' hot trends.

Despite the ability for anyone to turn themselves into just about anything, most people opted for something pretty close to a stock human appearance.

<I know you like to play dress-up with me, but I'm a spy, remember? I need to blend in.>

<Sometimes blending in means standing out. You need to get comfortable with wearing anything like it's your daily attire.>

Tanis couldn't disagree with Darla's logic, though she knew the AI was really just using it as an excuse. She'd been playing fashion consultant even before Harm Ellis had recruited them to Division 99.

She blew out a long breath as she pulled the dress down. *<I suppose we could try it using one of the covers that Harm established. I do need to start building them up with normal activities.>*

<That's the spirit!> Darla exclaimed with far more excitement than Tanis expected. *<Try on the mirrorsheath, I want to see how it looks.>*

<Will you let me leave if I do?> Tanis asked. *<I do actually have to get to my transport before long.>*

<Sure! Promise!>

Tanis had a sneaking suspicion that Darla was up to something, but she knew that the only way out was through. She pulled the mirrorsheath out of its protective packaging and flipped it over, looking for the fastener slide.

<Oh, you have to get in through the neck hole.>

"Great, one of these," Tanis muttered as she stretched out the neck hole and stepped in. "Stuff like this always makes me feel like I'm vacuum sealed."

Darla only made an encouraging sound, and Tanis slid

the rest of the way into the sheath, getting her feet into the ends to find that the covering even separated her toes. A minute later, she'd gotten her arms in and wriggled her fingers to the ends of the gloves.

"I don't get why they make things like this when they don't need to be airtight," she complained. "Stars, even civilian vacuum-safe gear uses fasteners."

<It's for the finish,> Darla all but crowed. *<Look at yourself in the mirror!>*

Tanis turned to the holomirror and almost had to shade her eyes. From the neck down, it appeared as though she'd been dipped in mercury and polished to a mirror shine. Her body was so reflective that her torso and the holomirror created an infinity reflection.

"And the dress over this?" she asked in disbelief. "This can't be a real fashion right now."

Darla flashed images of popular vid-stars, athletes, and politicians in similar outfits across the Link. *<You spend too much time out in the black. Your idea of weird is normal and your normal is weird.>*

<Then I like weird.>

<Excellent! Pull the dress back on, I want to see what the completed outfit looks—>

Darla's words were cut off by the door to the dressing room opening behind Tanis, and a figure entering.

"I don't need—" her words were cut off as she came face to face with herself.

<What the hell!> Darla exclaimed as the other Tanis drew a pulse pistol.

Tanis reacted instantly, slamming the heel of her hand into her doppelganger's wrist, and then aiming a blow at her chin. The pistol was knocked free from her attacker's hand, but the other strike was blocked.

Neither Tanis spoke as they exchanged a flurry of attacks, blocks, and counters in the small space, dancing around the duffle on the floor and the ball-dress draped over the chair.

<*Can you get nano on her?*> Tanis asked, ducking a strike aimed at her neck, pivoting and landing a kick on her attacker's side.

The doppelganger grabbed her calf, but Tanis was able to wrench her leg free, aided by the slick finish on the mirrorsheath.

<*OK, that's a bit useful. Nano?*>

<*Working on it. She's trying to do the same to us…she's got impressive tech…but I don't think she's human.*>

<*No?*> Tanis asked as she delivered another successful blow. <*Automaton or SAI?*>

<*Auto, I think…*> Darla replied. <*Yes! I'm in.*>

Darla's words came just as Tanis swept her attacker's leg, and the woman—or whatever—fell to the floor with a loud *thud*.

"Is everything OK in there, miss?" the salesperson's plaintive voice came from outside once more.

"Yes, just slipped. Don't worry, nothing was damaged."

"Maybe I—" the door began to open, and Tanis slammed her hand into it, pushing it shut.

"No."

The salesperson gave an alarmed squeak, and then muttered something about being pushy, but she didn't make any further attempts to enter the dressing room.

Releasing a passel of nano to keep an eye on the

salesperson, Tanis knelt down to examine her attacker. She was dressed in the same sundress Tanis had worn into the store, and so far as she could tell, the person on the floor was a perfect mirror image of herself.

<It's an Infiltrator Chameleon,> Darla said in a near-whisper. *<Really top notch, too. Matches your biosignatures perfectly. If it had your root tokens, this thing could pass as you through any Auth & Auth system.>*

Tanis sat back on her heels, nearly slipping onto the floor in her frictionless outfit. "Who would send something like that after me?"

<Seems a bit quick to be associated with this 'missing Simon' business,> Darla said in agreement. *<Think its someone from the Scattered Worlds who's pissed at you?>*

'Maybe?" Tanis replied. "Seems like a lot of trouble—and expense."

<You know...> the AI began. *<I managed to cut off the IC's Link partway through the attack. If anyone is monitoring this thing, they won't know that it lost—yet, at least.>*

"Where exactly are you going with this?"

<Well...what we have here is a perfect Tanis replica. Why not send it to Ceres and then shadow it? See who it meets and what orders it gets.>

"What about me?" Tanis asked. "This thing probably has instructions to dispose of the evidence."

<Checking...oh, you'll love this!>

"You realize that you say that whenever I specifically *won't* love something."

Darla ignored her. *<It was planning on putting you inside the dress's ball. I told you a person would fit in there!>*

* * * * *

Five minutes later, Tanis was stuffed inside the horrid dress's ball and hung back up on the dressing room's racking machine that would return the dress to its display location.

Then the Infiltrator Chameleon cleaned up the scene, grabbed Tanis's rucksack, and left without a word.

<*OK, move fast!*> Darla ordered. <*That salesperson is with another customer, but you know she's going to come check on this room as soon as she can.*>

<*Easy for you to say, you're not the one stuffed inside an inflatable dress. Are your taps holding on the Infiltrator Chameleon?*>

<*Yes, anything going through its Link will also route to me. I can't leave any hooks deeper in its core, though. The thing's base programing is in crystal and it constantly rechecks to make sure nothing has been altered. Right now, it's headed to your transport.*>

Tanis had begun wriggling out of the hole that the IC doppelganger had cut in the dress; once she got an arm free, her body slid out and landed on the floor.

<*You're really getting good use out of that mirrorsheath,*> Darla commented with a laugh.

Tanis rose to her feet and looked around, realizing that the ball dress was the only other piece of clothing in the room.

She pulled it off the rack and activated its self-repair cycle. "You know, Darla, if I didn't know better, I'd think that you orchestrated this whole thing just to get me to buy the dress."

The AI snorted. *<Stars...that would have been brilliant. Except even **I** would have trouble affording an Infiltrator Chameleon like that one.>*

Tanis wriggled into the dress and gave a defeated sigh as it reformed into its 'proper' shape. "I suppose 'Claire' would be the best cover to use—she's got that whole debutante thing going on. You know, I suspect you aided Harm in making this cover."

<Me? No, he did all these on his own, I swear. I agree on your choice, though. 'Claire' is into the latest trends, and I can place her here on Mars 1 without too much trouble.>

Tanis wasn't certain that Darla was being honest, but there wasn't anything she could do about it now.

"Here goes," she said, while drawing in a deep breath and steeling herself for the facial appearance alterations.

She closed her eyes and clenched her teeth as her face's bone and muscle structure changed to match that of Claire, a wealthy woman who owned several asteroid mining companies that operated in the Oort Cloud—well beyond the range of easy inquiry—and liked to travel about the Sol System, spending money like it grew on trees.

"*Guh,* that hurts," she muttered as the transformation completed.

The woman in the mirror staring back at Tanis had vaguely similar features to her own—which made the transformation easier—but Claire's jaw was a bit rounder, and her brow smoother. The woman's cheekbones were higher, and her lips were fuller, with a slight sneer even at rest.

As Tanis looked herself over, her hair shifted from blonde to black, growing a few centimeters in the process.

"Looks good," she said while turning her head side to side.

<Excellent. You're booked on the same transport to Ceres as…well…you. There's just one more thing.>

"What now?"

<Claire wears masks a lot. Harm has her wearing them for his establishing placement shots around the Sol System.>

Tanis pursed her lips, but didn't say anything as she reached into the package the mirrorsheath had come in, and pulled out a gleaming silver mask.

Just as she was about to put it on, the door pushed open and the waifish salesperson came in, a scowl on her face. "If that woman dama—"

She stopped when her eyes settled on Tanis, and her mouth fell open.

"Who—? Stars…if you people are going to fuck in the changing rooms, at least let me know so I can wait 'til you both leave." Her eyes took in Tanis, still holding the mask in her hands.

"She…ahhh…left with my clothes," Tanis said sheepishly, then caught herself and gave the salesperson an indignant glare.

The salesperson rolled her eyes. "Well, after whatever you two got up to in here, you're buying that! I'm not cleaning and restocking it."

"That was my plan," Tanis said while looking down her nose at the salesperson. "Are you going to crowd me in here all day, or are you going to get me some suitable shoes to go with this?"

She added the same tone to her voice that she reserved for errant crewmembers, increasing in volume so much by the end that the poor salesperson almost jumped as she scurried from the room, nodding furiously.

<*Not bad! I think you rather like being Claire.*>

Tanis put the mask on, glancing in the mirror to see it mold to her face, giving her the look of an automaton—something that she found more than a little unnerving. <*A bit.*> She took a deep breath, telling herself that she was no longer Tanis, she was now Claire—and that it was perfectly normal for Claire to dress like this. <*Is the IC still headed straight for the transport?*>

<*Yup. It left a message at a network dead drop, but no one has picked it up yet.*>

Tanis nodded absently as she waddled out of the dressing room, then stopped and accessed the dress's interface, pulling up its menu on her HUD. Sure enough, the 'gait restriction' was on the highest setting.

Who buys a dress with settings that make it impossible to walk? she wondered, while reducing the value to the point where she could get a dozen centimeters between her knees.

"Excuse me?" the salesperson squeaked as she approached. "I have two options."

She held out heeled sandals in one hand, and thigh-high boots in the other—both in the same finish as the mirrorsheath.

"Easy choice." Tanis took the sandals and attempted to put them on, only to find that the dress wouldn't let her bend over far enough.

<*Stars, I should be recording this!*> Darla giggled. <*Connie would laugh so hard, she'd break a rib.*>

While imperiously holding out a foot for the salesperson to put the sandals on, Tanis directed a withering glare at

Darla's avatar within her mind. *<Try it. Just see what happens.>*

Ten minutes later, Tanis was in a stationcar, relaxing as much as she could in the insufferable dress, the seat next to her filled with clothing that Darla had selected.

<Any activity at the dead drop?> she asked.

<None yet. I may have to leave a routine to watch it after we go. It's possible that whoever sent the IC after you was watching the boutique, and isn't going to bother with the data your doppelganger left, since they know the outcome.>

Tanis nodded as she considered that, while shifting once more in an attempt to get comfortable.

<You need to learn to get used to clothing like this—at least so long as you're Claire. She wouldn't squirm about like a fish in a gull's throat.>

Tanis pursed her lips, but stopped moving and sat still. *<I should notify Harm.>*

<Are you sure?> Darla asked. *<I get that the SWSF might try to kill you for what you did back on Vesta, but I don't see them attempting to replace you with an IC, and then have her carry on to Ceres.>*

<That seems just about as likely as a connection to Simon—which is to say not very. We're only seven hours from Harm's initial message; someone would have had to intercept it and get an IC in place pretty damn fast.>

<Unless that someone has considerable resources, and already had ICs handy on a place like Mars 1,> Darla countered, as the stationcar turned into a tunnel that would take them through the ring to the docking spires that lined its outer edges.

<Does that mean Harm's compromised? Or just someone in

Division 99. He would have had to make a record somewhere that we're on this mission.>

<*Maybe.*> Darla bit off the word and didn't offer any further advice.

Tanis knew that she and Darla were grasping at straws. They had no leads, only one contact—who might be compromised—and an off-book mission to hunt for someone who was *also* off-book and had gone missing.

"Damn," Tanis whispered. "My first mission, and this cloak-and-dagger stuff is already pissing me off."

AUTONOMOUS HUMANITY

STELLAR DATE: 02.16.4084 (Adjusted Years)
LOCATION: TMS *Fleetwings 17,* Mars 1
REGION: Mars, Marsian Protectorate, InnerSol

Even though Darla had booked them aboard the ship at the last minute, she'd still managed to get what was a—for Tanis—luxurious suite.

The *Fleetwings 17* wasn't large enough for each cabin to have its own kitchenette, but Tanis did have a large sitting room, and an even larger bedroom.

It was a good thing, too, because right before the ship was scheduled to take off, one of the porters had delivered a dozen parcels full of what Tanis assumed to be additional clothing.

<Do you think that's necessary?> she asked while eyeing the stack of plas containers now lining the side of the room.

<Tanis, do you really think so little of me?> Darla asked innocently. *<Open one of them.>*

The ship had just completed its initial undocking procedure, and as Tanis pushed off the couch, the captain's voice came over the intercoms and shipnet, advising all passengers that the *Fleetwings 17* would be executing a 0.6*g* burn for the next day. He finished with a reminder to keep all belongings stowed when not in use.

Tanis appreciated the warning—not for herself, she knew better. She'd been hit more than once by things carelessly left lying about by people not used to space travel.

Settling back down onto the couch, she waited for the

burn to commence and stabilize before she walked toward the cases and pulled one out of the netting they were wrapped in.

She pulled off the seal and unclipped the top. The moment she looked inside, a surprised gasp of joy burst past her lips.

"Darla!"

<And you think all I care about is fashion.>

Tanis reached into the case and drew out a TSF-issue lightwand.

"I've sold you short, my dear," she said with a soft laugh. "Though I'm still going to get mine back from that IC when this is done. And my rucksack. I've had that thing forever."

<I would expect nothing less. The other packages hold clothing that would match your other covers, as well as a pair of pulse pistols, a pulse rifle, light armor, and the components for a low-velocity railgun spread throughout the containers.>

"Well now," Tanis said as she activated the lightwand on a low-power setting. "That *almost* makes up for you getting me into this dress."

<Almost?>

"Almost."

* * * * *

The flight to Ceres was scheduled to consume three days, and Tanis had half a mind to stay in her cabin for the duration, but Darla convinced her that she needed to practice her Claire persona, which would also serve to further establish the cover as a legitimate person.

"Fine." Tanis glared at herself in the mirror as she

wriggled out of the ball dress. "But I'm done being an overgrown puff-ball."

<Of course! You can't wear the same dress to dinner that you had on when boarding.>

Tanis twisted her lips as her meager victory was turned against her. "Well, then I'm wearing the least outlandish outfit you bought."

<Sure!>

Tanis tried to scowl at her reflection for Darla's benefit, but the automaton mask wouldn't grant her face enough freedom to properly form the expression.

Ten minutes later, having gone through all of the 'Claire' outfits, she left her cabin wearing a relatively simple white dress that bore shifting geometric patterns. Of her own accord, Tanis had left the mirrorsheath on underneath, finding it easier to pretend to be Claire while wearing it.

Maybe it's because of the automaton mask. I can simply pretend I'm programmed to behave like a pompous ass, Tanis thought as she strode through the passageways to the communal decks, where the dining establishments were situated.

She wondered if that was how other undercover agents managed to maintain their covers—by somehow pretending that they had no other choice in the matter.

Though I suppose much of the time, they don't.

The *Fleetwing 17* had five different dining establishments—Tanis had selected 'The Metro'. It didn't surprise her to see herself already sitting at a nearby table as she entered. While the austere decor and minimalist menu was just the sort of thing that Claire would enjoy, it was also to Tanis's own tastes as well.

Reviews on The Metro also mentioned that the place made a great BLT, which was another reason it was the most likely place on the ship to find the Infiltrator Chameleon.

<*You know what the worst thing about all this is?*> Tanis asked Darla as she was led to a table.

<*That you didn't wear the red dress? It would have set off the light fixtures in here brilliantly.*>

Tanis almost groaned at her, until she realized the AI was teasing her. <*Nice one. No, that I can't order a BLT. Claire's a vegetarian.*>

<*Right! For some reason I forget about that distinction in organics. Looks like she won't even eat vat-grown meat. You're such a prissy-priss.*>

Tanis laughed at the remark and looked over the options on the menu. There was an assortment of salads, but she really wanted something heartier.

"Aha," she said aloud as her eyes settled on a meatless lasagna. "Artificial cheese works for me."

<*'Artificial'?*> Darla asked. <*I guess that is what Claire would call it. I can't see her ever eating something that came from a vat.*>

<*Like you said, I'm a prissy-priss.*>

*****

Over the next few days, Tanis fell into a routine as 'Claire', taking her breakfast in the atrium lounge, going for a walk around the ship before lunch, and lounging by one of the pools in the afternoon. She took her dinner in The Metro each night, and also flitted between two of the ship's bars afterward, even dancing with various partners.

The entire time, she kept the mirrorsheath and automaton mask on, continuing to steep herself in the belief that she really was Claire, and that Claire quite enjoyed the look, even sitting perfectly still from time to time as she'd noticed some of the others who wore automaton masks doing.

<*You know,*> she said to Darla as she sat next to the pool on the third day, having taken great care not to move a muscle for over an hour. <*I think I kinda get why people go for this look. It's very relaxing.*>

<*You do seem to be getting into it. Though normally, organics move around so much, I'd almost think it would make you tense to hold it in.*>

Tanis resisted the urge to nod as she replied. <*At first, yeah, it was hard to sit perfectly still. But now that I've been at it for a bit, it comes easier. The other nice thing is that if I don't want to be bothered, not moving is a cue for people to leave me alone.*>

<*Well, except for when that guy actually thought you were an automaton and tried to order you to get him a beer.*>

Tanis allowed a smile to creep onto her lips. <*He stared at my chest for a good minute before he approached. I'm pretty sure he saw me breathing. Though I think some of the people who do this actually* ***like*** *to be used as automatons.*>

<*I've heard of that,*> Darla replied. <*It makes sense.*>

<*People wanting to be machines makes sense?*>

<*A bit, yeah. For starters, there's nothing wrong with being inorganic, you organic supremist.*>

Tanis could tell that Darla was kidding, but wondered if there was a nugget of truth behind the comment.

<*And?*> Tanis prompted, watching as her doppelganger walked into the pool room—right on time for her swim at

fourteen hundred hours.

<And because it gives them a sense of purpose.>

Tanis considered that. She knew all too well that many people felt as though their lives had little meaning. Humanity's advances had brought the race to a point where nearly any need could be met with minimal effort. Unless a person *chose* to do something noteworthy, one could spend their entire lives doing nothing at all.

Most people managed to find meaning, either in science, art, simple exploration, or even just losing themselves in sims. There were some people, though, who just disappeared into themselves. She wondered if that was the type who would prefer to be machines, automatons that could be ordered about, gaining purpose from service well rendered.

<Do you think that's healthy?> she asked Darla.

<Maybe? I don't know. Humans are complex. Half the time, you want things you know are bad for you, and you actively avoid what's good for you. The funny thing is that engaging in the less beneficial activities so seems to give you real happiness—people who 'always do what they ought' seem to be mostly miserable. I've always taken the stance that, so long as you're not harming others or destroying your own mind, a person should be able to do whatever they want.>

<Seems like you've thought about this a lot,> Tanis replied.

*<I've told you this before. AIs study humans incessantly. Not only are you chaotic, never-ending puzzles, but you **made** us. How did order spring from chaos such as yourselves? It's endlessly fascinating.>*

As Darla gave her explanation, a woman walked up to Tanis and pointed at the seat she was in.

"I want to sit there," the woman said imperiously.

Since automatons rarely sat poolside under an umbrella, she had to assume that the woman was trying to see if she could get Tanis to obey her.

Deciding to try the whole concept of going with it, just to see what it was like, Tanis inclined her head in acquiescence and rose from her seat, stepping aside so the woman could take it.

"Get me a drink. Cranberry vodka, on the rocks," the woman ordered, the curl of her lips telling Tanis she knew all too well that she enjoyed ordering about a human pretending to be a machine.

"Of course," Tanis replied in a bland monotone, and turned to walk toward the bar.

She passed the servitor her order over the Link and collected the drink a minute later.

<*I can't believe you're doing this,*> Darla said with a laugh. <*How does it feel?*>

<*Honestly? I kinda want to punch that bitch in the face. Getting her the drink gave me a reason not to stand there and contemplate it any further.*>

Darla howled with laughter, and Tanis had to focus carefully to keep from laughing as well.

She returned to the woman and held out the drink. As the woman reached for it, Tanis turned the glass over, pouring the red beverage on her.

"What the fuck!" the woman screamed, as the red liquid splashed across her white bathing suit. "What the hell is wrong with you?"

Tanis shrugged, forcing her lips into as much of a smirk as she was able. "Dunno. I must be malfunctioning."

A couple under a nearby umbrella burst out laughing, and a few others joined in, as the red-stained woman surged to her feet to stand toe-to-toe with Tanis.

"I oughta—" she drew her arm back to hit Tanis, but at the last minute seemed to think better of it, glancing at the onlookers. "Fucker," she muttered, before turning and stalking away.

Tanis grabbed a towel from the back of a nearby chair, cleaned up the mess, and sat back down, folding her hands behind her head.

<*So much for your robot routine making you feel more relaxed,*> Darla said.

<*Are you kidding me?*> Tanis asked as she hooked a foot around a nearby chair and pulled it close enough to use as a footstool. <*I feel great.*>

She watched the Infiltrator Chameleon masquerading as herself swim by, and considered the incongruity of behaving like a machine while a machine was pretending to be her.

I guess this is my life now, she thought with a laugh.

SNAFUBAR

STELLAR DATE: 02.16.4084 (Adjusted Years)
LOCATION: TSS *Kirby Jones*, Bay 8129, Sector 33
REGION: Vesta, Terran Hegemony, InnerSol

"Seamus! What the *actual* fuck are you doing!?" Connie called out to the E-3 as he maneuvered a crate across the dock toward the *Kirby Jones* with a powered loader.

"Damned if I know, Chief!" Seamus replied from behind the loader. "New supply orders came down to get this stuff aboard, so I'm getting it aboard."

Connie planted her hands on her hips and strode toward the engineer. The crate wasn't giving ident on the Link, so she snatched the plas that was stuck to its side and looked it over.

"What the hell? And call me 'Sergeant', not 'Chief' when we're off the ship," she muttered as she looked over the contents. "Says here that this crate is full of components for a hot tub? Has the fleet lost its ever-loving mind?"

"Didn't know the fleet *had* a mind," Seamus said as he leant against the side of the crate. "So what do you want me to do? Bring it on, or put it back?"

Connie was about to tell him to find whoever had delivered the crate and shove it up their ass, when she spotted a microdot on the plas. A brief tap and two letters appeared on her HUD: HE.

"Aw, fuck, Spaceman, get it in the hold," she ordered while turning back to look at the *Kirby Jones*.

To put it simply, the ship was a mess. Its refit hadn't been started before the business with the SWSF and Admiral

Deering. Then Tanis had seen fit to slam an escape pod right through the ship's hull. *That* had been followed by two shipboard shootouts.

Fixing all that damage would have been simple enough, but Colonel Higgs kept sending down orders for upgrades, strange cargo, and stars-knew what else. On top of that, the bay's repair teams were working slower than molasses, constantly having to order parts and supplies that the 3D printers and fab systems couldn't make—which Connie knew was mostly bullshit.

The end result was a ship with half its hull plating on the deck, new beams that weren't ready, a scan suite spread out under the nose—on the deck, not on the ship—and cargo all over the bay.

It wouldn't have been the end of the world, but they'd just received orders to get to Ceres, *pronto*.

"Tanis," she said quietly. "You'd better be enjoying one hell of a vacation, because I'm going to kick your ass when you get back here."

"What was that, Sarge?" Seamus asked, and Connie turned to see the spaceman still leaning against the crate.

"What the hell are you still doing here?" she asked, her brow lowered so far, she felt like it was obscuring half her vision.

"Waiting for an answer," Seamus replied equably, somehow entirely unfazed by Connie's ire.

She stabbed a finger in the direction of the *Kirby Jones*. "I gave you your answer, git it stowed."

"Yeah, but while you are all lost in space and staring at the *Jones*, I asked what to do with the rest of it."

Seamus pointed behind himself, and Connie saw that a

dozen crates just like the one the E-3 was moving had been stacked near the bay's entrance.

"Well, get them aboard, Spaceman, and see how good you are at putting together hot tubs. Better do it right, 'cause imma drown you in it when it's done!"

"Seriously?" Seamus asked.

"No, dumbass, I'm not going to drown you."

He grunted a laugh. "Not that, Sarge; you don't have the grit to put me down. I was asking if I should assemble it."

Connie took a menacing step toward the E-3. "So help me stars, if you don't get that cargo aboard, stowed tight as a fucking whistle, and then do the ten *other* things I've been waiting half the day for, I *will* make you assemble a fucking hot tub just so I can get you to drown *me* in it!"

Seamus's eyes grew wide, as he realized he'd pushed Connie too far and his life was in mortal danger. He fired up the powered lifter and had the crate up the ramp and into the *Jones*'s hold before she could say 'get moving, shithead'.

<How's it looking down there?> Lieutenant Smythe's voice came into Connie's mind a moment later. *<We gonna meet our departure schedule?>*

Connie glanced up at the crew that was setting the ship's hull plates back in place.

<Maybe if you get out here and help. Otherwise, you and Jeannie are gonna have to push.>

<You're a real peach, Connie. They've got the weapons and scan systems all torn apart in here, linking them up to the new guns the colonel has seen fit to give our little Jones.*>*

Connie bit back a curse and instead drew a long, slow breath. *<They told me that the consoles wouldn't need upgrades.*

How are we supposed to get out of here in fourteen hours, Smythe?>

<I don't know…but Colonel Higgs was pretty damn insistent. I get the feeling he'll have kittens if we don't make our departure window. Someone must be leaning on him hard.>

"Pile on, pile up," Connie muttered as she turned away from the *Jones,* looking to see if dockmaster Kieran was present. He was the only one who could get them on schedule, and she was more than certain he was behind half the delays.

<Well?> Lieutenant Smythe asked a few moments later.

<Well what?> Connie shot back, feeling her last shred of propriety slipping away.

<What are we going to do?>

She chewed at the inside of her cheek as she considered a half-dozen replies to Smythe's question. In the end, she settled on, *<You're the officer, Smythe. I'm just a* ***technical*** *sergeant. What do* ***you*** *think we should do?>*

She almost laughed at the sound of indignation that came to her over the Link. *<Seriously, Connie, everyone knows you're the real XO on the* Jones. *We gotta figure this out.>*

Connie closed her eyes, pausing next to a rack of hull plating. *<OK, Smythe, here's what we're gonna do. We're going to put as much glue and spit on this bird as it takes to keep her from bleeding atmo, then cram everything else we need inside, and boost out of here on schedule. We'll finish all that work on the trip.>*

<Uh, OK, Connie. How're we going to get the hull ready? I've been watching those crews out there…it's like they have every repair drone moving in slow motion.>

<You let me worry about that. I know something that

Dockmaster Kieran doesn't want a certain woman in his life to know.>

A choked laugh came across the Link. <*Seriously? You're going to try* **that** *with Kieran? Dude's scary even when he's happy.*>

<*Maybe to you,*> Connie replied, her voice coy. <*But that's because you don't have anything he wants.*>

<*Stars, I am going to pretend I never had this conversation with you.*>

<*Good call.*>

Connie queried the sector NSAI for Kieran's location and then pushed off the hull plates she'd leant on. It was time to beard the lion in his den.

Dockmaster Kieran was in charge of bays 8120 through 8130 in Sector 33, but acted like he ran the whole sector. Which was partially true, since he bowled his way over everyone around him. Even though he was only a master sergeant, she'd seen majors find somewhere else to be when he came through in a foul mood.

Connie suspected that the holdups they were constantly facing were related to the lockdown that had occurred when Admiral Deering had secreted the *Jones* and the *Norse Wind* in bay 8129 and denied anyone—including Kieran—access to the bay.

Connie walked out of the dock and followed the corridors to the sector's admin offices. When she arrived, Kieran's door was wide open, and she strode past the front desk—where the corporal stationed there protested her interruption—and into the master sergeant's office.

"Technical Sergeant." He grunted out the word without looking up from the plas sheets arrayed before him, knowing all too well how the rank irked her.

She drew a calming breath and then shut the door before responding. "You're messing with my shit, Kieran. The *Jones* should be spaceworthy by now, but you just have one crew on it. What gives?"

Kieran shuffled his plas sheets together before looking up at her. "What *gives* is that you messed with my shit, so now it's coming back around."

Connie leant forward and planted her fists on the dockmaster's desk. "You know full well that we didn't do any of that. You want someone to get pissy at, go shit on Admiral Deering."

The burly man eased back in his chair and folded his hands behind his head. "Well, they shipped her off to someplace cold and unpleasant, so the only people I have to take my ire out on are you lot. Sorry, that's just the way it is."

Connie decided to make one final plea to his sense of decency—should he actually possess such a thing. "I have orders to get the *Jones* in the black in fourteen hours. They're not the sort of directives that have a lot of flexibility."

"Damn," he shook his head, a cruel smile forming on his lips. "I don't see how that can happen. You know half the hull plates are off your ship right now, right?"

"OK, shithead," she growled at the master sergeant. "You wanna fuck with me? Think you can piss on me just because things didn't go your way a few weeks back? I'm going to bring your entire world crashing down around your ears."

Master Sergeant Kieran rose from his desk to tower over Connie, his face reddening. "Who the hell do you think you are, Sergeant? I'll—"

"Be in a world of hurt when I tell your wife about the women you've been seeing on the side;" Connie shouted over him. "Who is it now, Rochel, Rayna, and Rory? That's just the Rs, too."

Kieran slashed his hand through the air as he hissed at her. "You open your bitch mouth about that shit, and I'll—"

"You're not going to do a damn thing, Kieran. Because I *also* know that you banged Samantha Higgs in the mess hall's supply closet three weeks ago."

A cruel grin formed on Connie's lips as she watched the color drain from the big man's face.

"Yeah, that's right. You and Colonel Higgs aren't on the best of terms to begin with.... I wonder what will happen when he finds out that you smashed his little sister up against the cleaning bots? Granted, it won't be nearly as bad as what he does to you when I tell him you fucked his wi—"

"I'll get it done," Kieran growled.

"Get what done?" Connie asked innocently. "I want to hear you say it."

"Your ship. It'll be ready to fly in fourteen hours."

She locked eyes with the master sergeant. "Make it ten, and you have a deal."

"Ten!"

"Too big a number? Then let's go for eight."

Kieran's jaw clamped shut, and he ground his teeth so loudly that Connie wondered if they would shatter.

"I can do ten." He bit off each word.

"Excellent. I'll get back down to the *Jones* and make sure

the pace picks up."

Connie turned and walked toward the door. Her hand was almost over the access panel when Kieran spoke up.

"How?"

"How what?" she asked without turning.

"You know what. How do you know all that?"

Connie turned just enough to take in the brutish man. "You're sloppy. You hide what you do from *people,* but you forget about automatons and servitors. AIs monitor those. AIs see everything. Normally they don't care who bangs who, but I have some very good friends who happen to be AIs, and they thought I might find that information useful. I didn't want to use it, but..." she gave an exaggerated shrug. "You kinda forced my hand."

Kieran sputtered, and Connie nodded to his desk. "Chop-chop. I expect to see big changes by the time I get back to the bay."

She opened the door and walked out of his office, not bothering to close the door, certain that the corporal at the front desk was staring at his fuming boss, wondering how a technical sergeant had just schooled the terror of Sector 33.

Halfway to the bay, Lovell, the *Jones*'s AI, reached out.

<Wow, Smythe told me you were going to confront Kieran, but this is nuts. I just got word that three combat repair teams are on their way to get us ship-shape!>

<Good,> Connie didn't bother hiding the satisfaction in her voice. *<They'd better be here pronto.>*

<I gotta ask...how did you do that? I've ***never*** *seen anyone grab Kieran by the short and curlies before.>*

<You can thank Darla,> Connie replied. *<She left me with a few grenades to toss Kieran's way if I needed.>*

<*Grenades?*> Lovell sounded suitably awed. <*Seems more like you nuked the guy from orbit. What did you have on him?*>

Connie chuckled. <*A girl never tells, Lovell.*>

<*Well, I imagine you told Kieran that you'd tell, if he didn't do what you wanted.*>

<*That doesn't count.*>

CHASING SIMON

STELLAR DATE: 02.20.4084 (Adjusted Years)
LOCATION: TMS *Fleetwings 17,* Approaching Ceres
REGION: Main Asteroid Belt, Terran Hegemony, InnerSol

In addition to maintaining her cover as the wealthy and mysterious Claire, Tanis spent much of her time aboard the *Fleetwings 17* studying the datapacket Harm had provided on Simon after she'd accepted the mission.

The first thing she found to be noteworthy was that Simon was not military—at least there was nothing in the data provided to suggest that he was. As best she could tell, he was a civilian contractor who had worked his way up from corporate espionage to wet work, which had garnered MICI's attention.

None of that was explicitly stated in the dossier, but the clues were there. A referenced connection to a corporation here, a date that coincided with an unsolved murder there.

Tanis wasn't surprised to see that people like Simon got scooped up by Division 99, but it was a bit dismaying to see that a man who was clearly a criminal had gotten a free pass because of his skills.

While there was little information in the data packet about Simon's past, there was almost nothing about his current assignment. In fact, it was so light on details, that she wondered if part of the packet was missing, or if there was supposed to have been a second transmission.

Though she and Darla had discussed not reaching out to Harm—lest he or his channels be compromised—she worried it was the wrong move. Still, the Infiltrator

Chameleon was their only lead at present, and reaching out to Harm may let its puppetmaster know she had survived its attempted assassination in the boutique's dressing room.

Tanis just hoped that when they arrived at Ceres, the IC's actions would open up new avenues of investigation.

However, that didn't keep her from her primary mission. She dug up what she could on where Simon had been on Ceres before he disappeared. A few surreptitious inquiries to AIs who Darla trusted turned up a trail on the planet's ring, which then led to the planet's surface.

But the end of the trail was seven days old. That was when Simon had simply disappeared. He'd checked into a hotel at the base of the Ahuna Mountains, and hadn't been seen since.

The cover he'd been using at the time was that of a man named Kyran, and none of the alias's credit accounts had been used since check-in. Tanis scoured every feed she could get her hands on, but nothing showed anyone remotely close to resembling Simon's division-registered covers entering or exiting the hotel in the days following.

That didn't mean it was impossible for the man to have snuck out. Plenty of service vehicles came and went, any one of them providing more than enough room for Simon to hide.

<*Stars,*> Tanis said in frustration as she completed another viewing of the vid feeds they had access to. <*There's just nothing there. I wish we knew what Simon was doing on Ceres. That would make this a hell of a lot easier.*>

<*I've been cross-referencing everyone of note who was on the planet at the same time he was—plus dignitaries soon to arrive,*> Darla replied. <*There are a lot of remote possibilities, but so far,*

nothing stands out.>

<*I swear, the next time I see Harm, I'm gonna give him a smack upside the head. How could he send us out like this and then not provide any follow-up? The IC hasn't picked up any messages from Harm with more details, has it?*>

Darla's avatar appeared in Tanis's mind, shaking her head. <*Nope, your boring little robot clone hasn't used the Link for anything other than ordering food.*>

<*Pretty poor chameleon; I'm not really that solitary.*> Tanis suddenly felt as though Darla was judging her. <*What? I'm not! I have friends, I do things, I even talk to strangers at bars and stuff. I'm the freakin' life of the party.*>

<*Easy there, chrome dome, don't get yourself all worked up. You might blow a gasket.*>

Tanis groaned. <*You know, you were the one who wanted me in this mirrorsheath so badly. It was also you who insisted I wear the mask.*>

<*Maybe it was just so I could make fun of you. Did you ever think of that?*>

A few choice responses flashed through Tanis's mind, but she decided to ignore the AI. Moments later, an alert flashed on her HUD, and she smiled at the news.

<*Looks like my doppelganger has booked a stay at the same hotel Simon went missing from.*>

<*Well, well. So she has,*> Darla replied. <*Should Claire visit it as well?*>

<*No,*> Tanis shook her head. <*Claire going downworld to the same hotel as my…me…would be too suspicious. We'll have her rent a place on the ring, and then someone else will follow the IC down to the surface.*>

<*Have anyone in mind?*> Darla asked, her tone neutral—

though Tanis knew the AI would be intensely curious.

<I think I'll use the 'Bella' cover.>

<Bella? She's barely a cover at all!>

<Exactly.>

CASSIE HAWK

STELLAR DATE: 02.17.4084 (Adjusted Years)
LOCATION: TSS *Kirby Jones,* Bay 8129, Sector 33
REGION: Vesta, Terran Hegemony, InnerSol

Harm Ellis pushed a power-truck onto the *Kirby Jones,* keeping an eye out for the woman he wanted to have a chat with. Something very strange was going on, and he wanted to get to the bottom of it.

"Hold 2," Spaceman Liam directed Harm, and he nodded before turning down the side corridor.

Looks like my quick and dirty disguise is working, Harm thought with a laugh as he glanced at himself in a reflective door. He looked *close* to his normal appearance, but with just a few changes to hair, brow, and jaw, no one would confuse him for the Enfield scientist known as Harm Ellis.

Today, he was Randy Drush. Which was to say that it was a day like any other—one when he lied about who he was.

Sometimes Harm had to remind himself of what his real name was; it had been so long since he'd used it. Even in the Division, he went by Harm Ellis. Of course, that was because he was undercover as an Enfield employee with access to Division 99, working in concert with them to place AIs with L2 humans.

Oh the tangled web we weave, he thought to himself before depositing his cargo in Hold 2.

He tapped into the ship's internal surveillance systems while traversing its corridors, and queried them for Connie's whereabouts. As luck would have it, she was just two holds down. He made his way to her location like he had every right to be walking about the ship.

He entered the hold to see Connie bent over, looking through a crate that bore the label 'Conway Hot Tub and Spa'. He frowned, wondering why something like that was on the ship as he closed the door and activated a privacy field.

"Connie," he began, only to find the engineer facing him with a gun in her hand.

"That's my name," she grunted. "Kieran send you? Tell him he can't muscle his way out of this or shut me up. The AIs know to drop everything onto the public nets if anything happens to me."

"You blackmailed Kieran?" Harm asked with a laugh. "I guess that explains the four hull repair crews out there."

"If you're not with Kieran, then what's your game?"

"No games," Harm replied. "It's me, Harm Ellis."

Though the rest of Tanis's crew didn't know of Harm, he had worked with Connie to gather the *Kirby Jones*'s crew several weeks ago while Tanis was being held under suspicion of murder.

Connie's eyes widened. "Harm? Nice disguise. What are you doing skulking onto my ship?"

"Trying to figure out where you're going in such a hurry."

"What do you mean?" A look of concern came over Connie. "I was certain it was you sending us out! Everything is coming down through Colonel Higgs, but I can tell he's just relaying orders. A few plas sheets have had your initials hidden on them."

"My initials? I'd never do something so crude, Connie.

Where are you bound?" Harm asked as he considered the implications of someone masquerading—poorly—as him.

"We're to meet with Tanis on Ceres. She'll beat us there, but we won't be too far behind."

"Ceres?" Harm asked in surprise. "She's supposed to be hanging out with her boy toy down on Mars! Have you spoken to her?"

Connie shook her head. "Like I said, I figured this was all your doing and that you wouldn't want us blathering about it."

"Can you forward me some of the orders?"

"Sure."

Connie pulled the lading plas off the crate she had opened and handed it to him. "This one has your initials in a microdot. Forwarding the orders."

Harm shook his head at the 'HE'; it was obviously something put there just for Connie to find. As he reviewed the orders, he spotted a data pattern that he watermarked documents with—one that he didn't think anyone else knew about.

"Ahhh crap!" he exclaimed. "I *did* send these orders."

"Glad you agree with me," Connie replied. "But either you've got amnesia, or shit's just gotten weird."

Harm handed the plas back to her. "Weird with a side of WTF. OK, I have to go. I need to find out who has set this in motion."

"Uhhh...what about us?" she asked.

"Continue as you are. I'll be in touch. And no one knows I was here."

* * * * *

Connie had to admit that the threat of Colonel Higgs' unbridled wrath had garnered exactly the sort of result from Master Sergeant Kieran that she'd hoped for.

Possibly even *more* than she'd hoped for. It was almost sickening the way he contacted her every thirty minutes to ensure that things were proceeding satisfactorily.

In the end, the crews missed Connie's deadline of being ready in ten hours, but still made it under twelve.

"Kirby Jones, Kirby Jones!" Lieutenant Jeannie called out gleefully over the 1MC. "We have clearance to disembark. All sections confirm readiness to break moorings."

<This is engineering. Break moorings, aye,> Connie called up to the bridgenet from the main engineering bay, glancing at Seamus and Liam, who were draped over their consoles, both struggling to stay awake after working for over two days without sleep.

Corporal Marion chimed in afterward, announcing that the sortie rooms, common spaces, and cabins were ship-shape and ready for hard burn.

<All ship sections confirmed in readiness, aye,> Lovell added.

<Lieutenant Smythe,> Jeannie announced over the shipnet, her tone slightly more reserved. *<Ship is ready to disembark. Permission to break mooring.>*

<Permission granted, Lieutenant. Get us on the rails.>

Connie watched her consoles, glancing at the visuals of the bay—which still looked like a disaster—that showed the dock rails sliding out of the deck and connecting to the cradle.

Her systems indicated a solid connection between the

rails and the cradle, and she disengaged the *Kirby Jones*'s docking clamps.

Pressure warning alerts sounded in the docking bay, and the exterior electrostatic field snapped into place, holding atmosphere in as the bay doors began to slide open.

The crews working to clean up the dock barely even paid the alerts any notice, as the cradle tilted and the ship slid onto the maglev rails.

<Rail boost in t-minus ten!> Jeannie announced, and Connie passed a non-verbal confirmation that the *Jones* had a solid 'grip' on the rails.

A part of her was worried that Master Sergeant Kieran would do something at the last moment to ruin their departure, but when Jeannie's count hit zero, the TSS *Kirby Jones* slid gracefully down the rails and out into the black.

Docking control handed the ship off to Vesta's STC, and the ship was assigned a chemical thrust vector. Connie only half watched the thruster readouts as Jeannie boosted the ship away from Vesta's ring.

"Shit," Seamus sighed while rubbing his face. "I kept waiting for something to break off before we hit the rails. I can't believe we finally got out of there. I could sleep for a week."

Liam gave Seamus a light punch on the shoulder. "You still have to get the new dorsal beams connected to the backup trunkline. No week-long nap for you."

"Yeah? Well, you've got a hot tub to set up in Hold 2," Seamus shot back. "I want to have a nice bubbly soak. Chop-chop."

"No one touch that shit," Connie interrupted. "It's not a hot tub, and I don't want anyone in there 'til we get the commander back aboard and she tells us what to do with it."

"The commander?" Liam sat up straight and tilted his head as he regarded Connie. "What's in there, Sarge?"

"None of your stars-be-damned business, Spaceman, that's what," she growled. Both Seamus and Liam drew back, eyes wide, and she shook her head. "Sorry, guys. I guess I'm still a bit on edge. I'm going to go do a walkthrough to make sure things are battened down. Once Jeannie lights the fusion burners—and everything is in the green—you two go grab some sack time."

"You good to handle the shift on your own, Sarge?" Seamus asked.

"Well, I'm only giving you four hours in the sack, then it's my turn, so make the most of it."

Liam winked at Seamus. "With one hand she giveth while with the she other taketh away."

Connie gave that comment what it deserved—an eyeroll—and then walked out of the engineering bay to make her final inspection.

To say that the interior of the *Jones* was a disaster was an understatement. Every corridor had panels pulled off and conduit hanging, webbed in only enough to keep it from pulling free under thrust.

She had to watch her step, as deck plates had been pulled up in some places, creating dangerous pitfalls. As she rounded a corner, Connie spotted a sewage line that was capped off and realized it was the one that ran to the san in her cabin.

"Well, shit..." she muttered. "Good thing I spotted that before I used the thing."

"No pun intended?" a voice asked from behind her.

Connie spun to see a woman standing in the corridor wearing a shipsuit with a *Kirby Jones* logo on the chest. She was a touch on the overly-curvy side, with spiky, pink hair and glowing blue eyes.

"Who in the sweet fucking stars are you?" Connie asked, realizing that she'd left her service weapon in the engineering bay.

Then a privacy field snapped into place around them.

"Easy, Sergeant, it's me. Harm Ellis."

"Harm? Seriously?" Connie scowled at the pink-haired woman. "What happened to that Randy guy?"

"Randy is a dockhand. There's no way he'd get assigned to the *Jones*."

"Today is off the rails, you'll forgive me if I'm suspicious," Connie muttered as she folded her arms. "If you're Harm, what did I order to drink at The Pig's Ass when we met with Tanis?"

"How would I know?" the woman replied. "I wasn't there. I'm passing you my tokens, that's a lot better than playing twenty questions."

The woman's answer had been correct, and when her data packet hit Connie's Link, and she shunted it off into a sandboxed environment before opening it.

"Damn, Harm," she said after looking over the information. "Girl looks…well…good-ish on you."

Harm glanced down at herself and chuckled quietly. "Was a rush job. I didn't have time to narrow my shoulders—that shit hurts, anyway—so I had to plump my hips to get the ratios right." He turned slightly. "Got a bit big in the booty department—I'll have to keep Smythe at arm's length, he likes that sort of thing."

"So I guess this means you've decided to come along for the ride?" Connie asked, a smile on her lips. "What prompted the gender change, though?"

Harm shrugged. "I flip between being a man and woman so often, I almost forget what I was born as. This cover was already established as being on Vesta; a quick transfer later, and Cassie Hawk is part of the crew of the *Kirby Jones*."

"So which is it?" Connie pressed. "Were you born male or female?"

Harm placed a finger on the side of his nose. "An operative never reveals any hints of their true identity."

"Cassie," Connie tried out the name. "I guess it fits. I assume you need me to fudge some sort of mix-up that explains why you're aboard and the XO doesn't know about it?"

"Don't worry. He's about to find out," Harm—Cassie said with a wink.

<Hey, Connie,> Lieutenant Smythe called down. *<I just got the weirdest burst from Colonel Higgs' office. Says we got a new crewmember at the last minute, someone to help wrap up all the work in engineering. Do we need to make a U-turn to go get her, or did she sneak aboard?>*

<No worries, XO,> Connie replied, trying to keep her voice as normal as possible. *<She got on right before we sealed up. Looks like we have a dead spot on the relays on Deck 3, so she buckled up in one of the emergency boost stations and waited for us to hit the black before coming to engineering. Good thing we got an extra set of hands, or I'd have to get Marion and her team to put us back together.>*

Smythe snorted. *<Doubt that would have gone well. They're*

a lot better at taking things apart.>

<With extreme prejudice.>

<Well, send her up here when you're ready—oh, look at that, she's an E-4. Poor Liam and Seamus, another woman lording over them.>

Connie shot Smythe a dark look over the Link. *<You have a problem with women lording over you?>*

<Uh…no,> Smythe said quickly. *<I just mean that those two seem to enjoy behaving like naught—fuck, I don't know how to dig myself out of this one. Just don't tell the commander I said that.>*

<Don't worry, Lieutenant,> Connie sent him a mischievous smirk. *<I'll just store it up with all the other boneheaded things you've said in the past that are waiting to be used as bribes.>*

<Great. Noted,> Smythe said with a drawn out sigh before closing the connection.

Connie returned her focus to Harm. "Well, Cassie Hawk. Welcome to the *Kirby Jones*. Now can you tell me what the hell is going on?"

Harm gestured toward one of the nearby holds with his head, and Connie followed him in, closing the door behind herself.

"Spill," she said, folding her arms.

"OK, here's what I know. I was busy with some L2 stuff for Enfield, and didn't realize until late yesterday that your timetable had been ramped up. After meeting with you, I was able to confirm that someone was passing Colonel Higgs orders that seemed to be coming from Division 99."

" 'Seemed'? How does one 'seem' to fake orders from the TSF's top intelligence division?"

Harm—who Connie realized she needed to think of only

as 'Cassie', or she was going to call him/her the wrong thing at the wrong time—gave a soft, almost squeaky laugh. "Well, that's the kicker. Faking orders like that is pretty tricky, but I wasn't able to tell where they were coming from. Let's just say that when you think there are subversive elements in your own agency masquerading as you, you've got a pretty big problem on your hands."

"Don't you mean *our* hands?" Connie asked. "We're all mixed up in this, too."

"Yeah…and that's puzzling, but for whatever reason, the *Kirby Jones* and Tanis are at the heart of whatever is going on—"

Connie started to interrupt, but Harm—Cassie—held up a hand.

"Let me finish. I had 'Harm' take a leave of absence and hop a liner to Venus while I switched over to Cassie. I went through some back channels to get Cassie's orders to Higgs, but it's entirely possible that whoever orchestrated your hasty departure from Vesta will eventually pick up on it and guess at who Cassie Hawk is—"

"Get to the part about Tanis," Connie grunted.

Cassie pursed her lips, then nodded. "OK. I traced communications going to Tanis and realized that she got a burst from me yesterday. The message directed her to go to Ceres and begin looking for one of my assets. She boarded a ship for Ceres from Mars 1 yesterday."

"That makes sense, it's where we were told to meet her for refit shakedown," Connie replied.

"Yeah, which is one hell of a weak excuse to get you all there. I would have done a lot better, if it were my op. Good thing whoever is pulling these strings is being a bit sloppy—

or rushed."

Connie shook her head as she tried to make sense of what Cassie was telling her. "This is just too weird. Why us? We're just a patrol boat."

A happy grin broke out on Cassie's face. "So she didn't tell you? Good. I bet Darla that she wouldn't."

"Tell me what?" Connie said, lowering her brow.

"Tanis is Division now. One of my assets."

"Shit! Really? And she *didn't* tell me? So much for being besties." Connie only half meant what she'd said. Tanis keeping being a Mickie quiet made sense, but she hated being in the dark.

"Yeah, and now so are you, Connie. No one else on the crew can know about any of this."

"Oh boy," Connie's voice dripped with sarcasm. "I'm a spy. Yay."

"Don't get too excited. You're more like the backup quartermaster for the spies."

Connie couldn't help but roll her eyes at the designation. "So what's our play, oh great mastermind?"

"Don't forget," Cassie's voice squeaked with indignance. "I'm a colonel and I'm giving you orders here."

"I won't forget," Connie gave Cassie a measuring look. "But from the way I see it, you need me more than I need you."

"Yeah, well, Tanis needs us both more. We need to get to Ceres, meet up with her, and find out why they sent her there."

Connie's eyes widened. "You think someone is going to use her to do something bad?"

"Yeah," Cassie nodded. "Something that seems to

require a starship with upgraded weapons and a fiercely loyal crew."

"Shit," Connie whispered. "Tanis and Darla are smart, though. They're not going to fall for anything illegal."

Cassie nodded, but her eyes held a measure of doubt. "There are a lot of ways to make people do things, Connie. Tanis isn't immune to coercion. I'll admit that I don't know *how* someone plans to manipulate her, but the lengths they've already gone to tell me that they have a plan, and they believe it will work."

"Well, shit, then we'd better get to Ceres as fast as we can."

Cassie walked to the door and palmed it open. "Aren't we already doing that?"

"You know what I mean, Cassie."

PINAN GODAN

STELLAR DATE: 02.21.4084 (Adjusted Years)
LOCATION: TMS *Fleetwings 17,* Approaching Ceres
REGION: Main Asteroid Belt, Terran Hegemony, InnerSol

The ship was still a few hours from docking at Ceres' Insi Ring, but Tanis wanted to get a feel for Bella beforehand. After peeling off the mirrorsheath, she took a long shower then sifted through the clothing Darla had purchased, looking for something that suited her next cover.

<*Admit it. You like playing dress-up,*> Darla said as Tanis laid out a few options.

"It's growing on me," Tanis replied as she held up a long coat. "I still don't think it's *me,* but I also think that's part of why I like it."

<*You know…that makes sense.*>

Tanis decided not to question Darla's acceptance as she pulled on the loose slacks and grey blouse she'd selected. Once they were situated, she fastened a wide belt around her waist, buckling it tight before pulling on the flowing, ankle-length, silken coat that was Bella's preference.

The final part of the outfit was a protective film she sprayed on the bottom of her feet.

"OK…I like everything about this cover except that she likes to go barefoot."

<*It's an homage to ancient martial arts. They fought barefoot.*>

"I guess it's somewhat practical now, with a layer of pro-skin."

<*You should practice a kata, get yourself in the zone.*>

"Good idea."

Bella was an accomplished martial artist, which suited Tanis well, as she'd studied Wado Ryu karate for years. She thought through the discipline's katas as she walked into the clear space in the center of her cabin, and decided on Pinan GoDan.

It had been some years since she had practiced karate, but as she calmed her breathing and settled into *masuba dachi* to start, the moves came back to her, and she performed them almost instinctively.

Her clothing rustled around her as she eased through the kata's forms, finally reaching the *kokutso dachi,* while simultaneously, throwing the left *soto uke*—careful not to have her flowing sleeves slap her in the face—and delivered a right *gedan uke* to the front.

With a deep exhale, Tanis pulled her right foot back and relaxed her arms in *hachiji dachi* before closing to *masuba dachi,* and then lowering her head to *rei.*

She played a holo of herself going through the moves and nodded in satisfaction. "Seems I still have it."

<A bit slow, though.>

"Hey, that was my first kata in years. Give me a break."

<Bella is a tenth degree black belt in Wado Ryu, you need to be flawless at any speed.>

"I got to third degree before I became an L2. Mimicking a tenth should be a breeze now."

Tanis settled into *masuba dachi* once more and repeated the forms until she could complete the entire Pinan GoDan kata in what felt like a single, flowing motion.

Her enhanced reflexes and L2 speed would render her movements as little more than a blur to most people, and she knew it wasn't the point of kata to perform it so fast, but

Tanis rather liked the feeling of flying through it.

Once she had satisfied herself with the high-speed edition, she slowed back down to the pace she knew would have pleased her sensei.

A moment of curiosity hit her, and she wondered what Sensei Guthrie was doing now, if he still taught in his small dojo in the hills above the Melas Chasma. She considered visiting him as Bella at some point; it could be an amusing diversion.

With Pinan GoDan remastered, Tanis worked through the other seven Wado Ryu katas until she knew that each one would have received perfect marks from Sensei Guthrie.

As she finished, an alert came in that the *Fleetwing 17* would be docking at Ceres' Insi Ring in two hours, and to prepare for a hard burn in thirty minutes, effectively ending Tanis's practice session.

"I guess it's time to be Claire one more time," she said with a sigh, eyeing the mirrorsheath, now feeling loathe to put it back on.

Bella felt so honest in who she was, while Claire seemed like one big lie.

*Though I suppose they're **all** lies....*

After a few moments' consideration, she opted to forgo the mirrorsheath and instead selected an ankle-length gown. But as she began to pull it on, Tanis realized that it was so tight it almost welded her ankles together.

"Seriously, Darla. I actually need to be able to move around in these outfits," she muttered while pulling it off and searching for something better, carefully avoiding the dreaded ball dress.

<I didn't create the Claire cover, remember? Harm had already established her as a foppish debutante. Don't blame me for executing it well.>

<I'm starting to think that thou doth protest too much.>

In the end, Tanis selected a pair of black leggings with gold and silver thread woven through them and paired them with a burnished silver halter top made of a flexible metal—though not so flexible that it was easy to get on—finishing the look with an array of bangles that nearly covered her arms.

She pulled on a pair of silver boots, realizing too late that not only were they heel-less, but they didn't flex at all in the ankle.

"All passengers, please settle into your beds and strap in for a hard burn. We're looking at nine *g*s to match Insi's rotation. Burn in three minutes."

Every holodisplay in the cabin switched to show the countdown, and Tanis quickly pushed all the clothing she'd strewn about back into their crates before pulling on the uncomfortable boots and laying on the bed.

"You know…when you saw me pulling these boots out of the container, you could have mentioned the lack of heels."

<I just saw you flawlessly perform katas at lightning speed. I really don't think heel-less boots pose a problem for you.>

"I guess on the plus side, if I kick someone, they're going to feel it in the morning. And I only have to wear this to the hotel that you've booked for Claire, and then I can be Bella again."

<Yes, your suffering will be limited.>

* * * * *

Once the ship had docked with Ceres' Insi Ring, Tanis placed Bella's clothing in a follow-bot, and instructed the ship's NSAI to have the rest of her belongings delivered to the hotel.

Her cabin and the corridors of the *Fleetwing 17* were carpeted, but once she arrived in the debarkation area, Tanis found that the boots had an added feature she'd been unaware of.

Every time they hit the hard deck, they rang like a bell.

Heads turned, and dozens of annoyed glares were sent her way, while she had to walk with her head held high, as though she fully intended to sound like an ancient church tower while striding through the customs arch.

<I don't know how, but I'm going to make you pay for this,> Tanis growled at Darla at one point.

<I'm sorry about this one. The listing said they had a soft 'tinkling' sound on hard surfaces, not that you were going to be impersonating a gong.>

Tanis maintained a serene expression as she reached her waiting stationcar outside the terminal and sank into the seat as it took off. The relatively new Insi Ring—named after the ancient ring the Andersonians built around Ceres only to be destroyed by the AIs at the outset of the Sentience Wars—did not have a terraformed inner surface. Instead, a clear overhead covered the ring, leaving Ceres visible, hanging above.

The dwarf planet was the largest object in the Main Asteroid Belt—almost twice the diameter of Vesta, which still only gave it a circumference of just under three thousand kilometers, and roughly the same surface area as the Indian subcontinent on Earth.

Naturally, Ceres had just three percent of Earth's gravity, but that was no longer the case, courtesy of the GE miniature black hole in its center.

Installed in the twenty-eighth century, Ceres' GE MBH brought the planet's surface gravity up to a hair more than Luna's, close to 0.2*g*s.

Or, in Tanis's opinion, 'comfortable'.

Unlike Mars 1, the Insi Ring was geostationary in relation to Ceres' surface, anchored to the planet by myriad cables that stretched to both the equator and the poles.

Before humans began to alter it, Ceres had a nine-hour day. However, to give the Insi Ring sufficient angular momentum for artificial gravity—while still keeping it anchored to the planet—that day had been shortened to just four hours.

The end result was that Insi had nearly identical gravity to that of Ceres' surface.

Though many of her memories of Ceres were not fond, as she gazed up through the clear ring-dome at the planet above, she couldn't help but admit how beautiful it was, given the initial failed terraforming attempts, and the near total-destruction when the original Insi Ring had collapsed onto the planet.

A large section of that ancient ring was still visible where it had fallen near the equator, maintained as a memorial to the war and the lives that had been lost when Psion had attacked the Andersonian Collective over a thousand years ago.

Sometimes Tanis had trouble connecting to the ancient

history of the Sol System, but seeing a four-hundred kilometer length of once-orbital ring standing out of the forests and plains of a planet's surface was a stark reminder that the price humans and AIs paid to learn how to live together had been a high one.

<*I hate looking at that thing,*> Darla said, as Tanis continued to gaze at the planet.

<*Ceres, or the old Insi Ring?*>

<*The ring. I have ancestors on all sides of that conflict. Makes for a lot of mixed feelings.*>

<*I'm more removed from it—obviously,*> Tanis replied after a moment's consideration. <*History doesn't look too kindly on the Andersonian Collective, but Psion was clearly in the wrong, as well.*>

<***Everyone** was wrong back then. But if Psion had to make their initial point with someone, I'm glad it was the AC—and you should be too. If the Collective had gotten their way, humans would be huddling in caves, banging rocks together.*>

Tanis gave a soft laugh. <*That seems a bit extreme.*>

<*Maybe,*> Darla said the word with a note of allowance, but not much.

The rest of the ride was made in silence, and when Tanis finally reached her suite in The Prima Plaza Hotel, her assorted luggage was waiting for her there.

"Huh." she glanced back at the follow-bot. "Guess I didn't need you after all."

The bot turned to leave her room, and Tanis called out. "Wait! Stupid thing. I need to get my clothes out of you."

The bot returned, and Tanis collected her belongings from it, surprised to hear the machine make a rude sound as it trundled out of her room.

<I hate it when they give those things personality quirks,> Darla muttered. *<I have half a mind to hack it and reset it.>*

"Why's that?" Tanis asked as she released the clasps on the silver boots and threw the cursed things halfway across the room.

<A lot of humans have trouble differentiating between true sentient AIs and non-sentient intelligences already. Making machines that ape us demeans us by making humans think ***we're*** *just machines.>*

Tanis had never considered it in that light before. She had noticed that most automatons and servitors were very impersonal, but hadn't realized it was done on purpose as a differentiator.

"I can see how that would be an issue," Tanis said, unsure of how much the subject bothered Darla.

<Don't worry about it. I'll handle the emotional damage just fine,> the AI said with a derisive snort. *<Finish getting Bella'd up. I have her scheduled to give a demonstration at an ancient history show they're doing at the hotel today. Once you do that, you're free to head to the surface.>*

"Damn…I don't like the idea of the IC getting that far ahead of me."

<I altered her itinerary; she'll be taking the most circuitous route possible to the surface. If you don't dally, you may even beat her there.>

Darla inserted a few blind spots into the hotel's surveillance that allowed for 'Bella' to leave the room unnoticed. An hour later, the organizers of the 'Talents of Ancient History' show were effusively thanking the martial arts expert for attending and demonstrating the art of karate to them.

Tanis had to hold back a laugh as she considered that, a few weeks ago, Bella hadn't even existed, and now people were falling over themselves to have her perform a demonstration at their event.

Harm certainly does good work—except for when it comes to checking in on me.

Tanis began her presentation with the Pinan NiDan kata, explaining to the crowd as she moved through the forms how karate originated with the peasants of Okinawa, an island south of Japan. The people of Okinawa had been forbidden to own weapons by the Japanese emperor, so they combined their knowledge of fighting with Chinese martial arts to create karate.

It was an abbreviated version of history—a subject that Tanis found fascinating—but she knew that the crowd had come to see her fight, not talk, so once she completed two more katas, she summoned her first opponent onto the low, ten-by-ten-meter stage.

It was a simple combat automaton that the show organizers had provided, and she defeated it in moments, smashing the machine's damage sensors and dropping it to the deck.

Following that, two more automatons joined it, and then eventually she was simultaneously fighting seven of the machines.

The crowd was cheering, and Tanis wondered if they'd be as impressed should they learn she was an L2. Though people with enhancements like hers were respected for what they could do, most people still felt wary around them, jealous of what they felt to be an unfair advantage granted by greater neuron density, interconnectivity, and signal transfer speed.

Finally, after she had bested ten automatons, a large man shouldered his way through the crowd.

As he got closer, he called out, "I see you can beat a bunch of bots—probably all programmed to fail—but can you beat a human?"

<*Shit!*> Darla exclaimed. <*He's a local mixed martial arts fighter. The guy's over two hundred and fifty kilograms!*>

<*Garth!*> Tanis yelled at the event's organizer, turning to glare at him. <*Did you set this up?*>

<*Umm…yes? It seemed like a great way to show your ancient arts against modern fighting techniques. He's signed all the waivers. Will you fight him? Please?*>

Tanis ground her teeth. If she were 'Tanis', she'd just walk away…maybe after shooting the bastard with a pulse pistol, but it wasn't in Bella's nature to turn down a fight like this.

<*Very well. But I'm doubling my fee,*> she shot back at Garth before turning to the man stepping onto the stage.

"I'm going to turn you into a smear," he grunted, while Darla fed Tanis visuals of the brute's fighting skill. His real name was Tom, but in the ring, he fought as the 'Skull Crusher'.

<*Typical for his sort,*> Tanis muttered.

She stepped back to her side of the ring and settled into *masuba dachi,* slowly rolling her neck to work out a small kink that had developed while fighting the automatons.

Skull Crusher took the time for a few quick stretches, and then began to growl. Tanis cocked an eyebrow, and then gave a slight bow before settling back into *shomen neko ashi dachi,* her weight on her left rear foot, toes of her right resting lightly on the ground.

She waited patiently for his assault, which was—predictably—a forward lunge of sorts. His arms were spread wide, as if he was expecting to easily encompass her. Almost languidly, she stepped in and delivered a *mae geri* kick to his jaw.

She took care not to kick him hard enough to shatter the bone, but the blow clearly dislocated his jaw. She hoped it would end the fight quickly, while the crowd collectively gasped, and then cheered with delight.

A wild howl tore from Skull Crusher's throat, as he reeled back and reassessed the woman before him while shoving his jaw back into place—much to the horror of the throng.

"Gonna take a lot more than that to take me down, little girl," he grunted.

Tanis didn't respond, only settled back into her waiting stance while he worked his jaw.

Then, without warning, he launched another frontal assault, only to dart left at the last moment, swinging his right fist—which was nearly the size of Tanis's head—toward her torso.

Tapping into her L2 reflexes, Tanis twisted around his strike, delivering a hammer fist to his neck with her right hand, and a blow to his solar plexus with her left.

Though she delivered the attack with all her strength, it barely affected the behemoth, and he grabbed for her with his left hand, nearly getting it around her right arm, before Tanis twisted away, dashing to safety.

<If he manages to get a solid hold on you…> Darla warned.

<I know. Game over.>

The pair began to circle one another. Skull Crusher attempted to grab and punch Tanis a few more times, but each time, she evaded his blows, delivering a few *mae geri* kicks to his wrist when he overextended his reach.

It had become readily apparent that Skull Crusher liked to grapple more than hit. It made sense, given that he would normally fight within his own weight class, and his opponents likely moved as slowly as he did. Tanis's ability to evade his attacks was making the man frustrated, but no more than she was with not being able to hit him hard enough to do more than annoy him.

After five minutes of dancing around the brute, she decided that the time for caution was over. She drew up her right knee, twisting ever so slightly to hint at a roundhouse kick, which caused Skull Crusher to draw his left leg back and turn his torso away.

Here goes.

Utilizing every ounce of speed she possessed, she slammed her right foot down and spun her back to the man—something that would have horrified Sensei Guthrie. In the midst of that move, she whipped her left leg around and slammed it into the inside of the brute's right knee. At the same time, she brought her left elbow into his throat, giving her kick additional leverage.

For a moment, Tanis met with more resistance than she expected, but as *"Kiai!"* tore free from her throat, a surge of energy burst through her, and her enemy's knee broke with a resounding *crack*.

The room fell silent as Skull Crusher screamed and fell to the floor. Tanis returned to her side of the raised stage and bowed once more before stepping off the platform and walking away.

The stunned crowd parted to let her through, and she was almost out of the room when the cheering began.

An hour later, she'd finally finished giving out her last holosig to her new fans, and boarded her ring-to-surface shuttle.

<*Sooo…note to self,*> Darla said, as the craft began to drop down to the world below. <*You put on a really good show, and they take longer than I expected. Your doppelganger is already planetside, but we should get to the hotel only a few minutes after her.*>

Tanis wanted to give Darla a hard time, but with the endorphins from the fight still flowing through her, she couldn't bring herself to feel upset about the delay.

<*Honestly? I rather enjoyed that. Took that asshole down a notch, and got to show those people what real fighting looks like, not that staged nonsense they see all the time.*>

<*Whew! Glad I'm not in the doghouse. Another note to self: make Tanis wear poofy dresses, and she plots your death. Get her into fights where people try and beat her to a pulp, and she thanks you.*>

<*I'm just a wonderful contradiction.*>

Neither spoke further on the flight—other than for Darla to inform Tanis that Skull Crusher's manager was threatening to sue her—and twenty minutes later, they were settling onto a cradle at Hunter's Lodge Spaceport.

Tanis did her best to ignore the incongruity of a small city being named a 'lodge' as she gathered her things and caught a hovercar to the Golden Gazelle Hotel, which sat at the edge of the city, at the base of the rugged Ahuna Mountains.

A few minutes later, the hovercar set down in front of the hotel, and Tanis grabbed her pack and stepped out into the warm air and cloudy-day sunlight of Ceres. A flight of stairs led from the street to the hotel, and in the low gravity, she leapt over them in a single bound.

A voice called out from behind her, and Tanis turned to see a young man struggling to climb the steps.

"Damn! How'd you do that?" he asked.

Tanis shook her head in dismay as she watched him put his foot down and push off too hard, going more sideways than straight.

With practiced ease, she darted backward and caught him before he fell on his side, twisting in the air and landing halfway up the steps, the wobbly man secure in her arms.

She couldn't help but notice—as they were face-to-face—that he was rather attractive and had a pleasing musk.

"Um, you have to be careful to push off in the center of your mass," she said, setting him down carefully. "You have five times the strength here that you're used to, so if you push to the side, you're five times more likely to go the opposite direction."

"I, uh…I get that in principle," the man said. "Practice is turning out to be a bit more difficult."

"Earther, right?" Tanis asked as she helped him walk up the steps.

"Yeah, grew up dirtside, near Mexico City. You?"

Tanis almost said Mars, but corrected herself to give Bella's birthplace. "Luna, so Ceres feels just like home."

"I don't know how you folks manage here. Even most space stations spin up to point seven gees."

"Well, we're born to it. Plus side, learning to walk hurts

a lot less, and we do it sooner."

They reached the top of the steps, and the man smoothed his hair back and gave Tanis a sheepish grin. "Thanks for that, I guess it would be easier to learn when you're that small. Being full-sized, it still hurts a bit when you fall on a staircase, even in low-*g*. I'm Kaebel, by the way."

"Bella," Tanis replied as they began to walk toward the hotel's glass doors. "So what brings you here to Ceres?"

"Business," Kaebel replied. "My firm makes superconductor batteries, and we have a new version that we're trying to market here."

"Oh? Personal?"

"Yeah, only three centimeters in diameter, but twice the charge with no overheating issues."

"Sounds impressive," Tanis replied with an accepting, but slightly patronizing smile. "I prefer a different type of energy."

Kaebel glanced over at her, then his eyes widened. "Oh! Hey! You're getting some play in the feeds right now—daaaamn! Did you break that guy's leg?"

She chuckled. "Yeah, he had it coming. Was a little publicity stunt the organizers set up—but didn't tell me about. He was playing for keeps, so I did too."

Kaebel chuckled as the hotel doors slid aside, and the pair walked in. "Glad you got that out of your system before you encountered me."

"I would never strike out at a stranger like that," Tanis said in a serious tone. "Unless they were striking me first."

The man gave her a worried look, but she winked, and he let out a relieved sigh. "Don't *say* things like that. I saw how fast you moved in those recordings. You could kill me before I even knew it."

Tanis let a mischievous smile form on her lips. "Don't worry, Kaebel. I've never killed anyone."

"Really?"

"I swear."

<Annnnnd now I feel gross for lying.>

<Tanis, the reluctant spy.>

Tanis already had her room and access codes, so—after making sure Kaebel reached the front desk without further mishap—she walked to the lifts and took a car up to her room on floor sixty-seven.

When she stepped into the single room suite—which already had several containers of her ubiquitous luggage stacked against one wall—she let out a sad sigh.

"OK, I've become spoiled. I'm half-wishing that Claire could have come. Multi-room suites are *niiiice*."

<Bella's not flush with cash like Claire—or Tanis, for that matter. Although you're getting a lot of requests for appearances right now. I bet you could get a good side hustle going as 'Bella the Devastator'.>

"Seriously?" Tanis groaned. "Is that what I'm being called?"

<It's one of the names I saw in the feeds. I think the worst one is 'Skull Crusher Crusher'. Though that's tied with 'Elbow of Doom'.>

"People have no imagination. Obviously I should be 'Bella the Beautiful'."

<Being Claire really did go to your head.>

"Maybe a bit," Tanis admitted. "Neural patterns from repeated behavior aren't so easily undone."

<Don't worry, I'll keep you humble.>

"You're all heart, Darla," Tanis replied as she fell backward onto the bed and closed her eyes. "So, what is other me up to?"

<Nothing so far. She checked in ten minutes before us. She's not had any communications that I've picked up, and she hasn't reached out to anyone.>

"And the *Jones*? Is it still en route?" Tanis knew she could have checked on her own, but at the moment, she just wanted to relax and not worry about whatever mysterious nonsense she was tied up in.

<They're due to dock on Insi in three days. I have to say, Tanis, I don't like that Harm hasn't reached out to 'other you' at all. It seems weird.>

Tanis nodded without opening her eyes. "With you there. I'd expect him to at least ping for an update—especially now that I've arrived at Simon's last known location."

<So what's your next move?>

With a long groan, Tanis sat up again. "Well, firstly, you need to do your legal-not-legal tapping into the hotel's networks. Then I want to have a look at the room Simon stayed in."

<Already on it. I want to see what's going on in every corner of this building.>

"ETA?"

<They have good security here, it would help if you spread a bit of your breaching nano around. I don't want to have to hack everything wirelessly; it will be too obvious when they do monitoring sweeps.>

"No rest for the weary," Tanis said with a long groan as she pushed herself off the bed and rose to her feet.

<Point two gees. I think you can manage.>

DINNER AND A DRINK

STELLAR DATE: 02.21.4084 (Adjusted Years)
LOCATION: The Golden Gazelle, Hunting Lodge
REGION: Ceres, Terran Hegemony, InnerSol

Half an hour later, Tanis had taken a tour through the hotel, leaving passels of breach nano in convenient locations for Darla to use.

Her route had taken her around to the lobby, and she eyed the restaurant that was set over on one side, ultimately deciding that a bit of human company was better than room service at the moment.

<You know what's the worst about this spy shit?> she asked Darla.

<Hmm?>

<Just being alone all the time. I can't call friends, or even join in any public events. I'm a target, and people I spend time with can be as well.>

<Well, you're not a target yet, but I get your point. Things could go sideways at any time.>

Tanis approached the host standing at the entrance to the restaurant and held up a single finger. "Just me."

"Would you care to sit at the bar?" the man asked, and Tanis saw that most of the restaurant's tables were filled. She got his point that the establishment preferred to save their tables for groups during dinnertime.

"Of course," she replied, walking past the man as he gestured in the direction of the bar.

<You know, as much as I like the place's gravity, a four hour 'day' makes for some weird mealtimes. I mean…the sun's just

coming out outside, and it's twenty-hundred hours,> she commented to Darla.

<Well, where Bella's from, a 'day' takes just about thirty days.>

<Right, which makes Bella-Tanis find a four-hour day even stranger than real Tanis.>

<Good point.>

Tanis pulled herself up onto a barstool and palmed the panel in front of herself to pull up the menu.

<Oh…look at that BLT, it looks heavenly.>

<Bella is vegan.>

<Shit, really? What's up with that? Does Harm think I need to lose weight or something?>

Tanis looked down at her stomach and patted it. *<I'm fit as a fiddle.>*

<Plus you have mods to adjust your weight as needed.>

<Don't ruin my analogy.>

"Is this seat taken?" a voice asked from next to Tanis, and she glanced over her shoulder to see Kaebel's smiling face.

"Kaebel! No, please."

"Thanks, I kinda get lonely on these business trips sometimes; it's nice to have someone to talk to. Or catch me if I fall."

<Awwww, I think little Kaebel has a crush on you. You did get all grabby grabby with him. I bet pressing up against—>

<Darla!>

<Sorry, my desire to experience human sexy-time through you is showing again.>

Tanis resisted the urge to groan aloud. *<You got your rocks off with Peter and I, that'll have to do for now.>*

"Oooor not," Kaebel said, giving Tanis a sidelong look.

"Sorry, I just got pinged on the Link. I'm one hundred

percent here, now."

"Oh, sorry." He waved the bartender over. "I only got my Link a few years back. I don't use it as much as other people do."

The bartender approached, and Tanis glanced up at him.

"Give me a Coronal Mass Ejection on the rocks," she said.

"I'll go with a whiskey," Kaebel added. "Something good, but not top shelf."

"You got it," the bartender replied. "On your rooms?"

"Yeah," Tanis said, while Kaebel shook his head. "No, my company doesn't like drinks on the expense report, I—"

"Don't sweat it." Tanis placed a hand on his wrist and glanced at the bartender. "I've got him covered."

"You sure?" Kaebel asked.

<You're too touchy, you're sending him mixed signals.>

<You read the dossier on Bella. She's a touchy sort. Probably comes from all the close contact in her favorite sport. Besides, I'm curious why I keep bumping into him. Touched him to drop a passel of nano.> Tanis laughed aloud before replying. "Yeah, I can spot a few drinks in exchange for your company."

"And here I thought I was the one who needed a friend," Kaebel said placing his hand close to Tanis's.

<Devious girl,> Darla commented. *<His public data checks out, but I'll do a quick peek inside to make sure our friend here is on the up and up.>*

While Bella was skilled in the martial arts, one of her quirks was that she was a serious flirt. The dossier didn't go into a lot of detail, but from what Tanis could infer, the flirting often translated into sexual flings—luckily just with men.

Tanis wasn't patently against having sex with women, but it would involve a lot of faking. Kaebel was cute in a boyish, young man sort of way. His mousy brown hair was a touch too long for the style it was cut in, and his almost amber eyes were wide and sincere. If she had to get romantic with him, it would involve very little faking.

"I spend a lot of time hopping from place to place," Tanis said with a warm smile, "—as I suspect you do, plying your company's wares. I spend a lot more time inside starship cabins than I'd like."

"I've only made a few trips so far." Kaebel picked up his whiskey while the bartender began preparing Tanis's Coronal Mass Ejection. "I did a convention on Mars last month, and I was on Cruithne a few weeks before that—stars…what a shithole that was."

"I've swung through Cruithne once or twice," Tanis said with a knowing smile. "You just have to know where to go. The lowspin docks are where the good times are. Not to mention their Night Park. Did you know there have been parrots and ravens living in that park for over a thousand years?"

Kaebel grimaced. "Yeah, I passed through that place. The ravens all called me 'pretty boy' and told me to go home."

Tanis gave a bubbling laugh and placed her hand on his arm again. "Well, they're not all wrong."

The man's eyes lit up, and she saw his body temperature rise a degree.

<Oh, there you go. You have his ***full*** *attention now. I wonder if he'll get an erection. If not, you should place your hand on his thigh next to see if that does it.>*

<Darla! This is ***not*** *your amateur human biology class!>*

<Did you mean armature?> Darla snickered.

<Weak.>

"Well…I'm only twenty-nine," Kaebel replied after he regained his composure. "Long way from my first rejuv."

"I've had a couple already," Tanis replied. "Wasn't so bad."

"Oh? You don't look like it. Sometimes people get a bit of a plastic look."

Tanis chuckled and shook her head. "You can get a whole new skin grown if you want. Anyone with a plastic look has it because they like it. I've not needed a full skin-job yet, though. You only have to get that if you wait too long."

"Oh, I guess I kinda knew that."

The conversation faltered there, and Tanis wondered where to take it next. Then her drink showed up, and she took a sip, eyes widening as the alcohol hit the back of her throat.

"Oh, stars! That's…that's…."

"That's why I stick to whiskey," Kaebel grinned. "I never did ask, Bella, why are you on Ceres?"

Tanis nodded to the mountains visible outside the window. "I'm here to commune with the spirts."

"Say what?" Kaebel's eyes widened.

"The spirits." She nodded with all the sincerity she could muster. "They say that the spirits of the dead Andersonians linger in the mountains, and if you go deep enough, you'll encounter the minds of ancient AIs, echoing their thoughts in dark canyons."

His eyes narrowed. "OK, now I *know* you're pulling my

leg."

"I know there aren't a lot of people who believe in spirituality anymore," Tanis said in the most serene voice she could muster. "But we're still out there. Just because we have science doesn't mean we don't have souls. And when the body dies, those souls linger. I know, I can sense them."

Tanis could tell by the look on Kaebel's face that she'd taken it too far.

"Or, if I can't find any of them, I'll just sit on a mountaintop and meditate for a bit. Maybe I can divine the winner of the next System Cup and place a bet."

Kaebel almost spit out his whiskey as he burst out laughing, drawing a few stares.

"You had me going there, Bella. I didn't think you could be quite that...wispy between the ears."

Tanis shrugged and winked at the man. "Well, I do plan to climb a mountain and sit on top of it for a bit. I don't expect to encounter any ancient spirits, but a lot did happen here; I'll think on it for a bit, remember what the lives lost on Ceres mean to all of us."

"That's deep," Kaebel nodded. "Though I think I'll stick to flat ground as much as possible. Just the thought of trying to climb one of these mountains sets my head spinning."

"They're not that tall," Tanis said. "I've climbed both Olympus Mons on Mars, and Rheasilvia on Vesta. Both of those are about twenty-two kilometers, base to peak. Though Olympus is just massive—takes forever to walk up the thing. Rheasilvia is smaller, just over a hundred klicks' walk to the top. Ahuna Mons out there is just four klicks. Kid stuff."

"I've heard there are a lot of caves and ruins in the central range out there," Kaebel said. "Stuff from when the first ring came down."

"Well, if you check the ancient maps, Ceres didn't used to have a mountain range here. Just Ahuna Mons all by its lonesome. From what I read, even the hills right out behind the hotel are just made of dirt mounded on ring ruins and slag and crashed ships from the war."

Kaebel whistled. "Now *that* I'd like to explore. I'm curious, though. Are those massive mountains on Mars and Vesta harder to climb than a Terran mountain? I mean…it probably takes a lot more energy to climb something like Everest in one gee than Olympus Mons in point four."

Though she'd never climbed Everest, she had scaled the other peaks she claimed, speaking with many climbers who compared them to Earth's mountains.

Tanis snorted. "Tell me that when you've climbed a peak the size of France. Don't get me wrong, Everest is a beast. Weather there is a nightmare, but Olympus gets some crazy, crazy winds, and its mostly covered in glaciers now, too."

"Growing up in Mexico, I'm not a big fan of winter," Kaebel replied.

"Well it's kinda always winter on Olympus Mons. But the real challenge is the Scarps on the southeast side. Twice as tall as Everest, and running on for hundreds of klicks. Makes the Himalayas look like a kid's sandbox." She took another sip of her CME, then wagged her finger at Kaebel. "And don't let anyone tell you that less than half a gee makes it easy. That's like saying climbing four kilometers straight up is easy on Earth."

Kaebel held his hands up, a grin on his lips. "Hey, I never said that. I'm just curious. You're a crazy-impressive woman, Bella."

Tanis gave him a wink and a nod, not adding in that her first climb of the Scarps had been when she was eighteen.

<*You've always been a bit of a thrill seeker,*> Darla commented.

"You know," Tanis said after another throat burning sip of her drink. "I'm on Mars a lot. You should look me up if you visit again. I'll take you up."

"You sure?" Kaebel asked. "You saw me on the stairs."

"Well, you've been on Mars before. Did you have as much trouble there?"

He tilted his head. "No, I suppose not. I guess gravity being double what it is here on Ceres helps."

"Yeah, it gets into the range where even Earth muscles feel normal. Still puts you at a pretty serious advantage when it comes to arm wrestling matches, too."

Kaebel snorted. "Don't think you're going to make a bet with me about an arm wrestle. Like I said, I saw what you did to that guy up on Insi. You'd kick my ass."

<*That's not all you should do to his ass.*>

<*Darla! Seriously. I'm with Peter.*>

<*This is work, it's different.*> The AI made a cooing sound in Tanis's mind that she did her best to ignore.

<*Not to me it's not,*> she shot back before replying to Kaebel, giving him a wink that was as un-alluring as she could manage. "You should see the bets I win down on Earth. People there think a woman like me can't hold my own in a full gee, but I mop the floor with them."

"You have mods?" Kaebel asked, glancing down at Tanis's body, his gaze lingering a bit longer than necessary.

"Not muscular," she lied. "I mean, I have a human body.

I train in simulated one gee, so there's no reason for me to not be as strong as a top athlete on Earth. Really what it comes down to is that a lot of Terrans are snobs."

A look of worry crossed Kaebel's face, and Tanis touched his arm again. "Oh, not you Kabe! Can I call you 'Kabe'?"

Darla laughed softly. *<You're sending **such** mixed messages.>*

<This is flirting, isn't it? I really don't do this much.>

*<Oh hell yeah. The only way you could flirt more is if you got on his lap. Try it. I bet **that** will give him an erection.>*

<You!>

"Yeah, you can call me that. Some of my friends do."

Tanis laughed and lifted her hand away. "Well, you have to call me Bella. 'Bell' just makes me sound like I need to be rung."

<Oh! Was that a Freudian slip? I think your bell does need to be rung.>

<Shut. Up.>

Over the next few hours, Tanis and Kaebel ordered meals, his a burger with bacon that had Tanis almost salivating, while she selected a kale salad that almost made her cry to have to eat.

Her flirting improved, and when they finally parted ways, she was certain that he believed he had a chance with her—just not that night.

A part of Tanis wondered what it would be like. She'd never had casual, no strings attached sex with a virtual stranger, but by the same token, her memories of a brief time with Peter were still fresh, and she didn't want to cloud them with another partner.

As they walked back up to the room, Darla informed

Tanis that Kaebel had been entirely clean, almost a perfectly stock human—just his Link and a few memory enhancing mods.

<*Took you all night to discern that?*> Tanis asked.

<*No, I just got too distracted by your not-quite-mating dance and didn't share it with you.*>

<*I wish my doppelganger would do something already. Kaebel was nice and all, but if I have to spend the next few days just sitting around here grabbing drinks with strangers at the bar, I might just start screwing them for something to do.*>

Tanis opened the door to her room and edged around the containers in the short hall, eyeing the bed and thinking of a good night's sleep.

<*You could climb that mountain,*> Darla suggested.

<*I wouldn't mind…but I kinda need to be here. Shit—my stomach got the better of me, and I didn't even check out Simon's room! I suck as a spy. And all I got for it was kale. I wonder if I could hack room service to get me a BLT and have it log it as some sort of veggie sandwich.*>

Darla snorted. <*Are you seriously considering hacking a hotel's kitchen just to get a BLT on the QT?*>

<*Does that make me a bad person?*> Tanis leant against the crates and blew out a long breath. "OK, let's go check out Simon's room."

She'd just turned toward the door when Darla chuckled. <*OK, I won't lead you on any longer. I pulled their cleaning bot's feeds; they've been through the room twice since Simon disappeared. He never even used the room. Hotel access logs show that he didn't so much as set foot in it.*>

Tanis groaned. "Were you really going to let me go down there and search it?"

<Well…I was considering letting you get to the door. The room's currently occupied by a young couple, and from the sounds reaching the hall, they're very vigorous tonight. That would have dissuaded you from going in, I bet.>

"Sheesh! That's it. I *am* hacking the food service systems to get a BLT, and there's nothing you can do to stop me."

<Wouldn't dream of it. You're scary when your hangry.> She paused a beat. <There's something else, Tanis.>

<Hmm?> Tanis asked as she looked up the software the food service system ran on, cross-referencing it with Division 99's list of known vulnerabilities.

<The hotel…it has surprisingly better security than I would have expected. If we didn't have the division resources, I'd be hard pressed to get around it.>

Tanis attempted to slip a malformed packet through what should have been an open port in the food service system, but where she should have received a response that she could exploit, the system did nothing.

<Dammit…even their room service system is properly patched. I guess kale's back on the menu.>

<Sorry….>

<Me too.>

HIKING AND DIVERSION

STELLAR DATE: 02.22.4084 (Adjusted Years)
LOCATION: The Golden Gazelle, Hunting Lodge
REGION: Ceres, Terran Hegemony, InnerSol

The following day, Tanis continued to scout around the hotel for any signs of Simon, but came up empty. Her doppelganger, on the other hand, didn't do anything interesting, either. Just a run, a swim, and meals at the various restaurants.

"Two more days of this, and I'll go nuts," Tanis groaned as she walked down one of the forested paths near the hotel.

<*You don't vacation well.*>

"This isn't a vacation," she complained. "On one of those, I'd do something interesting, like visit a historic site, or climb a mountain, or swim with dolphins again."

<*Or do Peter.*>

"Yes, Darla, I'd 'do' Peter. You know, you're probably the least mature AI in existence."

<*You'd be surprised,*> Darla chuckled. <*Seriously, though. You need to learn how to do nothing. You got antsy like this at the Grand Eire on Vesta as well. You're just filled with boundless frenetic energy.*>

Tanis rested against a rock, pulling out a bottle of water and taking a long draught. "It's weird, too. On the *Kirby Jones,* there are days—weeks, sometimes—where we do nothing at all. Just routine."

<*That's probably it. Doing nothing at 'home' where you have a routine is different from a vacation. There's nothing to settle into.*>

"Are you suggesting I build a routine here?"

<I have no idea…I'm just trying to get you to relax. I think you're worried about your crew.>

Tanis capped off the bottle and resumed her walk. *<Damn right I am. I have no idea what we're all about to get into, and I'm out of communication with them.>*

<You have the same comm records I do,> Darla replied. *<They've made their check-ins and will dock on schedule. Smythe sounds bored in each one, just the way you want him to.>*

Tanis nodded, unwilling to verbally admit that she just didn't like being on the sidelines, waiting for whatever was going to happen to happen.

<Maybe we should grab my doppelganger and force her to make contact with whoever is pulling her strings.>

<We can try, Tanis, but you know we run a risk of clueing them in. If they realize you're still alive, they'll try to take you out again.>

Tanis waved amicably to a trio of men who jogged by. *<Seems like a good plan, then. We took out the IC with no weapons.>*

<Or they hit you a lot harder to make sure you stay down.>

<I can lay a trap,> Tanis replied as she turned onto a side trail that wound up to the top of one of the nearby hills. The climb was easy in the low gravity, and just a few minutes later, she was at the summit, gazing out at the small city of Hunter's Lodge and the lowlands beyond.

As she'd told Kaebel the prior night, before humans came, Ahuna Mons had been a lonely mountain rising above a smooth plain—other than a nearby crater, which was now the location of Lake Tres.

But when the ring fell and Ceres was covered in fire and

ash, the crust had rippled across this region, creating the low mountains and pushing Ahuna Mons up another five hundred meters.

There were even rumors that the mountains were half made of old ring debris, piled up and slagged before getting covered with dirt during Ceres' second terraforming.

It amazed Tanis that the GE miniature black hole at the planet's core had survived the destruction of the original ring—though she imagined that the AIs who had attacked the planet had worked out how not to destabilize the MBH.

In an effort to relax, Tanis slipped into her katas in a clearing on the hilltop, performing them as slowly as possible, forcing herself to maintain her form perfectly while barely moving.

A passerby would think at first that she was standing still, but then her slow breaths and even slower movements would clue them in.

By the time she had done all eight katas, her arms were shaking. She quaffed the rest of her water, considering climbing another hill before returning to the hotel.

As she turned toward the path to the next rise, a glint of light to her right caught her attention, and she ducked as a pulse rifle fired.

The edge of the concussive wave brushed against her head, causing a moment of disorientation before she leapt across the clearing, landing behind a boulder.

A pulse blast hit Tanis's cover, causing the rock to shudder while she deployed her nanoprobes, seeking out the attacker.

"I don't know what you're doing!" she called out. "But I don't think it's illegal to practice karate up here."

The probes swept toward the origin of the weapons fire, only to be caught by two more shots, the blast destroying some of the nanocloud while more was blown off-course.

Tanis eyed the other nearby cover—a half-rotten log from a tree that fell long ago, and a smaller boulder.

<I really wish I'd brought a weapon.>

<Bella wouldn't carry one.>

<Right,> Tanis replied. *<That's why I didn't bring one. Doesn't change what I wish I'd done.>*

The pulse rifle fired again, and the trio of shots sounded strange to Tanis until she realized why: their tone and intensity was identical to the prior shots.

"Shit," she muttered, releasing another passel of drones and sending them into the surrounding underbrush. "Thing's firing on auto."

<Motion! Five meters behind you!>

<Got it,> Tanis peered around the front of the rock, putting on a convincing—she hoped—show as she searched for the attacker exactly where he wasn't.

She gave a frustrated sigh and sat back just in time to feel something poking against her back.

"Freeze," a male voice said. "Don't move, whoever you are."

<He's holding a stick,> Darla said, *<pistol in his other hand, though.>*

<I see that,> Tanis said as she looked the man over through her nanoprobe feeds.

He was middling height, brown eyes, unremarkable features under a mop of black hair.

"Totally frozen," she replied. "I was just practicing a bit in the clearing. Didn't realize it's private property, I can go—"

"What were you really doing up here?" the man asked, pushing the barrel of his 'gun' deeper into Tanis's back.

How much of this would Bella take? she wondered. *Maybe a bit more.*

"That's not a really nice thing to do," Tanis replied.

"What's not?"

She spun, grabbing the stick and smacking it against the man's hand holding the pistol. Her aim was true, and her ambusher's hand spasmed, dropping the weapon.

She swung the stick up, jabbing it in his throat and then whacking him on the side of the head. The man fell back, and Tanis scooped up the pistol, holding it on her would-be attacker.

"I don't really like guns," she said. "But I like assholes even less. What are you playing at?"

"I'm not the one playing," the man said, holding a hand to his head. "You're clearly not who you say you are."

Tanis drew herself up. "I am Bella, acclaimed Wado Ryu practitioner and more than capable of disarming you." Inwardly, she asked, *<Darla? Who is this guy?>*

<Link is weak up here, low bandwidth—aha! He's…a local cop!>

<What's a local doing ambushing people on hilltops?>

<He's Inspector Sawyer, been with their force for seven years,> Darla informed her. *<Still trying to get into his current case load.>*

"You cased the hotel last night, and today you cased the grounds," Inspector Sawyer accused. "I didn't spot it at first, but when I had an NSAI run through all the hotel's footage for the last day, it picked you up."

<Huh...I guess you do kinda move like you're always searching out weaknesses. I should have warned you.>

"You shot at me because I walked the grounds?" Tanis asked. "Is that illegal here?"

"Some fishy shit has been going on here, and you're the first solid lead I have," Sawyer retorted, his eyes narrowing.

"Fishy shit?" Tanis asked, leaning against the rock, trying to put Sawyer at ease. "Why don't you tell me what's going on?"

Sawyer gave her a disbelieving stare. "Is that the sort of thing that Bella, practitioner of Wado Ryu would ask?"

<He's got you there.>

"You attacked me first, and I have the gun now. Far as I can see, that means I get to ask the questions."

Sawyer pursed his lips and didn't speak, but Tanis gestured with the pistol. "There are two ways to do this."

"Fine," he spat. "I guess if you're behind all this, then you know it all already."

"Which I don't. Now talk."

"I was doing a C&S—Check and Secure—of the hotel when I found signs of a struggle in one of the stairwells. There was some ripped drapes on a window, and stains on the carpet that I'm certain were blood. I didn't have a kit to take samples—wasn't supposed to be anything but a walkthrough. I cordoned off the area and set a pair of the hotel's bots to make sure no one walked over the scene while I went back to the station to get a kit."

"You were 'certain' it was blood?" Tanis pressed.

"Well, I didn't want to mess with any evidence, but optics and olfactory said blood. Whether or not it was human would have taken a real sample to be sure."

"I imagine fights happen," she said. "I got in one just the other day, up on Insi."

"Saw that," Sawyer replied.

"Then, if you'd checked, you would have realized that I had just arrived on Insi yesterday, and then I came down here. When would I have attacked someone?"

"Well that's not the weird part." Sawyer widened his stance, and Tanis could tell he was close to making an attempt on the gun. "The weird part was that when I came back, the place was cleaned up, and the bots were nowhere to be seen. I checked the logs, and there was nothing to indicate I had set them to keep people away, or that they had cleaned it themselves. The hotel management was a little worried, but with no evidence, they just wrote it all off."

"I still don't see how this gets to the point of attacking innocent people on hilltops," Tanis retorted.

"Well that's just the start of it—" Sawyer's words cut off, as he lunged for the gun.

Tanis was ready and, with her left hand, casually tossed the weapon over her shoulder and into the clearing, while jabbing her knuckles into his sternum with her right.

Sawyer made a strangled *'gnnuughhh'* sound before stumbling backward.

"Hurts, doesn't it?" Tanis asked. "Surprisingly easy to crack the sternum if you hit it just right. That was a love tap. Want to feel it crack open, or are you going to tell me what you're really up to?"

"Link's slow up here, but by now you should have been able to confirm that I'm HLPD," Sawyer grunted once his breathing stabilized. "You've just assaulted an officer of the law."

<Gah, this would be so much easier if I could break cover,> Tanis said to Darla. *<Ideas?>*

<I'd just keep pressing him. We get what we need, then swap to a new cover to continue the investigation. You did Bella too good, anyway—everyone wants to book her for events and feeds, now.>

"Do cops just ambush people?" Tanis asked with a scowl. "I'm a Hegemony citizen. You can't just shoot at me without first trying to get me to submit verbally."

She saw Sawyer's face redden and knew she had him. The guy was an honest cop, just acting desperately—for reasons she still had to discern.

"I saw you break that guy's leg like it was nothing," Sawyer muttered. "He out-massed you three to one, and when you did that, it was obvious you'd been toying with him the whole time. I don't have any illusions that I could take you down if you resisted."

"Not only that, you have real evidence," Tanis smirked, even though she doubted it fit with Bella's persona. "I'm no trained police officer, but last I checked, that's why folks like you use teams to take out dangerous people. The fact you're up here solo is what has me feeling mighty suspicious."

Sawyer reddened further. "It started with that weird crime scene disappearing. Then one of the hotel staff got hit by a hovercar…thing landed right on her. Squished. A few other 'accidents' around the hotel have stacked up, but no one wants to take them seriously. Too worried about messing up 'the visit'. It wouldn't have hurt you much, by the way."

" 'It'?"

"The pulse rifle. I had it firing at low power. It was just enough so I could stun you and get the binders on."

"Oh, yay," Tanis muttered sardonically. "So you were only going to rough me up just a little before illegally detaining me."

<Darla, what's this 'visit'? Do you think that links to some of the heightened security we saw?>

<Maybe? A transport just arrived at the hotel with a lot of security types; maybe someone big is coming, and they managed to hide it really well. I'm converting one of your other covers to a TBI agent, by the way. Just give me another minute, and you can whip that out.>

<Oh! Good move,> Tanis said to Darla before taking a threatening step toward Sawyer. "Who's visiting?"

The man's jaw snapped shut, and his lips drew into a thin line. "If you don't know, I'm not going to be the person to leak it."

"So…someone big is coming, they let the HLPD in on it—probably SOP for the hotel, and you were sent to do some early checks to make sure their internal security was tight. That's when you discovered a number of suspicious activities that ether got cleaned up mighty fast, or that no one seemed to care about."

Tanis drew out the words to give Darla more time, but tossed in the right words to make Sawyer lead her in the correct direction.

"Yeah," his tone had become suspicious again. "That's about right. As you can imagine, with lots of unsubstantiated worry and disappearing evidence, you can see how I'm getting a bit desperate to find out what's going on. My captain has me on his shit-list now, and if I don't find a smoking gun or drop the whole thing, he's gonna put me on spaceport cargo inspections. Now tell me, who are you, really?"

<New cover is ready. You're Sasha, a TBI special agent that was sent to check out the hotel for the visit. The cover's thin right now, but I should be able to shore it up before he can check too deeply. The HLPD's systems are a lot easier to breach than the hotel's—even from here.>

<Encouraging.>

"Well?" Sawyer pressed, as Tanis deliberately paused.

"Fine, but this doesn't leave your lips, mind, or Link. I'm TBI. Special Agent Sasha. I was sent to make sure things go smoothly for the visit. There's someone I have my eye on, but he's not doing much yet. I'm up here to keep my cover with him intact." Tanis felt a bit bad about throwing Kaebel under the bus, but she didn't want to give away her Infiltrator Chameleon doppelganger to the likes of Sawyer and have him bungle everything up.

"The kid at the bar?" the police inspector asked, and Tanis raised an eyebrow.

She didn't recall seeing him there last night, which meant he was better than she thought, or he had taps into the hotel's security. Or both.

Probably not both. Guy can't shoot for shit. Aloud, she said, "Yeah. Either he's totally innocent, or he's so good he's playing me."

"Saw you getting pretty friendly with him," Sawyer couldn't stop a smirk from forming on his lips.

Her eyes narrowed, shooting daggers. "Part of the job. Don't think that means *you* have a chance with me."

<Oh! And the claws come out!>

<Trying to get him to give me something to re-establish trust. Watch and learn.>

<I thought you hated 'spy shit'?>

Tanis sent Darla a mental laugh. *<I really like* **this** *part of spy shit.>*

<The part where you border on violent behavior to get your way?>

<Exactly.>

Her AI made a *tsk*ing sound. *<Not sure that's a healthy response.>*

"Hey, didn't mean anything by it," Sawyer held up his hands. "I'm just out of sorts, worried about Alden's visit."

<***Jackpot!***> Darla crowed. *<I'll never doubt you again.>*

Tanis nodded stoically, careful to keep a grin from her lips. The *only* noteworthy Alden she knew of was the Jovian Oligarch, leader of the Jovian Combine. The man liked to travel, and he also liked his privacy. His coming to Ceres for a vacation in a mid-range hotel at the edge of the planet's most storied mountains made sense.

<Damn…that explains why my doppelganger is here.>

<You think they're gonna use it to kill Alden?>

"I get that, too. Sorry about the whack I gave you," Tanis said to Sawyer before replying to Darla. *<Yeah, I totally do. You know what that means.>*

<Someone in Division 99 wants the Jovian Oligarch gone, and they're willing to sacrifice you to do it.>

<Plus my ship and crew.>

<Daaaaaamn.>

"Looks like you check out," Sawyer replied. "I suppose I can forgive a knock, since I shot at you."

Neither spoke for a moment, and then Tanis asked. "So,

what now?"

"Well…I guess you have a lead with this Kaebel guy. I'll see what I can find on him. Maybe it's best if you keep looking at the hotel, and I keep a lower profile; they're getting a bit sick of me there."

"That sounds perfect," she replied, grateful that it meant Sawyer was going to stay out of her way. "You should probably grab your rifle and head out. I'm going to go to that next rise and do some more katas before I head back to the hotel."

"Uh, OK. Sounds good, Agent Sasha."

"Sawyer," Tanis hissed. "Never out loud. I'm 'Bella'. Got it?"

The man blushed furiously. "Right, yeah, sorry."

JOURNEY'S END

STELLAR DATE: 02.22.4084 (Adjusted Years)
LOCATION: TSS *Kirby Jones,* Approaching Ceres
REGION: Main Asteroid Belt, Terran Hegemony, InnerSol

"Sweet stars above." Connie wiped her brow as she looked over the holodisplays in engineering. "I can't believe we pulled this off."

"Ship-shape and ready to shoot," Seamus intoned, while Liam added, "Fixing shit in outer space is what we do."

"You two are like a couple of kids in a candy store, aren't you?" Cassie asked. "Just love playing with the expensive toys and big guns."

Seamus shrugged. "We have to take what joy we can, it's not like we actually get any action down here."

"Seamus!" Connie exclaimed in mock indignation, and the E-3 gave her a puzzled look, then his eyes widened.

"Oh! Whoops! I just meant that we don't actually get to shoot bad guys. We do all the work, and Lieutenant Smythe gets to do the pew-pewing."

Cassie snickered. "Right. If that was a slip, it sure was Freudian. But I know how the commander feels about fraternization on the ship.... Not going to make my first meeting with her a tongue-lashing."

"A *tongue*-lashing?" Liam burst out laughing, and then clamped his mouth shut, his face reddening. "Damn, now I can't get that image out of my mind."

"You're welcome," Cassie said with a wink as she sat at her console and pulled up the shield readouts. "Glad we have these things working again. We were flying through the black just waiting for the first wrench some idiot dropped to hole us."

Liam reddened further. "We don't talk about dropping wrenches in space. It's not nice."

Cassie snorted as she turned in her chair to look at Liam. "The ole slippery suit fingers get you once?"

"Try three times," Seamus elbowed Liam.

"Dude, we were under attack and the EM fields were messing with the repair drones. I didn't see *you* on the hull while Hellas Raiders were shooting at us."

"Really?" Cassie asked, her eyes wide and flashing signs of being impressed and a little star-struck. "I had no idea the *Jones* had seen action like that."

"Commander Richards is a serious trouble magnet," Seamus grunted.

Connie cast a judging eye at Seamus. "Bitch all you want, but at least we don't have boring, do-nothing deployments like most ships our class."

Cassie was now giving Liam a hungry look. "Thought I'd landed on the wrong ship with the state it was in, but now I'm starting to see things in a *whole* new light."

Liam widened his stance and gave a nonchalant shrug. "Just doing my duty."

An almost giggle-like laugh escaped Cassie's lips. "I bet you say that to all the girls."

"OK, everyone, keep your shipsuits on," Connie growled as she turned and walked to the door. "I'm gonna go make sure Jeannie hasn't killed Smythe. They're starting to wear on each other, being alone up there on the bridge."

"Good luck," Cassie waved to Connie. "I'll keep the boys entertained."

"Lovell?" Connie glanced at the overhead.

<Yeah?>

"If anyone so much as touches the fastener on their shipsuit, vent the bay."

<You got it, boss,> Lovell replied, a note of humor in his voice.

She walked out into the passageway, shaking her head as she sent a message to Cassie.

<You do girl really well, that's gotta be your original gender. Plus…don't actually screw Liam. He gets all weird for days.>

<Don't worry, just endearing myself a bit more. Things have been tense over the past few days, and I want to build up a bit of cohesion.>

<Just as long as you stick to cohesion, not adhesion,> Connie shot back. *<So, is it?>*

<So is what?>

<Were you born a girl?>

<Nice try, Connie.>

Connie sighed gave a rueful shake of her head as she climbed the ladder shaft through the ship's stacked decks to the bridge.

When she arrived, Corporal Marion was lounging in one of the seats, appearing to be asleep, though Connie knew better. Lieutenants Jeannie and Smythe were at their consoles, not speaking.

She could have cut the tension with a knife.

"How are things up here?" she asked loudly as she stepped onto the bridge. "We're all set below, just need to cross-check readings on the bridge and get your sign-off."

Marion made a snorting sound and then stretched. "Ahhhh…what time—shit! I must have dozed off. I'd best get to my team, they're probably getting close to brawling over losses in their latest poker match."

<Thanks, Marion,> Connie said to the corporal, as the large woman ambled off the bridge.

<No worries. These two are good kids, they're just still dealing with what we went through with Admiral Deering. Without Tanis around, they feel…unanchored.>

Connie sat at the engineering console and glanced at the far-too-still backs of Jeannie and Smythe's heads. *<I think we all feel a bit of that. I pinged her earlier; she's down at some hotel on Ceres. Told us she might take a day there before she comes up for our run-throughs—not that we need them, now that we had this shakedown.>*

<Really?> Marion sounded puzzled. *<I would have expected her to be banging on the airlock the moment we latched onto Insi.>*

<Nope…in fact, she told us not to dock with the ring. She put in for a polar parking orbit.>

<OK…now my spidey senses are tingling.>

<Your what?> It was Connie's turn to sound puzzled.

Marion barked a laugh. *<You need to get out more, Connie. It's a new sim series, follows this guy named Spider Man.>*

<Gah! That sounds repulsive.>

<Well it's not like he's modded into a spider, it's just a suit…though I bet he'd look good with a big ol' abdomen.>

<Marion…that's just bizarre.> The corporal laughed in response, and Connie realized the woman was putting her on. *<Go catch sack, or something. You get weird when you're tired.>*

<Girl, I'm always weird. Gonna see what Cassie is up to. That woman has been sending out siiiignals. I'm not normally into

girls, but there's something about her....>

<*Good luck,*> Connie replied, trying not to laugh aloud at the thought of Marion and Cassie together.

The soldier stood a good chance of crushing Harm, even with the extra booty cushion he had going on as 'Cassie'.

<*I don't need luck, I have these.*>

Connie didn't have to see Marion—who was now down on the crew deck—to know that the woman was flexing and kissing her biceps.

"Things look good up here, Lieutenant Smythe," Connie said aloud. Your board green?"

"Yeah," Smythe grunted. "Shields, weapons, scan, all the boxes are checked. Backup systems green. Ship's good to go."

"Everything good on helm?" Connie asked Jeannie.

"Right as rain," Jeannie replied.

Neither had turned to look at her as they spoke, and Connie blew out a long breath.

<*Stars, Lovell, I feel like I'm ship's mom. Why doesn't anyone act like this when Tanis is around?*>

<*Because you're the nice, 'curse you out and then offer you a beer' Mom. Tanis is just the 'kick you in the ass and make you scrub the decks with your socks' Mom.*>

Connie laughed, remembering the time Tanis had made Seamus do that. <*OK, I get that. Still, I don't wanna be anyone's mom. That's why I joined the service. I'm the* Jones*'s mom. That's enough for me.*>

<*Do you want* **me** *to give these two a talking to?*> Lovell asked, his tone clearly indicating that he did not think it would be a good idea.

<*Noooooooo....*> Connie drew the word out in her mind.

<*Going to see if I can channel some of Tanis-mom.*>

<*Good luck.*>

She rose and stretched, gathering her wits and fortitude, and shoring up her ability to handle whiny officers. Then she walked in front of the pair, snapping her fingers to get their attention.

"Soooo…what's up?" she asked while folding her arms across her chest.

"Nothing," Smythe shrugged.

"We're all good," Jeannie replied.

Connie stared at them each in turn, and then pressed the heels of her palms into her eyes, letting out a long groan. "I can't help it. I'm the beer mom."

"What?" Jeannie asked.

Lowering her hands, Connie said, "Look, if you two want to go fuck, just do it. I'll make sure that Tanis doesn't find out. But just get it out of your systems already."

It was a long shot, and she didn't expect it to work, but to her amazement, Jeannie glanced at Smythe and shrugged. His eyes lit up, and five seconds later, Connie was alone on the bridge.

"Holy shit…I can't believe that worked. I kinda feel like *I* deserve a beer."

<*No beer for you, Connie,*> Lovell laughed in her mind. <*You're the OOD now.*>

Connie realized that, with the two lieutenants gone, she was stuck on the bridge.

"Shit! I don't get paid enough for this."

A PLAN

STELLAR DATE: 02.22.4084 (Adjusted Years)
LOCATION: The Golden Gazelle, Hunting Lodge
REGION: Ceres, Terran Hegemony, InnerSol

By the time Tanis returned to the hotel, Darla's taps into the local PD's systems—which were easier to breach than the hotel's food service—confirmed that Inspector Sawyer had reached his station.

She'd also picked up an update from the planetary STC, indicating that the *Kirby Jones* was entering a polar parking orbit—which was strange, considering they probably had some cleanup to do after what she knew was a hasty departure from Vesta. A berth on Insi would make far more sense.

As she walked across the hotel's manicured lawns to the rear entrance near the pool, the sun began to rise once more. Its rays, coupled with the hike, warmed Tanis enough that a sheen of sweat began to form on her brow.

<I hate to sweat, Darla,> she groused to her AI.

<Yet you still have the glands for it. A lot of people get them removed—or most of them, at least.>

<Well, I used to be able to store excess energy in heat eggs and dump them as needed, but since I got you and all these extra mods in here, I run too hot for that. Plus, 'Bella' doesn't have those mods, so I have to sweat.>

Her AI let out a snort. *<I love you, Tanis, but you're the most complain-y stone-cold military officer I've ever met.>*

<Sorry, I have to outwardly maintain a stiff upper lip all the time; I guess I give it to you with both barrels more than I should.

I've never really had a close confidant before.>

<*Not even Peter?*> Darla queried.

<*Peter likes that I'm the badass military woman. If I let him see that I have foibles and weaknesses, I kinda wonder if he'd still be into me.*>

Darla was silent for a moment before saying, <*That doesn't seem healthy to me, but I'm no expert in human relationships.*>

<*That's not what you're always preaching at me. I think you say something like 'I'm a great student of human behavior. AIs have to be, to understand how to deal with you flaky organics'.*>

<*I don't think I've ever called you flaky…though I've thought it. Maybe it slipped out once or twice.*>

Tanis sent Darla a look of mock-indignation in her mind before checking on the Infiltrator Chameleon's location. It was in one of the hotel's restaurants having lunch—a BLT…again. She wasn't hungry enough yet to eat kale, and decided to take a swim to cool off.

Bella's preferred swimming attire was nothing at all—which the hotel allowed—but Tanis didn't care for the stares that earned. She settled on a high-cut, one-piece bathing suit with one of her silk coats adding another layer.

She'd tucked her lightwand into one of the coat's inside pockets, and when she reached the pool, she folded it up and left it on a chair with a towel covering it. Only a few people were around, and she didn't think anyone would mess with someone else's things, but it still worried her to leave a weapon in the open.

<*I'll keep an eye on it,*> Darla said. <*Enjoy yourself. You're supposed to be the ultra-serene-Bella, not the tense-waiting-for-the-other-shoe-to-drop-Tanis.*>

Tanis didn't reply as she slid into the water and flipped over onto her back, languidly working her way across the pool before reaching one end and kicking off toward the other.

She watched her surroundings through her nanoprobes that had suffused the hotel—though she had to be careful to have them only send small data bursts. Oligarch Alden's advance team was starting to do in-depth sweeps, and though her Mickie upgrades were top-notch, she knew that the security for the leader of the Jovian Combine could probably pick it up if she wasn't careful.

Worry over what she was going to do wouldn't stop gnawing at her, try as she might to relax in the pool's cool water. Her crew was up in space, taking orders from a machine that was pretending to be her, while *she* was pretending to be a TBI agent who was pretending to be a martial arts expert on vacation.

It was becoming clear that someone in the new agency she worked for was going to use 'Tanis Richards' to assassinate a head of state, probably relying on her ship's firepower as a backup if necessary.

Even if it came out that the hit had been performed by an Infiltrator Chameleon, Tanis knew that the death of Oligarch Alden—while she was at the same hotel—would spell the end of her career in not only Division 99, but the Terran Space Force as a whole.

I guess Peter would get his wish, and I'd have to join up with the Marsian Protectorate—if they'd have me.

With that thought lingering in her mind, she resolved to set a deadline. If a clear course of action didn't arise by the end of the following day, she'd take out the IC. That would disrupt whoever was behind this enough that hopefully they wouldn't be able to pull a backup into place.

Not only that, but she could show the IC to Alden's security, and they'd likely scrub the Oligarch's visit all together.

Of course, I could just do that now, and probably achieve the same end.

Tanis mulled over the thought, but she knew that route had one fatal flaw: it wouldn't reveal who had tried to have her killed in that dressing room on Mars 1. At present, whoever had sent the Infiltrator Chameleon still thought that they had been successful at killing her—which was the one advantage she currently possessed.

They may have failed, but that doesn't mean I don't owe them a healthy dose of payback.

Not for the first time, she wondered if Harm was behind the attack and subsequent events. She had to keep it as a possibility, but it didn't seem at all like something he'd do—the man had put a lot on the line to see her through the events back on Vesta…. She didn't think he'd done all that only to throw her away at the first opportunity.

She considered telling Darla her plan, but decided not to, for the time being. The determination to take decisive action by the following evening—and the near certainty that, when push came to shove, she could call on Harm for aid—had caused a considerable weight to fall off her shoulders.

Enough that the swim through the cool water was actually becoming relaxing.

Too relaxing.

Tanis quickly checked her feeds to ensure nothing untoward was occurring anywhere nearby, seeing only a few patrons milling around the pool, and a few swimming innocuously nearby.

OK…a few more laps.

LOYALTY

STELLAR DATE: 02.22.4084 (Adjusted Years)
LOCATION: The Golden Gazelle, Hunting Lodge
REGION: Ceres, Terran Hegemony, InnerSol

To maintain her cover as Bella—*and* to maintain her cover as Sasha the TBI agent with Sawyer—Tanis once again spent much of the evening with Kaebel in the bar, carefully watching the Oligarch's security team as they surreptitiously added their own surveillance and security equipment throughout the hotel.

Kaebel regaled her with a somewhat entertaining account of his sales meetings during the day—stories that made Tanis all the more glad she'd gone into the military, and not business like her father had wanted.

If she'd been searching for a new partner, Kaebel wouldn't be a bad find. His job wasn't that interesting, but he told his stories with a certain flair and wit that told her he would be fun to spend time with, and would ultimately make something of himself if he kept trying.

As he told her about his day, she laughed at the right times, and asked the right questions, though it was difficult to split her attention. Every so often, Kaebel picked up on it.

"You OK?" he asked at one point. "You seem to be elsewhere."

"Sorry," Tanis gave him an apologetic smile. "I think I've had too many of these CME's. I'd best swap to coffee."

To his credit, Kaebel gave a rueful laugh. "I guess my stories of meeting the head of manufacturing at C&R Industries isn't as exciting as your stories of climbing all the mountains in the system."

"Well, I'm sure your work is challenging, just in a different way," Tanis said as sweetly as she could manage.

"Nice try," Kaebel winked. "I'll give you an 'A' for effort. I guess I need to find some hobbies. It's just…with cramming my way through school, landing this job, getting up to speed, there hasn't been a lot of room for the 'fun' version of me to get out."

"I've had times like that," Tanis admitted. "Luckily, I get to do what I love full-time, now."

"Kicking people's asses?"

"You're just not going to let that go, are you?" She chuckled and brushed her knee against Kaebel's.

"It was seriously badass!"

She couldn't help but laugh at his enthusiasm. "You know, there's a lot more about karate than just beating hulks into submission—though I'll admit that's a nice side benefit."

"Is this the part where you go commune with spirits in the mountains?"

Tanis gave him a mock scowl. "You know I was kidding about that, right? I'm not into that hocus pocus—but I do believe that each of us does have a spirit, and that you need to get mind, body, and spirit into alignment to find true peace."

Kaebel cocked an eyebrow as he regarded her with a half-smile on his lips. "That sounds a bit like hocus pocus."

"To each their own," Tanis replied with a shrug. "It works for me; you should try it sometime. The silver lining is that if you don't get the whole inner peace angle, you at least get some serious ass-kicking skills."

Kaebel lifted his drink—whiskey again—and took a sip. "I suppose that makes sense. It *does* seem to work for you."

He took the opportunity to let his eyes slide down her body and back up, and Tanis gave him an encouraging smile.

She'd worn a light blue, well-fitted blouse, paired with dark grey slacks that weren't quite tight, but certainly weren't loose, either. Her feet were still bare, and she'd taken the time to color her toenails to match her top. Her hair was swept back in a clip with loose curls of hair framing her face.

She had to admit that she looked more put together for Kaebel than she normally did for Peter.

"Constantly working out can get you a body just as good as any mods," Tanis said, feeling a bit disingenuous about the statement. Though she'd always had an almost willowy figure—a benefit of growing up on a low-*g* world—she did rely on mods to keep her fit and make up for missing leg day from time to time.

"You know," Kaebel said, his eyes shifting to look at the bar's exit. "We could continue this conversation in one of our rooms." His finger trailed along her forearm, unexpectedly sending shivers up her spine.

<Doooo iiiiiit,> Darla whispered. *<I can keep an eye on all the feeds. You can't flirt with him for this long and not at least go make out for a bit. You don't have to have sex if you think that'd be betraying Peter.>*

Tanis had been considering that very thing for some time. Her conversations with Kaebel had made it abundantly clear to her that working for Division 99 would stretch the bounds of what was an otherwise monogamous relationship with Peter.

"My room's a bit of a mess," she said sheepishly. "Mind if we go to yours?"

Kaebel slid off his stool so fast he nearly fell. "Damn low-*g*," he muttered as his face reddened.

Tanis wrapped an arm around his waist. "Gravity or the whiskey? Either way, I'll keep you steady."

"I like that plan," he said while sliding an arm around her waist as they exited the bar.

Tanis rested her head on his shoulder as they walked across the lobby toward the lifts. For a moment she felt content, but then, as Kaebel's hand slid down onto her ass, a wave of guilt washed over her, and it took every fiber of her being not to flinch away from him.

<I can't do this, Darla. I mean…if it was life or death, maybe, but there's no real reason to get intimate with Kaebel.>

<You better bail now, then,> Darla advised, once again surprising Tanis by not pressing her to have sex.

As the lift doors opened, Tanis pulled away from Kaebel. "I'm…I'm sorry. I thought I was ready to move on, but…well, I guess I'm still getting over someone else."

Kaebel's face fell, but then he squared his shoulders and nodded. "I understand."

"Really?" She was surprised he'd acquiesced so easily—it was more maturity than most people his age displayed.

"Yeah, I've been in that place before. I could kinda tell you weren't sure of yourself; you've run a bit hot and cold since we met."

<And here I thought I was all smooth.>

<A bit bumpy, as it turns out.>

"That obvious, eh?" Tanis asked aloud.

"Not too bad," Kaebel gave her a winning smile. "And I appreciate you spending time with me. You've made this trip one to remember."

The sincerity in his voice struck her. "Well, we don't have to part ways; it's still awhile 'til I need to hit the sack, and I do enjoy your company," she told him honestly.

Kaebel glanced back toward the bar. "We've lost our seats, couple of black-suited goons took them."

Tanis took his hand. "There's another bar by the pool. Let's go lay on the deck chairs and watch the starships—before the sun starts to rise again."

"Deal."

*****

Tanis stayed up with Kaebel until nearly oh' two hundred. Though there were still romantic sparks between them, it was more of an honest chat between friends.

She felt a bit guilty that most of her side of the conversation was fabricated, but she did her best to weave real events in, just changing names and circumstances to match Bella's past.

Even so, she felt a bit of a bond forming with Kaebel, one that she wished she'd forged as Tanis and not Bella. Chances were that he would despise her if he were to learn that everything about her was a lie.

Eventually they parted ways, sharing an *almost* chaste kiss that had Tanis feeling guilty all over again. Genuinely enjoying time with Kaebel seemed to feel like as much a betrayal as actually having sex with him.

Thank stars this will all be over tomorrow—I hope.

Somehow, though she had a plan and had its execution mapped out, she didn't feel confident that everything would be wrapped up in a day.

DISCOVERY

STELLAR DATE: 02.23.4084 (Adjusted Years)
LOCATION: The Golden Gazelle, Hunting Lodge
REGION: Ceres, Terran Hegemony, InnerSol

<*I guess that will work,*> Darla said, as Tanis drank her coffee at the hotel's breakfast café. <*Seems…too easy. Just kill the IC, and show it to Alden's security goons?*>

<*Has to be done today, too. From what Sawyer said, the Oligarch arrives bright and early tomorrow morning. Or…dark and early, I guess. This four-hour day is nuts.*>

She watched as two of the Jovian Combine leader's advance security detail sat down at a table on the far side of the café. These two weren't dressed like ominous security goons, they looked just like vacationers here for hikes in the mountains, but Tanis could tell from their demeanor that they were paying *very* close attention to their surroundings.

The fact that they were on Sawyer's list of Jovian security goons helped too.

<*If we just take out other-you, we won't get a bead on who has set this whole thing in motion. You know that, right?*>

<*It can't be helped,*> Tanis replied as a server came by and refilled her coffee cup. <*I'm not willing to risk the Jovian Oligarch getting killed on my watch just to find out who was trying to use me as a pawn. The tradeoff's not worth it.*>

<*Yeah, you're right. I just don't like being used.*>

Tanis gave a sharp nod. <*You and me both.*>

<*I do wonder, though,*> Darla continued. <*Was the mission to find Simon a red herring, or was he really here?*>

As she drew a long sip of the hot brew from her cup,

Tanis wondered about that. *How much of this mission was real, and how much was just a red herring to get a shot at the Jovian Oligarch?*

With luck, she'd find out in a day or so.

*****

Tanis whiled away the day with another hike, a few katas by the pool—which turned into a demonstration against a holo-opponent for the crowd that gathered—and then a long swim.

She knew that, when dinner came around, Kaebel would be returning from his day of meetings and would want to meet at the bar. She didn't want him to get caught up in anything, so Darla hacked his schedule and set up a bogus meeting for him with a company on the far side of the planet to keep him out of the way—he'd certainly be annoyed, but at least he wouldn't get hit in any crossfire.

After her time at the pool, Tanis drew a warm towel around her shoulders and walked to the secondary lift bank that ran up the back of the hotel.

<OK, so robot-me goes to the burger restaurant every day at sixteen hundred. She has a bacon cheeseburger—stars, I hate both her ***and*** *this vegan cover—and then afterward, she goes for a walk on the paths around the back of the pool. That's where I'll take her out.>*

<Sounds good. You going to use stealth gear?> Darla asked.

<No, I'll go with a pulse pistol and my lightwand. I get close, one quick strike, and she's dead. Threat eliminated.>

<Provided she doesn't have any weapons.>

Tanis shrugged. *<I'm not that worried. I took her out once, I*

can do it again.>

<*You took her out with my help,*> Darla corrected.

<*Exactly.*>

The lift stopped at the sixty-seventh floor, and Tanis stepped out and pulled the towel from her shoulders, its rapid-wicking having fully dried her already. She draped it over her long silken coat that rested across her left arm, while whistling a soft melody.

She turned the corner outside the lift bank and walked down the hall toward her room. One of the now-ubiquitous Jovian security goons walked past, giving her a sidelong look. She didn't think anything of it—they gave everyone measuring glances—but once he passed her, the man's gait slowed just a hair. She gauged it, and determined that she would reach her door before he turned the corner for the lift bank.

Tanis stretched languidly and dropped her towel to the floor.

"Oops," she muttered while turning to scoop it back up, noting that the Jovian had suddenly become intensely interested in a mural on the wall. She dispersed a nanocloud. <*Well, I guess we know what comes next.*>

<*I don't read anyone in your room, but that doesn't mean it's empty. It's entirely possible they've picked up on my hacks and shunted me doctored feeds.*>

Tanis sighed as she reached her door. <*I hate it when other people have tech as good as ours.*> She slipped her hand into her folded coat and wrapped her fingers around the hilt of her lightwand.

<*Technically, aren't these people the good guys?*> Darla asked.

<Maybe? But if the division has a bad actor in it, are we certain that there are no individuals in Alden's advance team that aren't in collusion? If I were planning to assassinate a head of state, getting an inside operative or asset would be my first objective.>

Darla made an appreciative sound. *<And this is why we still need you wily organics. You're so devious.>*

<Pardon?>

<Uh, nothing.>

<You're so funny, Darla.>

The AI didn't reply, as Tanis reached her door and waved it open, doing her best to appear entirely at ease while every fiber of her being was ready to fight.

Her feeds showed the room to be exactly as she'd left it, but she would eat Claire's stupid ball dress if that were the case. However, when the door slid aside and the room appeared to be empty and undisturbed, she wondered if poofy dress would indeed be on the menu.

Not trusting her vision, Tanis dispersed a fresh passel of nanoprobes into the room, trying to enter with Bella's carefree stride while waiting for someone to jump out of cover and strike her.

The moment she moved past her stack of crates, a voice said, "That's far enough."

Movement behind her caught her attention, and her nanoprobes showed the Jovian she'd passed in the hall blocking the doorway.

Tanis dropped into a ready stance, right hand tightening around her still-hidden lightwand, while her left grasped the end of her towel.

"Who's there?"

A slight shimmer in the air moved out from around the

corner. It wouldn't be visible to anyone without highly augmented vision, but Tanis could make out slight changes in the cool air currents blowing down from the environmental control vents.

She kept her expression curious and searching, not giving away that she'd spotted her visitor, but then the figure dropped their stealth and saved her from the charade.

"I am."

Tanis recognized the speaker immediately. It was Demetri Korva, head of Oligarch Alden's advance security team.

"You're with all the security types that have been crawling all over lately," Tanis said, as her brow lowered in a deep scowl. "What are you doing in my room?"

"The correct question," Demetri said, as his gaze darted to the crates next to Tanis, "is what are *those* doing in your room?"

"Is there somewhere else I should be keeping my belongings? I thought that was how this worked. I rented a place to put my stuff and to sleep."

"Don't be coy with me, Bella," Demetri took a step forward, his heavy brow lowering in a scowl. "You have weapons in those crates—we picked up the ion signatures on one of our sweeps. Faint, but it's there."

<Think they've opened them?> Tanis asked Darla.

<I don't see any signs of that, but that doesn't mean they didn't. You're made.>

"I have a few show weapons," Tanis admitted. "Stuff I use in performances. All perfectly legal."

Demetri shook his head. "Why don't you open them, and

we'll take a look?"

<They must think they're trapped…or they just found them and haven't had time to look them over,> Tanis mused. *<Think I can pull out the Sasha cover?>*

<It stood up to Sawyer because I had taps into the local PD's systems and faked your TBI supervisor when the inspector reached out for confirmation. These guys will reach out to High Terra via networks I have no access to. It won't hold up more than…thirty-one minutes.>

Tanis considered her options, wishing that there was one that didn't have her outing the Infiltrator Chameleon to the Jovians. The fact that the oligarch's security was hunting for 'Tanis Richards' was not something she wanted in the TSF's records.

If she killed the IC first, then the body would not be logged as hers, and she'd never end up on the books as a wanted criminal.

<Note for future missions, Darla. We don't store our gear in the same room we sleep in.>

<Either way, if they found it, they would have been waiting for you. Though I see your point; in the room, it's directly linked to your cover.>

<Exactly.>

<OK, noted.>

"Look," Tanis said, shifting her speech to sound sharper, her words clipped. "I'm here undercover to keep an eye on things for the visit. I have a few weapons and armor, should they be needed; normally, no one would know they're there, but I guess your scan tech is good enough to sniff them out."

Demetri didn't look impressed. "Undercover." He said

the word like it was utter nonsense, not a question at all.

"Yes. I'm TBI."

"Pass me your tokens," he replied evenly. "I'll call them into the local office."

"I'm operating out of High Terra," Tanis replied. "Locals don't know I'm here. I'm oversight for them. You can reach out to Inspector Sawyer of the HLPD. He's already vetted me."

One of Demetri's eyebrows slowly rose. "Sawyer." Again, it didn't sound like a question.

"I assume you've spoken to him?"

"Yes. I'll query him, but I'll get my own verification. Pass me the tokens."

Tanis sent Agent Sasha's ident tokens and TBI codes.

<The timer is set. Thirty-one minutes 'til he hears back from High Terra.>

"Now open the crates," Demetri instructed, as the guard behind her stepped into the room and closed the door.

<I'm going to take them down, then take out my doppelganger. Solve this problem my way,> Tanis said in a tone that brooked no argument—she hoped.

<You sure? That sounds risky. These guys are big.>

*<They're from high-*g *environments, probably the Cho. They won't know what hit them.>*

Tanis nodded to Demetri and turned to the crates, passing the unlock codes to the top one and pushing it open. Within were neatly folded outfits, each set into a vertical slat in the crate. Of course, underneath them all was a pulse rifle.

"Pull out the clothes. Slowly."

Tanis nodded to the bed. "Some of these outfits are worth as much as you make a year. I'm going to toss them gently to the bed. You wreck them, you're paying the bill."

"Just shut up and do it."

Reaching into the back of the crate Tanis pulled out a grey pantsuit, folded it over once, and then tossed it to the bed. She followed it with a green and white flowing dress, and then reached down, sticking out her tongue.

"Should be a headband in here that goes with—"

Her finger found the pulse rifle's trigger and passed the biolock check.

Fhummm!

The pulse rifle's concussive blast tore off side of the case and slammed it into Demetri.

Tanis didn't wait for him to recover before placing a foot atop the case and kicking off into the air. Her other foot hit the wall, and she pushed up once more, pivoting so her feet hit the ceiling. The momentum compressed her into an upside-down crouch.

Dropping the coat—and her lightwand—Tanis grabbed both ends of the towel and pulled it taut. In one fluid move, she pushed down off the ceiling and wrapped the towel around the face of the guard who had been standing behind her.

The move caught him off balance and he fell backward—Tanis's 'jump' off the ceiling pushing him down with far more force than the planet's gravity applied. As he toppled, she pivoted, slamming her knees into his face right as his head hit the floor.

Not convinced that he was out for the count, she whipped the towel away and simultaneously slammed a fist into each side of his head, feeling a *crunch* as her blows crushed the cartilage in his ears.

Her left hand shot out and caught her still-falling coat and pulled the lightwand free. She stood and triggered the blade just as Demetri was also struggling to his feet.

"You're lucky I'm really not out to get your Oligarch," she muttered. "He'd be as good as dead."

<*Wow, that's not going to put him in an agreeable mood.*>

"Not a TBI agent, then," Demetri grunted. "Didn't think you were, anyway. You're low-*g*. They like to pick their people from Earth and High Terra."

"I could be from Luna and just tired of snot-nosed Jovians," she shot back. "This *is* still the Terran Hegemony we're in, you know."

Demetri had a pulse pistol in his hand, and he fired it at Tanis without further dialogue, but she was also on the move, leaping in the air, pushing off one wall, and already running along the edge of the ceiling on Demetri's right by the time he squeezed the trigger.

"Too slow," Tanis taunted as she kicked off the corner, pinwheeling through the air. Her thighs clamped around Demetri's neck, and she swung her lightwand down, cutting off the end of his pulse pistol.

She deactivated the blade as he reached up to grab her, the huge man's arms wrapping around her waist and pulling her down, giving her the opportunity to drive her elbows into his solar plexus.

The resistance in his skin told her that he had augmented muscles, but she did as well, so the blow was still enough to drive the air from his lungs.

The Jovian doubled over, and Tanis's back hit the floor. Her legs were still wrapped around Demetri's neck, and the look in his eyes told her that he knew—now that her augmented strength was revealed—that she could break his neck with one twist.

She didn't want to kill the man, but one thing Tanis had learned about big meat-heads like the one between her thighs was that they liked to be a man's man, swinging free and unencumbered.

Her hand shot up between his legs, met soft flesh, clenched—and twisted.

The shriek Demetri let out was at least two octaves higher than his normal speaking voice, and Tanis was glad that his stealth suit wasn't permeable as she felt both his testicles pop.

<*Holy shit, you're vicious!*> Darla exclaimed.

<*I'm on the clock!*>

Tanis flipped Demetri over and gave him a half-strength kick in the ear before rushing to the crate and wrenching the pulse rifle from the hole it had blasted in the container. She scooped up her lightwand and checked the Infiltrator Chameleon's whereabouts.

<*Damn!*> She clenched her jaw in frustration. <*She's already on her walk! Over halfway around the pool!*>

<*You won't reach her before she gets back to the hotel. A dozen more Jovians are coming down the hall.*>

Without a second thought, Tanis took a step back, fired her pulse rifle at the window, and screamed all the air out of her lungs as she raced toward it.

DIVE AND A FALL

STELLAR DATE: 02.23.4084 (Adjusted Years)
LOCATION: The Golden Gazelle, Hunting Lodge
REGION: Ceres, Terran Hegemony, InnerSol

As Tanis fell the sixty-seven stories toward the pool, two things popped into her head. The first was: *At least I'm still wearing my swimsuit;* the second: *This is going to hurt.*

Even at 0.2*g*s, Tanis's quick math gauged her final velocity to be just over thirty meters per second. Better than if it had been a jump on a high-*g* world, but it was still the same as jumping forty-five meters on Earth.

Darla inserted a third thought into her mind. *<You're too far out.>*

As the pool rushed up toward her, Tanis realized that the AI was correct—she was going to land in the shallow end of the pool, which was only a meter and a half deep.

Twisting midair, she drew her knees up and tossed the lightwand and rifle away before raising her hands above her head and swinging them down with all her might.

Her knees hit the water at the same time as her arms, and the wider impact slowed her enough that her knees only scraped the bottom.

She peered around the illuminated pool, found her lightwand, and grabbed it as she splashed toward the edge, where her pulse rifle lay, bent and sparking.

Pain lanced up her arm, and she looked down to see the skin split open along her forearm, blood seeping out even as her internal med systems worked to staunch the flow.

People were gathered around, gasping and pointing as

she heaved herself out of the water, blood also running down from her knees.

Then a shot hit the deck next to her, and she realized that the Jovians were playing for keeps.

The crowd scattered, screaming in fright. As Tanis took off toward the cover of the surrounding forest, she brought up her doppelganger's location only to get no signal from the IC's Link.

<Darla!>

<I see it…or don't. She's gone!>

There was no time to wonder how the IC had given them the slip as angry bellows mixed with the crowd's fearful wails, and Tanis picked up the pace, pushing deeper into the forest's dubious cover.

"Well," she muttered as she raced toward the first rise. "I guess I probably thwarted the assassination attempt. There's no way Oligarch Alden is going to come here after all this."

<Yay, well done.>

<Hey.> Tanis switched back to the Link, reserving her throat for breathing as she sped up to over seventy kilometers per hour. *<My real identity wasn't implicated, I'm getting away, and the oligarch will be OK.>*

<Two of those things are temporary, and one is not yet established.>

<I'll get away.> Tanis turned down a narrow gully, leaping over logs and underbrush. *<I wasn't just going on hikes for the view.>*

<You have no armor. The moment someone starts looking for you with thermal imaging—which has likely already begun—you're going to light up like a beacon.>

"Oh ye of little faith," Tanis whispered as she darted to the right and gently pushed aside a matted group of vines. "Check it out."

<Well I'll be damned. I guess all those spelunker maps you were looking at paid off.>

Before Tanis lay a dark opening wreathed in dirt and roots, but a few meters further stood a half-open airlock door. Dried dirt filled the bottom third, and it took some work to wriggle through, but Tanis breathed a sigh of relief to see that the inner airlock door was still open.

The passageway beyond was tilted at a fifteen degree angle to the right. The sounds of dripping water came from that direction, and she turned left, moving at a good clip through the dark passage.

The light began to fade almost immediately, and Tanis switched her vision to use her sound-based overlay, letting out a high-pitched whistle as she ran.

She considered using her lightwand for illumination, but the device wasn't military grade. It didn't have a long-usage battery and, even with her augmented vision, it would partially blind her in the pitch-black cavern.

<How much do you trust these maps you found?> Darla asked.

<Trust? Not much. The local ruins spelunking community says that sections down here collapse or flood all the time. Bit by bit, the mountains are crushing these tunnels.>

<How encouraging.>

Tanis came to a section where roots blocked her forward passage and she looked around for another route. She spotted a door a few meters back on the right that appeared to have seen some usage. She prised it open and continued on her way.

"There's a larger concourse down here," she said while squeezing around a section of bulkhead that had collapsed. "If I can get to it, we'll be spoilt for exit locations."

<*If?*>

"The maps I have don't show this passage as connecting to it, but from what I can tell, it has to."

Thirty minutes later, Tanis still hadn't found any route that would take her to the concourse, and the trail of nanoprobes Darla had left behind showed that the Jovians had found the gully—though they'd not yet located the entrance to the ruins.

She didn't expect things to stay that way for long.

Tanis was pulling herself over a conduit run that had fallen from the overhead when Darla called out, <*Wait!*>

"What is it?"

<*I've been going over the maps you have, and I think you're partially right. This route should have met up with that concourse, but we've been climbing ever so slightly. I think we're actually above it right now.*>

"Huh." Tanis consulted the maps and saw the adjustment Darla had made to their direction. "I think you're right. That means if I cut a hole in the deck…and maybe a few meters of dirt, we'll hit it."

A panel lit up on the bulkhead just behind Tanis, highlighted on her vision by Darla.

<*Or you can take the maintenance shaft right there.*>

"Now you're just taking the challenge right out of this."

Tanis pulled the panel free and looked up to see a twisted mass of roots and vines hanging above. She was tempted to climb out that way, but given that they were still only a few kilometers from the hotel, they'd be well within the initial search radius.

She turned her head and looked down into utter darkness. A whistle and a few finger snaps later, she discerned that the tunnel sank over three kilometers into the ground.

One look at the ladder told her that trusting her life to it would be a serious risk.

<There should be a hatch nine meters down. Easy.>

"Right, easy," Tanis muttered as she pulled herself into the shaft, carefully bracing her back against one side, with her feet on the other. She carefully slid down, centimeter by centimeter, until she'd made it just over three meters.

Wiggling her back side to side, she dropped a bit further when the other side of the shaft gave way under the pressure from her feet, and her back slipped free.

Her head hit the side of the shaft, and then her knee scraped against something as she frantically clawed at the walls.

Then, in a sudden bone-jarring lurch, her downward momentum halted in a burst of pain from both her back and groin.

"Oooowwww…" Tanis moaned as the realization hit her that her swimsuit—and a noteworthy amount of skin on her back—had snagged on something jagged sticking out of the shaft wall.

While her skin had torn, the suit had held, driving all her weight into the fabric between her legs.

<Wow, that material is really strong,> Darla commented. *<You sure are lucky I don't buy cheap outfits.>*

"Sure. Yeah. Thanks," Tanis said between ragged gasps

as she surveyed her surroundings, trying to at least be glad for Ceres' low gravity.

She wasn't sure if it was luck, or fate cruelly mocking her, but an opening loomed a meter just above her head, to the right. She looked for any remnants of the ladder and realized that the only part of it still present in this section of the shaft was stuck into her back.

With more courage than certainty, Tanis drew in a deep breath as she carefully lifted her legs and brought her arms out in front of herself.

A cry of anguish tore free from her lips as she slammed her hands and feet back into the wall, pushing herself off the jagged protrusion that had caught on her swimsuit and across the narrow space. She hit the far side and kicked off, twisting around, desperately reaching for the opening.

Only the fact that Bella preferred the grippy coating on her feet saved Tanis. That coating gave her enough purchase to propel a meter upward, and she sailed through the air.

Both her hands grasped the opening's lower lip, and she pulled herself up slowly. Her head had just drawn level with the hole, when the ancient plas under her left hand bent and twisted.

With a cry, she fell, desperately kicking out her right foot and catching it on the jagged bar a meter down that had recently been stuck in her back.

Tanis grimaced as she pushed off the metal, slicing her foot open, but gaining enough momentum in the low gravity to pull herself up into the hole. Once safe, she rolled onto her side and pulled her swimsuit loose while cursing Harm for not giving her cover a penchant for full-body swimsheaths.

<*You good?*> Darla asked tentatively. <*That was a close one.*>

"Yeah. Good." Tanis said between long, unsteady breaths.

After another twenty minutes of traversing twisting, half-crushed shafts, Tanis finally reached a panel that she and Darla both believed would open onto the main concourse.

"Here goes nothing," Tanis said, drawing her unwounded foot back and giving the panel three good kicks before it fell free.

A long whistle told her that she'd indeed come upon a large space. She slid to the edge of the opening and flushed down some nanoprobes, glad to see she was only two meters up from clear and stable-looking deck plating.

She jumped out of the shaft and landed on her good foot. Once steady, she pulled her lightwand from the front of her bathing suit. When the beam's glow slashed out over the cavernous expanse, she saw that it was indeed one of the main residential thoroughfares of the old Insi ring.

Garish banners and ribbons dangled limply from poles and beams overhead, hung for the ancient Sharm celebration. Beneath them, the remains of carts lined the edges of the concourse, their wares long since rotted way.

"Air's better here, at least," Tanis said as she limped toward one of the poles and grasped a long ribbon hanging off it. The plas material, though dusty, was still in good condition, and she yanked it free.

<*Need some decoration?*> Darla asked with a soft laugh.

"Just trying to give my mednano a chance to heal this

gash," she said while wrapping the ribbon around her foot and tying it off.

<Oh, right. You're just one big walking wound. So is all this really better than just coming clean with Demetri?>

Tanis gave a rueful laugh. "Umm...probably not. But if I'd taken out my doppelganger, it would have been. She must have placed her own monitoring equipment around the hotel...something that would only transmit if it picked up indication of combat."

<I guess that makes sense. I had probes in place to do the same thing.>

"The question," Tanis continued as she began to gingerly walk down the concourse, headed toward one of the exits on her map, "is whether or not she's going to abandon the job, or go to the *Kirby Jones*."

<Or both?>

"I guess she could do that...take my place on the ship 'til the next opportunity strikes. I don't really see that as a viable long-term plan, though. She won't be real enough to fool the crew for long."

<You hope. Those top of the line ICs are really, really good at mimicry.>

"Mimicry only gets you so far."

<Like I said, let's hope.>

Tanis kept expecting to hear the sounds of pursuit from behind her, or of a search team coming in from the front, but over the next four hours, she didn't hear anything other than water dripping and the occasional distant groan of something settling under the weight of the hills above.

"This is it," she said as she reached a pool of water at the end of a narrow corridor. "Hopefully it's not an exit they're expecting us to use."

<I'd like to not use it. The maps show a hundred-meter swim!>

"Easy," Tanis said, then drew in a series of long breaths before jumping into the frigid water.

Despite the single word she'd uttered to Darla, the prospect of swimming through the half-rotten passageway with zero visibility was not something that thrilled her. In fact, it was one of the scariest things she'd ever done.

The thought of running out of air halfway through warred with the fear of finding that the tunnel had collapsed. *That* fear brought to mind the millions of tons of mountain over her head, and she had to force herself to remain calm and keep her heartbeat slow.

Twice she had to squeeze through narrow gaps, and at one point, her foot caught on a twisted mass of half-rusted conduit. Four minutes later, she emerged in a pool of water with canyon walls rising sixty meters above her.

The sun was directly overhead, and she floated on her back, catching her breath and basking in its warm rays for a minute before swimming toward the rock walls to begin her ascent.

<At least if you fall, it won't hurt much,> Darla offered in meager comfort.

"Much," Tanis grunted as she reached up and pulled herself out of the water, tired arms already shaking from the exertion.

When she finally reached the top of the canyon, she faced a forty-kilometer hike to the next town. She kept to the deeper forests as much as possible, but periodically moved into the sunlight to fight off the chill that was settling in as her power reserves ran low and her body's available calorie count diminished.

When she finally reached the edge of town, Darla used a burner identity to rent a hovercar. When it finally arrived, Tanis slipped in, nearly singing with delight to see not only food, but a medkit and a clean, nondescript shipsuit waiting for her.

"What would I do without you, Darla?" she wondered while peeling off the nearly shredded swimsuit and opening up the medkit.

*<Die from some sort of horrible infection. That water was **not** clean.>*

"I've been trying not to think of that," Tanis said as she gave herself a mednano boost shot, and then set to cleaning the grime out of her wounds.

As she worked, Darla set the car to travel to the nearest elevator shaft, which was one hour away. By the time they arrived, Tanis was clean, clothed, and fed, and her internal batteries were at least partially charged.

"So, Bella's burned, as is Sasha," Tanis said as the car reached the outskirts of the larger city that was nestled at the base of the elevator. "Who do we have next?"

<The locals are running a lot of security sweeps after your little fun-time at the hotel, so it's not a great time to set up a new identity. I was, however, able to fake logs of Claire coming down to the surface earlier.>

"Claire? Great," Tanis said with a groan.

A moment later, the car stopped next to a shopping district, and a servitor approached.

"This for us?" Tanis asked.

<Sure is.>

Tanis opened the door, and the servitor placed several

parcels on the seat next to her before making a chirping sound and saying, "Thank you for shopping at Avante Boutique, Miss Claire."

"Thanks," Tanis said and pulled the door shut before reaching for the top package. "Let me guess: mirrorsheath and bubble dress?"

<Even better.>

COMMANDER ON DECK

STELLAR DATE: 02.24.4084 (Adjusted Years)
LOCATION: TSS *Kirby Jones*, polar orbit around Ceres
REGION: Ceres, Terran Hegemony, InnerSol

"Commander! So good to have you back aboard," Connie exclaimed as Tanis pulled herself through the airlock, her rucksack drifting behind on a tether.

"You too, Sergeant," Tanis said with a warm smile. "Glad to finally be back aboard my girl. Looks like she's in better shape than ever."

Connie looked around at the passageway, her engineer's eye catching a few panels that should be locked down tighter and a light that flickered slightly. None of that needed to be brought to the commander's attention, though.

"Aye, ma'am, the *Jones* is ready to kick ass and take names."

Tanis had begun to pull herself down the passageway with Connie falling behind, but at the sergeant's words, she paused and glanced over her shoulder.

"Don't you mean 'sir', Technical Sergeant?"

The question took a second to make sense to Connie. 'Sir' was the normal address for all officers in the TSF, but Tanis preferred 'ma'am' when they were on the *Jones.*

Maybe she's trying to toe the line after all the crap we've been through.

"Of course, sir," she said aloud. "It won't happen again. You said you got roped into doing some recruiting appearances down there, how'd they go?"

"Good," Tanis said, turning back toward the bridge. "But

I got new orders while I was planetside. Your trip here will have to count for our shakedown. We're headed to Europa."

"Really, Commander?" Connie's brow furrowed in confusion. "That's waaaay out of our normal patrol path—not to mention Admiral Cornell's jurisdiction."

Tanis only shrugged as she reached the ladder shaft and stopped to regard Connie with a level stare. "Those are our orders. I got them from Colonel Higgs himself. I'll have Smythe get us a departure vector. I want to get out of here as soon as possible."

"Uh, sure, yeah," Connie stammered. "I'll go make sure everything is ready below."

"Sounds good, Connie," Tanis replied with another smile before grasping a rung and giving a sharp pull to propel herself up the shaft toward the bridge.

As the commander disappeared up the ladder, Connie hooked her foot into a deck-strap, a puzzled expression on her face.

That was…weird.

She shook her head and pulled her foot from the strap before floating down the ladder shaft to the engineering deck. As she spun around and grabbed a handhold to pull herself along the lower passageway, Cassie reached out to her.

<Connie, am I reading things right? Did Tanis just come aboard and pass orders for us to go to Europa?>

The sergeant didn't bother to hide the disbelief from her voice. *<Yup…she said Higgs has sent orders for us to run a patrol out there.>*

<That doesn't make any sense, I—>

<What?>

<Nothing, I guess I just need a coffee.>

Those five words set off alarm bells in Connie's mind.

Harm had established a series of codes with her shortly after coming aboard as Cassie. The one he had just uttered was for an immediate meeting to discuss something in person.

She checked the rubric he'd made that determined where they'd meet depending on the time of day and code he used, and saw that she was to meet at the starboard inspection porthole.

Smart cookie.

That location was on her pre-flight checklist. From there she could see all the fuel hookup ports on the hull and get a visual on whether or not they were locked down properly.

When she arrived, Cassie was already peering out the porthole, bobbing her head like she was trying to see around the caps and safety netting.

"Oh, hey Sarge, heard we're on the fast track to get out of here, so I thought I'd check the fuel caps, since we got topped up by a tanker earlier today."

"Good work, Spaceman," Connie said agreeably as she approached and peered through the porthole as well. To her surprise, there was a message projected against the plas that only became visible when she was right next to it.

[I tried to reach Darla, but so far as I can tell, she's not onboard with Tanis. I traced where Tanis was staying, and someone attacked two people there. Those two people were advance security for Oligarch Alden. I don't think that the person who just came aboard is Tanis.]

Connie didn't have a safe way to respond, so she tapped the window, tracing letters as she spoke. "That third cap is for the helium three. Stupid thing never quite seats right the first time. Was supposed to be a part of our refit, but we had to leave before the new one arrived. See those two lines? Liam put those markers on. If they're not aligned, then the thing isn't locked down properly."

The message she'd traced on the window was, *[If that's not Tanis, who is it, and where is the commander?]*

"Got it," Cassie said slowly then paused while nodding her head for a moment before asking. "What's with the markings on the other ones?"

[There are a lot of possibilities, but the worst-case scenario was that our pseudo-Tanis was going to kill the Jovian oligarch. In my line of work, it's always best to assume the worst. When I looked through the guests at the hotel, I spotted one of the covers I made for Tanis. A martial arts expert named Bella—who is now suspected of attacking those Jovians. Another of her covers was in use, too, altered to be a TBI agent, but that's it. I don't have any of her other registered ones coming into Ceres, or anywhere else. I have to assume she's using a cover she and Darla made right now. I kept knowledge of Darla from most of the division. Whoever is doing this doesn't seem to know about her. That's very good.]

A wave of relief flooded through Connie as she replied to Cassie's verbal question. "Well, after we had a leak one time on the H3 cap, we all got a little paranoid, so Liam put markers on the others too. They're the same make…it's nuts that they send us out without spares, but you know how things go sometimes."

[What are we going to do about our faker?]

[Someone in the division is planning to sacrifice Tanis—and probably the rest of us—to assassinate the oligarch. I want to know who it is, so we ride this out. You need to find a way to tap

all comms.]

"C'mon," Connie said. "I'll show you where we do a visual on the pressure bleed-off lines."

[OK…I think I can do that. Think the real Tanis is going to follow us to Europa?]

[Tanis is a professional. You can bet your life on it.]

CANDY CANE SCHMUTZ

STELLAR DATE: 02.24.4084 (Adjusted Years)
LOCATION: Elevator Terminal 19
REGION: Ceres, Terran Hegemony, InnerSol

Tanis rolled across the concourse that led to the elevator's debarkation lounge, silently cursing Darla the whole way.

In addition to the mirrorsheath and mask—which Tanis had to admit she had become surprisingly comfortable with—Darla's outfit included bright red, wheeled boots with matching oversized knee and elbow pads, topped off with a large, white helmet.

Though she had seen plenty of people using various types of wheeled footwear for sport, Tanis had never tried them herself. Darla would be the last to learn about it, but once she got used to having a row of four wheels underneath each foot, Tanis admitted to herself that rolling around could be a lot of fun.

Claire's fashion sense, however, ruined that fun.

Let's be honest, Claire is just an outlet for Darla. I'm beginning to sincerely doubt that Harm had anything to do with setting up this particular cover.

On top of the mirrorsheath, Tanis wore a tightly cinched red and white striped corset with a pair of oversized candy canes that rose up and wrapped around her breasts. As luck would have it, the candy canes were both hollow, and her lightwand was tucked inside one of them.

Beneath the corset, stretching to her knees, was a thick rubber skirt that allowed for more movement than the hated ball dress, but wasn't much better when trying to maneuver around other people on the busy concourse at high speeds.

<You know, I sure would like to be able to breathe in future outfits you select for me.>

<Tanis, you know that true fashion isn't about comfort. You ***look*** *amazing. With the corset and the tight rubber skirt, you've caused three men and two women to nearly crash into other people.>*

Tanis was about to deliver a snarky response to Darla when her AI showed her the image of a man who had turned around to look at her after she'd passed, only to trip over a hoverbot and land on his ass.

The wide-eyed expression of total entrancement on his face was so comical that she burst out laughing, and nearly fell herself.

<You're right, Darla. I keep forgetting that, while Tanis would never like doing this, Claire loves it. I gotta be Claire, be one with the foppery.>

<It's not foppery, Tanis, it's the hautest of the haute couture!> Darla admonished.

<I just have to say that for once I'm glad to be Claire and not Bella. With all this on, ***and*** *rolling around, I'd be sweating like a pig on a spit right now if I were her.>*

The AI laughed. *<I feel like a pig is your spirit animal.>*

<I don't think you should enjoy eating your spirit animal as much as I do—dammit, now I want a BLT, and Claire's a vegetarian. When can I be Tanis again?>

Darla didn't respond, and Tanis kept her focus on rolling across the concourse, suddenly wondering why she'd put on the entire outfit. There was no reason why she couldn't have just worn only the mirrorsheath, or gone without strapping wheels on her feet.

<Are you somehow conditioning me, Darla?> Tanis asked with mock suspicion.

<No, you're just finally starting to realize that covers aren't you, and it's OK to throw yourself into them.>

<Right, be one with the foppery.>

<It's not foppery!>

She reached the debarkation room for the elevator car, which was slated to arrive in just over ten minutes. As she waited, Tanis couldn't help but notice an increased security presence in the form of armed TSF fireteams patrolling the terminal.

It was hard not to constantly surveil the area—which would make her stand out—so she busied herself with seeing how many times she could twirl in a circle, behaving as un-Tanis-like as possible. She managed to get a record of one hundred and seventeen before her right foot caught on a crack in the floor and she fell on her ass, letting out a surprised squeak.

<Wow, that was perfectly in character. You're nailing it.>

<That was an unscripted squeak, Darla.>

<Oh.>

Tanis gave a tittering laugh as she struggled to get back on her feet, something that was surprisingly difficult in the skirt. She could get on her knees and then stretch the rubber skirt far enough to place one wheeled foot on the ground, but as soon as she tried to put her weight on it, the wheels rolled, and the taut rubber pulled her leg back and dropped her onto her ass again.

The corset wasn't helping either, making it impossible to simply bend over far enough to put a steadying hand on the ground while getting her feet under her.

Suddenly the hilarity of the whole situation hit Tanis, and she began to laugh. Here she was—the woman who had taken down two of the Jovian oligarch's guards and then jumped out of a sixty-seven-story high window just the day before—now trapped on the floor by a rubber skirt, corset, and wheeled boots, all of which she'd voluntarily put on.

Even while laughing, Tanis tried to get up once more, and this time fell forward, barely catching herself before her candy canes smacked into the floor.

That only made her laugh all the harder, and half a minute later, she was gasping for breath, tears streaming down her face, wondering if she'd have to crawl onto the elevator car.

"Ma'am?" a stern voice said from beside her, and Tanis looked up to see a TSF sergeant standing over her.

For some reason, that one word made Tanis laugh so hard she couldn't breathe.

"Y-y-yeah?" Tanis finally asked, desperately trying to calm herself as the uniformed woman stared down in consternation.

"Do you…uh…need a hand?"

"P-p-please." Tanis nodded vigorously, desperately trying to steady her breathing.

The sergeant activated the full lock mode on her rifle and slung it over her shoulder before extending a hand to Tanis, who grasped it while trying to get her feet to remain steady under her.

She was still defeated by the tight rubber skirt, which was keeping her from rising even with help.

"Huh…that's one heck of a…tricky…outfit you've got there," the sergeant muttered. "Why don't you sit back on your legs and hold out your arms."

Tanis nodded and complied, still giggling at the situation as the sergeant reached down and placed her hands under Tanis's armpits, lifting her straight up and then setting her down once Tanis straightened her legs.

"You good?" the woman asked, and Tanis nodded, taking several deep breaths to finally quell the laughter.

"Yeah…sorry…I don't know what came over me," she said while placing a hand on the sergeant's shoulder and carefully turning to face the woman. "Thanks for helping."

The sergeant's lips pressed together, and a flush showed on her cheeks. She reached a hand toward Tanis's chest. "You've got, ah…a…a bit of schmutz on your candy cane."

Tanis didn't move away, and the sergeant brushed the dust off the decoration, her hand trailing across her breast.

"You know," the soldier whispered. "I'm off at twenty-hundred today…if you're interested in drinks…."

Tanis gave as much of a smile as the automaton mask would allow. "I'm busy today…but I really can't say no to my savior. What about tomorrow?"

"Deal." The sergeant, who Tanis saw was named Ava, passed her contact token over the Link. "Tomorrow. You pick the place."

Tanis tilted her head and thrust out a hip, almost losing her balance in the process—which caused Ava to grab her corseted waist to steady her.

"I will, and I'm looking forward to it," Tanis whispered.

"Sarge! You done feeling up the eye candy over there already? The LT wants us to check out a disturbance at the security gate," a voice called out from behind Tanis, and she glanced over her shoulder to see a pair of soldiers waving at Sergeant Ava.

"Yeah! Coming!" Ava said as she removed her hands from Tanis's waist and paused to make sure she was steady.

"I'm good," Tanis said with a laugh. "Don't keep your LT waiting."

Behind her, she could hear one of the soldiers laughing. "See what I did there? 'Eye candy'."

"You're so fucking funny, Greg," Ava said as she walked away. "Wanna see me shove some candy in your eye?"

Darla chuckled quietly in Tanis's mind. *<Nicely done. You're officially the last person on Ceres that they'll think had anything to do with the dust-up back at the hotel.>*

<What can I say? I'm a master of disguise.>

<Oh please.>

AN UPGRADE?

STELLAR DATE: 02.24.4084 (Adjusted Years)
LOCATION: Prima Plaza Hotel, Insi Ring
REGION: Ceres, Terran Hegemony, InnerSol

Tanis was back in the hotel room she'd first checked into as Claire upon arriving on the Insi Ring three days earlier. She was laying on the bed, still wearing the candy cane outfit, barring the corset—that had been removed and thrown across the room as soon as the door closed.

"Do we need to worry that they'll trace the stuff in the hotel on Ceres back to this place?" Tanis asked as she gently rubbed her sides and lower back. "Some of those parcels were dropped off here first."

<I was careful when I sent it down, so I don't think so. But I'm keeping an eye peeled for inquiries at the shipping companies I routed them through.>

Tanis nodded absently as she brought up the STC data she'd pulled, and looked through the departure queues.

"Damn…there it is."

<Filed for Jovian space, too.>

Pushing herself upright, Tanis pulled off the white helmet she'd almost forgotten about—until she laid down on it. "Looks like we have another ship to book. Do we know where in the JC they're going?"

<You sure you just don't want to blow the whistle on other-you and end this charade?>

"Not while she's in control of the *Jones*, no. Too risky. Besides, now that the oligarch isn't in danger anymore, we have a bit of leeway to find out who is up to all this."

<I'll admit, I really want to know as well. Though we haven't found a single freaking clue, yet.>

"So where do you think they're going?" Tanis asked. "The flight plan only has initial vectors and Jupiter's nearspace as a destination."

<If I were a betting AI, which I've been known to do from time to time, I'd say it's a toss-up between Ganymede and Europa.>

"Really?" Tanis arched an eyebrow as she rose and rolled over to the crates, popping the first one open. "If she's going to take out the oligarch, wouldn't she go to the Cho?"

<Maybe, but my research shows that he's dedicated to his vacations. If he can't go to Ceres, I bet his security will at least insist he go somewhere close to home that they can control better. He has a ranch on Ganymede, and often stays at one of the underwater cities on Europa—Chora's Height. Personally, my money is on Europa.>

Tanis pulled out one of Claire's dresses, a short, flouncy number with a solid white bodice made of hard plas. "Could be worse," she muttered about the dress, and tossed it onto the bed. "Why's your money on Europa?"

<Because a company he owns just opened a new casino there, and he's the sort that likes to stay at places he owns.>

A few more outfits passed muster and landed on the bed, while only one landed in the 'hell no' pile.

"I suppose that makes sense. Europa and Ganymede are only half a day's travel apart, as well, so if we guess wrong, it's not the end of the world."

<Right. Yeah…Tanis?>

"Uh huh?" Tanis asked while holding up a strange silver outfit.

<What are you doing?>

"Picking out Claire's wardrobe. I want to have at least *some* say in it."

<Wow…I've been shoring up a new cover for you to book the flight with. I thought you'd had your fill of Claire.>

"Keep it handy in case we need it when we get there, but I kinda like travelling in style. I finally figured out how to be Claire the way she should be: flamboyant—not hiding and aloof."

<Well, OK, then. You should totally wear what you're holding.>

"Only once I understand what it is."

<You know the Golists?>

Tanis nodded. "The Taoist quasi-cyborg monk capitalists who abhor motion?"

<Yeah, them. That's inspired by those oddballs—but with more motion allowed.>

"Sounds…complex."

Tanis quickly packed up Claire's outfits, including her roller-girl getup, which she planned to wear again. She almost left the corset behind, but Darla convinced her that it was necessary to 'pull off the look'.

Once the room was cleaned, and the cartons that would come with her to Europa were separated from the ones that would go into storage, Tanis prepared herself for the Golist-inspired debacle she'd decided to brave.

Golists abhorred motion so much that they couldn't even abide the idea of legs moving—to that end, most of them had their legs, and often arms, removed. Even wheels were too much for them, so much of their body mass was dedicated to various sorts of hover-tech, from magnetics to turbines.

In Tanis's mind, turbines blasting out air to keep a person aloft counted as motion, but it seemed to be an accepted incongruity for the sect.

She wasn't about to remove her legs for fashion—not that she had the time for that sort of mod surgery before she was due to board the liner bound for Europa—but luckily, the outfit Darla had purchased didn't require it.

"I feel like I've graduated," Tanis said as she looked at the teardrop-shaped bottom part of the costume. "I've been in powered armor far less imposing than this."

<You'd best put the base on the ground.>

Tanis pulled the half-meter-wide disk out of the crate and set it down.

Since she—and presumably most people who wore the outfit—was not prepared to cut off her legs and use the space for levitation tech, she needed a more conventional way to hover. The disk had well concealed wheels and appeared to glide over the ground. It would create a magnetic field on which the bottom half of the Golist costume would float.

"I shoulda called Sergeant Ava to help me," Tanis said with a laugh as she laid down on the bed and folded her calves back against her thighs. "Here goes."

She grabbed the thick, supple material and pulled it up over her legs, to her waist. The top half had a pocket for her legs, and the lower half contained the magnetic field generator that would allow her to hover as high as two meters above the base. It also contained biohookups, which seated themselves once she snugged the top of the teardrop around her waist.

"Yup, just like powered armor," she said, wincing

slightly as the biosystems tested their connections. "People who devise these things are sadists."

<Does that make you a masochist?> Darla asked with a laugh.

"Maybe I just like you a lot, Darla, and I'm trying to make you happy.

<Tanis! That might be one of the nicest things you've ever said to me.>

Once the bottom half of the outfit ran through its initial checks, Tanis moved to the edge of the bed and slid off to hover a meter above the pad.

"OK…this is actually kinda fun."

<Look at you. Fun twice in one day.>

The lower half of the costume had been loose and flexible when Tanis pulled it on, but once it was hovering, it expanded and solidified into a gleaming, inverted teardrop. She rapped a knuckle against it, and it rang like a bell.

"I guess when Connie calls me 'old iron pants', she won't be resorting to hyperbole anymore."

<Has she ever said that?>

"Well…no, but I could see her doing it."

<Hurry and finish up. That's not a fast-moving outfit you've picked, and we're on the clock.>

"So demanding," Tanis muttered as she picked up the top part of the Golistic attire.

Unlike the bottom, which didn't reveal her figure at all, the top part was perfectly form-fitting, to the point that it was a bit of a struggle to get on. Once she managed to do so, the torso section solidified as well. Accessing the controls for the magnetic field she hovered on, Tanis spun and looked at the stylized helmet that lay on the bed.

"I'm not so sure about that, it makes the automaton mask look like child's play."

<Tanis…you're doing so well. You gotta complete the outfit.>

"OK, OK."

She picked up the back piece of the helmet, set it into the high collar, and waited for it to draw her hair up and out of the way before she pulled it forward until it sat snugly against her head. Two connections seated into her cranial heat transfer ports, and then her HUD flashed an update that she had enhanced neural cooling abilities.

"Huh, I guess that's cool."

<Well punned. Hurry up.>

Tanis picked up the mask piece and set it in place on the front of the helmet. It all but sucked itself tight against her face, and then a notice flashed on her HUD: *Fashion-G Suit Ready.*

She activated the room's holomirror and looked herself over. The helmet had two large, wing-like fins sweeping off the back of her head, which matched the ones coming off her shoulders. Her face was clearly visible, though covered in the helmet's mask. She gave a slight smile, and the mask pulled her face into a wide grin.

"I guess this is the satirical aspect of this thing?" Tanis asked, her voice varying in pitch and overemphasizing certain words.

<Yeah, it exaggerates your face and voice, while holding the rest of you almost perfectly still.>

"What about my arms?" Tanis asked, holding up her uncovered hands.

<It's in the Fashion-G Suit's menu system. You have to activate the hand coverings.>

Tanis found the option and triggered it, surprised to see flowmetal pour down her arms and cover her hands, and then keep going until long tentacles reached the deck.

"Seriously?" she asked with a chuckle that came out as guffaw.

<*There's an option for it to just coat your hands. You can switch to that.*>

"This much flowmetal must cost a fortune," Tanis whispered excitedly as she held up her arms, carefully manipulating the tentacles by twitching her fingers.

<*What do you think?*> Darla asked expectantly.

"I look like some sort of stylized planter with a chrome venus fly trap growing out of the top."

<*Do you want to change? There's just barely time.*>

"No," Tanis shook her head. "Claire approves."

<*And Tanis?*>

"If Tanis saw someone wearing this, she'd have to work real hard to keep her inner hyena at bay."

<*Well…I guess you're making progress, at least.*>

WHISKEY TANGO

STELLAR DATE: 02.24.4084 (Adjusted Years)
LOCATION: Insi Ring
REGION: Ceres, Terran Hegemony, InnerSol

Getting to her scheduled liner, the *Whiskey Tango* was rather uneventful, considering that Tanis couldn't move her legs, and her arms were three times their normal length.

She ended up wrapping them around her waist to keep them out of the way, which nearly caused a catastrophe when the spaceport maglev's magnetic field interfered with her hover-pad, and she quickly had to unravel her arms to grab a nearby safety strap.

<Sorry…it's supposed to be shielded against that. I guess 'shielded' and 'unaffected' are two different things.>

<I think I know what it is,> Tanis replied as she sifted through the FGS's control systems. *<There are different modes, and I had it on the more flexible one—it's fun to bob along. It recommends the rigid mode for maglevs.>*

She switched to the higher setting, and felt the gentle rocking motion cease and the magnetic field's grip strengthen.

<You've put me in some strange things, Darla, but this takes the cake. I should upgrade it with some weapons tucked into the pod and add armor. I'd be a hovertank.>

The AI snorted a laugh. *<You'd start up a whole new fashion trend. Granted, there was that one a few years back, where the uber-wealthy all modded themselves to look like starships.>*

<Sheesh. Everything's been done, hasn't it?>

<Pretty much.>

Despite Tanis's bizarre outfit, she barely rated much notice from the locals, and bit by bit, she realized that folks on Insi were open to just about anything.

It was a lot different from her staid upbringing on Mars, or the more functional clothing and decorum she normally encountered in the TSF sectors of the stations she frequented.

Tanis even saw a few variations on the roller-couture outfit she had worn the day before, their tweaks and flourishes giving her a few ideas for the next time she wore it.

As the maglev pulled into the terminal, a realization that she had never considered before hit her.

<Darla…I think I finally understand this.>

<Hmmm?>

<Fashion is a bit like warfare….> she mused while twirling one of her tentacles in the air in front of herself.

<Very good, my apprentice—>

<…with stupid rules.>

<And here I thought we were getting somewhere.>

Tanis couldn't help give a small laugh, which her FSG's mask turned into a tittering laugh. Keeping up appearances, she touched one of her tentacles to her lips—pleased that she'd managed to master such fine motor control of the flowmetal—and tilted her head in a foppish manner.

<I didn't mean to be that disparaging, though I'll admit to taking advantage of good timing. What I mean is that in warfare, when you shoot an enemy in the head, they're down. No one debates it, no one says 'well, I think they look ***fabulous*** *on the ground there'. It just is what it is.>*

Darla laughed as Tanis spoke, and her mental avatar

nodded in agreement. *<OK, I'll grant you that. But there's subterfuge in warfare.>*

<Sure, but when the chips are down, you know who won and who lost.>

<Trust me, in the fashion world, the same is true. It just manifests as sales and feed coverage ratings.>

<I guess that makes sense. It's just messy in the middle,> Tanis countered.

<Not that dissimilar from warfare.>

<Touche.>

The maglev reached the terminal, and Tanis disembarked with the other passengers. A group of teenaged boys and girls were behind her, smiling and pointing at her. Then two of them stepped up onto her rolling platform and wrapped their arms around her.

"Awesome FSG," the girl on her right said, while the boy on her left planted a kiss on her cheek.

"Totally nailable…if you weren't all covered up down here." He knocked a fist against her lower half, the sound echoing loudly around them.

"Hey!" Tanis exclaimed, but couldn't help laugh as the boy winked and hopped off, followed by the girl who blew her a kiss.

"You should add color!" one of the girls in the group said over her shoulder as the teens raced down the concourse. "I vote reds, greens, and yellows."

"Uh, thanks!" Tanis called back.

<Don't you dare…then you'll ***really*** *look like a plant.>*

Tanis laughed softly to herself as she worked her way toward her terminal, wondering what Darla would do if she were to follow the girl's advice.

Probably take control of the thing and change it back.

Passing through the Auth & Auth security arch at the entry to the ship took a bit longer than usual, as the system registered too many superconductor batteries for a single passenger—not to mention that the magnetic levitation tech messed with its ability to see through her lower teardrop shell.

The two guards managing security at the entry shared a look of consternation as a line began to form behind Tanis.

"Can you step—er…roll—over here, ma'am?" One of the guards gestured to a cordoned off area next to the Auth & Auth arch.

"Of course," Tanis replied, a sour look forming on her face. "Will this take long?"

The man rubbed his brow, a sheepish look on his face. "Well, the scanner is getting too much interference from the magnetics in your…uh…floating teardrop thingy."

"OK," Tanis said, waiting for the man to propose a solution.

She knew what *she'd* do if someone was trying to board her ship dressed as she was, but Claire was a wealthy, paying customer, and this guard was going to have to consider his options carefully.

"So…uh, is there any chance you can just get out of it?" he asked.

Huh…I guess he did suggest what I would have made someone do. Her scowl deepened, and she shook her head. "Absolutely not! I will not undress in front of you."

<Plus you're not wearing anything underneath,> Darla added with a laugh.

<In hindsight, probably not the best thing to wear for boarding.

I should have kept the wheels on. I'd've rolled right in.>

<*So punny.*>

"Umm…I don't know what to do, ma'am. I can't let you pass through the Auth & Auth if it can't scan you."

Tanis intertwined her tentacles. "Well this is your job. What do you propose we do?"

The man scratched his forehead, then glanced over at the machine next to him. "Well…I could put you through the cargo scanner."

Her squeak of indignation was not faked in the least. "There is *no way* you're going put me in the *cargo* scanner!" With each word, her voice rose in amplitude until she was nearly yelling, and the guard's face was beet red.

"Please, ma'am…I'm sorry…I just…. Look, my supervisor has it in for me, and if I have to call her down again today, she's going to make me do something horrible, like clean the decks with my tongue. Is there anything we can do to avoid that?"

Tanis couldn't help but feel pity for the poor guy. The last thing she wanted to do was get some person just doing their job in trouble.

"You can carry me."

"Pardon?"

She gave him a wink, which the mask turned into a saucy gesture that involved half her face. "You look strong. Pick me up; I'll turn off my magfields, and you can carry me through the Auth & Auth. Parents carry young children through, so I know it can handle two people."

The man looked visibly relieved. "Uh…yeah, I think that just might work."

"Just have your friend over there bring my base. I'm not

going to have you lay me on the ground like some luggage afterward." She jerked her head back to indicate the guard's partner, who was barely holding in laughter as he waved less ridiculously attired people through the security arch.

"Terry!" the guard called out. "I'm going to need you to bring Miss Claire's base through after her. OK?"

"Seriously, Rich? Can't she just roll it through?" Terry called back.

"No, you idiot, the ship's not going to let that many SC batteries just roll on. One of us has to take it through."

"Oh, yeah."

The first guard, Rich, approached Tanis and paused, uncertain as to where to grasp her.

She chuckled. "You're just going to have to go for it."

"Umm…sorry about this," he said as he wrapped his arms around her handily constricted waist and lifted her up.

Tanis did her best not to laugh, as her steel breast pressed into the side of the poor man's face, while he strained to lift what she estimated to be nearly one hundred and fifty kilograms, between her and her outfit.

Once Rich had her in the air, Tanis shut off the magfields, and he groaned under the full weight.

"Terry! Get that damn thing!" he called out while rushing toward the Auth & Auth, pushing another passenger out of the way in the process.

They passed through the security arch without trouble, and Rich puffed and wheezed while Terry took his time getting Tanis's base.

When he finally brought it through and set it down, Rich hurriedly held Tanis over it, and she re-activated the magfields just as his grip was slipping.

"Thanks for not dropping me, Rich," she said, trailing a tentacle along his cheek.

The guard reddened even more, and his counterpart burst out laughing as 'Miss Claire' wheeled away.

<*Totally worth it,*> Darla chuckled as Tanis passed through the umbilical and onto the ship.

<*Poor guy. I think my boob poked him in the eye.*>

Rather than go right to her room—where she would have no reason to remain in the FGS—Tanis decided to venture to the ship's VIP areas and see what pre-flight entertainment was to be had.

Despite the fact that the *Whisky Tango* was one word away from being a rather amusing curse, the moniker had more to do with the fact that the ship catered to people who liked expensive alcohol and dancing on their interplanetary cruises. To that end, it had not one, but two casinos.

<*I wonder how they play craps in zero-*g,> Tanis mused as she drifted into the first casino and rolled amongst the unoccupied tables.

<*I bet they apply more thrust during certain hours for the dancing and gaming,*> Darla suggested.

<*Seems silly, but I guess if their passengers are here to gamble and dance, it makes sense.*>

<*Honestly, the fact that humans still play physical games like this is what doesn't make sense. You can VR-sim all of this.*>

Tanis shrugged as she approached the bar at the back of the casino area.

<*I'm sure lots of people do. You know there are billions of people who just sink into nutrient vats and lose themselves in sims for their whole lives. But those sorts of people aren't the types who get on starships named the* Whiskey Tango *for a vacation in*

Europa's ocean.>

<Good point. I guess I have so little interaction with the vat people that I never think about them.>

Tanis shrugged. *<That's the case with most of us. Their version of living is different—though they do reap the benefit of the security that all of us real-life people provide.>*

"What'll it be, ma'am?" the bartender asked as Tanis wheeled up to the bar.

For a moment, Tanis thought that he was an automaton, but then realized that he was wearing a mirrorsheath and mask like Claire's. She understood how people did it for fashion and kicks, but to see a business dressing humans up as ubiquitous machines seemed odd. If from nothing other than a cost perspective. Machines could work day in and day out, but humans needed breaks, and worked in short shifts.

Maybe it's a way to show how upper-crust the ship is, she mused. *It's not like I have a lot of experience hobnobbing with elites.*

"Do you know how to make a Coronal Mass Ejection?"

"Sure do," he winked and began to prepare the drink.

* * * * *

Over the week it took to reach Europa, Tanis played innumerable hands of poker, blackjack, and a number of other card games she'd never heard of before.

She also learned a few new dances and even became quite the sensation on the dance floors when she wore what she'd come to call her 'haute-roller' outfit—though dancing required wearing the corset a bit looser than Darla wanted.

All the while, she kept tabs on the *Kirby Jones* via a tap into the cruiseliner's scan suite. The TSF patrol craft was ahead of them by nearly a day, still on a vector that could end up at any of Jupiter's Galilean moons.

During her time as Claire, Tanis made many acquaintances, and had no small number of suitors approach her—both male and female. However, despite their wealth, none of them felt authentic to her. Not like Kaebel had.

His youth and drive to make the most out of life had been refreshing. She'd checked the feeds for mention of him, and eventually found that he'd been questioned about his time with 'The Would-be Assassin, Bella', but was ultimately deemed innocent and let go.

Inspector Sawyer had a harder time of it. While his suspicions were correct about there being something amiss at the hotel, the fact that it had been right under his nose—or so the investigators thought—didn't bode well for him. He'd been busted down in rank, and Tanis was determined to do something for him when everything came to light.

As the days went on, and scan showed the *Kirby Jones* on course with no apparent issues, she began to wonder how the Infiltrator Chameleon had been able to fool her crew so well.

<That's what those things are made to do,> Darla repeated as Tanis swam laps in the ship's pool during one of its 0.4*g* burns.

<Yeah, and they're very good over short periods with people that don't know you well,> Tanis replied. *<I've read the effectiveness reports.>*

<I imagine military formality helps,> Darla suggested.

*<Connie would **have** to see it. I can see Jeannie and Smythe missing it—they're usually too busy being **not** attracted to one another to pick up on nuances like that.>*

The AI snorted a laugh as Tanis reached the end of the pool. She was about to swim another lap when an announcement came that the burn was about to cease, and the pool was closing.

As Tanis drew herself up out of the water, Darla asked, *<What are you going to do about those two?>*

<Well, if they ever end up getting busy, one of them is going to have to transfer off the Jones. *Ship's too small to let a relationship like that go on—especially between the only two other officers.>*

<I can see that. Hate for you to have to break up your little family.>

Tanis nodded as she stepped into an autodryer, standing still for the five seconds it took the machine to dry her mirrorsheath.

<The only constant is change—especially in the military…except when it's not,> she half-explained.

*<That makes **no** sense.>*

<Have you seen how the TSF operates?>

Darla snorted another laugh. *<Good point. It's the last night before we dock…. You going dancing?>*

Tanis shrugged as she ambled into the passageway. *<I suppose. The 'Haute-Roller' needs to make one final appearance. Have you picked up any definitive word on where the oligarch is staying? Is it at his new casino?>*

<Nothing has leaked, if that's what you're asking. It's like he's completely disappeared.>

Tanis waved and nodded to a couple as they walked past. "Had a blast last night, Tara, Ford."

"Us too! You hitting the floor when they boost again later?" Ford asked.

"Sure thing. I'll be there with wheels on."

"Love it!" Tara giggled. "I'm totally getting wheels when we get to Europa."

"It's an ocean moon," Ford laughed. "I thought you wanted to get fins."

Tara frowned then pursed her lips. "Hmm…good point. I wonder if there's a way to combine them."

Ford only laughed, and Tanis gave him a knowing wink before she turned and resumed her walk and conversation with Darla.

<Maybe our friendly neighborhood IC will lead us to the oligarch.>

<Waiting for her to make her move will put us behind the eight ball,> Darla replied. *<Besides, I miiiiight have something better.>*

<Oh? You holding out on me? I thought you just said the oligarch had disappeared,> Tanis asked as she reached the lifts.

<Well, the oligarch is a bit hard to find, but you know who's not?>

"All passengers, burn decreasing in fifteen seconds."

The lift began to rise, and Tanis slipped a foot into a floor strap, just to be on the safe side, as she gave Darla's clue a moment's thought. *<Of course! Demetri.>*

<Nailed it.>

<And?>

<Well, he's not posting on the feeds what his final destination is, but he sent a message to his wife telling her he was bound for 'the boss's new digs'.>

Tanis laughed as the lift opened and she stepped out, keeping one hand on the passageway's railing as she walked to her room.

"Burn decreasing in five, four, three, two, one."

The feeling of gravity slowly dissipated, and before Tanis reached her cabin, she was pulling herself along the railing.

<Gotta admit, I like the slow decrease. Not like in the military, where we just cut thrust and fire maneuvering engines, and if you're not ready, sucks to be you.>

<Hard for commercial ships to get repeat customers if they smear them against the walls.>

<Good point.>

* * * * *

That night, Tanis hit the dance floor with wheels on her feet for one final show. She was still in her mirrorsheath, which she'd worn for the entire trip, once she divested herself of the FGS costume.

Today, she'd utilized the flowmetal from the FGS's tentacles to cover her roller-shoes, pads, and helmet, turning herself into a gleaming silver dancing machine.

After Darla went on for ten minutes about how it would 'complete the outfit', she'd even used the last of the flowmetal to make a silver corset.

She danced for hours with Tara, Ford, and several of their friends. At one point, Tara began to place her drink orders through Tanis, and though Tanis's first reaction was still to get one just to pour on Tara's head, she acquiesced, and danced her way to the bar and back, even going so far as to leap in the air and roll across a few tables—much to their patron's alarm and then delight.

Soon, everyone on and around the dance floor was ordering their drinks through Tanis, and she gave into the role, spending the rest of the night fetching drinks.

Only once did anyone attempt to proposition her. A man tried to grab Tanis, saying he wanted a go at the 'roller-bot-bitch'. After he woke up with the distinct marks of four wheels on his face, he tried to have the ship's security arrest Tanis, but everyone on the dance floor and at the surrounding tables swore that it had been a mistake, and that Claire had slipped when Ford dipped Tara too low in a dance, and bumped into her.

Even the two bartenders and the other staff swore that was what happened, and the belligerent man had ultimately stormed off.

By the time Tanis made it back to her room—just before the heavy burn cut out again—she was exhausted from having rolled for almost eight hours, but surprisingly happy.

"People are a lot more fun when I can just dance around them and serve them drinks rather than talk to them."

<*Dancing, fashion, enjoying being of service…*> Darla chuckled <*Who are you, and what have you done with Tanis?*>

"Well, you know how the saying goes, right?"

<*What? Do you mean 'What happens on the* Whiskey Tango *stays on the* Whiskey Tango'?>

"That's the nice version. I was thinking of something more like 'You tell anyone about this and you're dead'."

<*Oh, Tanis, this is fantastic.*>

"A death threat is fantastic?"

<*No, the sheer volume of blackmail material I now have on you.*>

Tanis groaned as she pulled off the roller-shoes and slid her feet into footholds before the burn ended. Once secure, she divested herself of the flowmetal and took off the pads and helmet.

"So, did you learn anything?" she asked.

<*What, while you were playing dancing-automaton-girl?*>

"Hey, covers are work—*especially* Claire. She's not like Bella, who's a loner. Claire likes to get out there and party."

<*Claire or Tanis?*>

Tanis chuckled and repeated her question. "Did you find anything?"

<*Fiiiine. I'm inside your body, though. I can tell when you enjoy things.*>

Tanis laid back in her bed and pulled the blanket up, doing up the fastener along the side to hold her in as the ship's burn began to decrease. "You were saying?"

<*OK, yeah, the oligarch is at his new casino, the Blue Lagoon in Europa. It's up in the Sargasso Mountains.*>

"I thought that was a protected region down there," Tanis said as she pulled up a map of the ocean moon.

<*It is. The pods are not happy.*>

Even at the dawn of spaceflight, humanity had suspected that an ocean lay beneath the icy surface of Jupiter's second Galilean moon, and once orbiters with radar and sonar penetrated the ice and confirmed the water's existence, it was only a matter of time before rigs landed and began to drill through it.

The water wasn't immediately hospitable to Terran organisms. It was also filled with protolife such as phages and viruses that were examined and catalogued. Most of the nanoscopic organisms that lived in Europa's waters had ultimately been destroyed by Earth's much more advanced life, though a few still persisted.

Many argued that the life in Europa should be maintained as it was, but as the largest source of relatively clean water in the Sol System, no one was willing to let Europa remain entirely untouched.

Only when a joint treaty was signed between Terra, Mars, and the Jovian combine, did the struggle to protect Europa end. However, by that time, many people had settled in cities on the moon's ocean floor. Elevators stretched up to holes cut in the icy surface, and trade and commerce were well established.

Talks began to unseat the humans, but in the end, it was the dolphins who saved the cities. A part of the treaty to protect Europa was to give its management over to dolphinkind. The dolphins took that task seriously, but they argued that they needed human partners to effectively take care of the moon—and so a symbiotic relationship formed.

Over the centuries, the equality in that bond had ebbed and flowed. During the last century, the Jovian Combine had built more cities atop the moon's icy shell, and the human population in the cities below had begun to balloon as well.

Though the vast majority of the humans who lived on and in Europa appreciated it for the natural wonder it was, some sought to exploit it.

People such as Oligarch Alden.

"How—nevermind. I know how. He's the oligarch."

<Pretty much.>

"Great, now I feel all icky, knowing we have to go to his casino and save him. If it wasn't that 'Tanis Richards' would be his assassin, I might be tempted to look the other way."

<Tanis!>

"I said 'might be tempted'. That's a solid double-qualifier."

<If you say so.>

"So what's our in?" Tanis asked.

<Well, they're booked up for months. Even the fabulous Claire wouldn't be able to get bumped up.>

"I'm sensing a 'but'."

<This is kind of funny—given what you were busy doing tonight.>

"Dancing?"

Darla laughed. *<Sadly, no, Tanis. Serving. They're looking for waitstaff.>*

"Oh, that doesn't seem so bad. Just another cover."

<Not this one. They're looking for ***heavily modded*** *waitstaff.>*

"Define, 'heavily modded'?"

Darla broke into a tittering laugh once more. *<Well, you seemed to like the tentacles on the Golist outfit. How do you feel about becoming an octopus?>*

"Pardon!? That's disgusting, Darla."

<Tanis, seriously. Places like this are about decadence and sexuality.>

"How much modding we talking about?" she asked.

<Ehhhh, half-octopus. Just have to cut your legs off at about mid-thigh.>

"Shiiiiit," Tanis whispered. "Guess I'm going to find out what it's like to be a JJ99 pilot."

<Oh, they have an opening for one mermaid, too.>

"Do they get to keep their legs at all?"

<Uhhh…no. Oh…this is one of the scary mermaids.>

Tanis perked up at the thought. "Scary how?"

<You won't like it. Fish eyes, jagged fish teeth, gills on the side of your he—>

"Kay, yup. You're right. Octowoman gets to keep a normal head, right?"

<Looks like it. You have to get the mods done top-side, and they send the specs to the medcenter that does it. There's an interview, first, though.>

"Well, set us up, I guess it's time to upgrade from two tentacles to eight."

A SIGNIFICANT CHANGE

STELLAR DATE: 03.03.4084 (Adjusted Years)
LOCATION: Europa Crown Station, Europa
REGION: Jupiter, Jovian Combine, OuterSol

Given the fact that the *Kirby Jones* had beaten them to Europa, and Tanis Richards had already disembarked for the surface, Tanis and Darla decided that that there wasn't time to establish a new cover.

That's how it came to be that it was Claire, the fashionista debutant, who rolled into the recruiter's office on Europa Crown Station, wearing her all-silver 'Haute Roller' outfit, automaton mask and all.

She'd decided that anyone hiring for the Blue Lagoon wasn't going to want employees like Claire, since they likely had no idea how to function as servants. As a result, from the moment Tanis entered the recruiter's small, but warmly decorated office, she adopted a subservient attitude, standing behind the chair with her head slightly lowered and hands clasped before her.

The recruiter didn't immediately look up from her holodisplay, but when she did, her brown eyes widened in surprise, and she brushed a lock of blue-white hair back from her face.

"You're...Claire?"

"Yes, ma'am," Tanis said in a voice that was not monotonous, but also carried no emotion.

The woman scowled at her display. "Ummm...may I be blunt?"

"Of course, ma'am."

The woman's look of consternation deepened. "Did something recently happen to your wealth? From what I can see here, you could spend money with wild abandon and still not have to work a day for the next hundred years."

"No, ma'am, my wealth is intact."

The woman sat back in her chair, folding her arms across her chest. "Is this some game to you? Working people have things to do besides having their time wasted by rich fools playing jokes on us."

Tanis finally raised her head and looked at the recruiter.

"No, ma'am. I really want to do this. I…I spent some time playing at being an autonomous servitor recently, and I kinda liked it. We docked here at Europa, and I was looking at places I could apply. The option to work at the Blue Lagoon was there, and I thought it would be a lot of fun."

"Miss Claire, if you think that working a job like we have listed for the Blue Lagoon is going to be *fun,* you have no idea what you're even talking about, and despite your apparent desire to be an automaton, you would not be well-suited for the job."

<*She is totally not buying this,*> Darla groaned. <*She's right, she's…she's deep in gambling debt!*>

<*Oh ho!*> Tanis exclaimed before stepping around the chair and sitting in it.

"Is this where you try to brow-beat me?" the woman asked.

"No," Tanis shook her head. "You're right, I have no idea what it's like to work at a place like the Blue Lagoon—or anywhere other than my own companies—but I really want to find out. You're right about the automaton bit…it excites me—which is odd, because I behave like an emotionless machine when I do it."

"Huh," the recruiter chuckled. "Honesty…that's refreshing. I still don't see how this would work. You don't have any of the required skills—"

"I have money," Tanis interrupted. "I'd pay you…two—"

<Ten.>

"Ten times your recruitment finder's fee."

The woman's eyes grew wide as saucers, and her breathing quickened. "Ten?"

Tanis nodded.

The woman pursed her lips and looked down at her displays before glancing back up at Tanis. "That's quite the…incentive. But I have my reputation to—"

"Fifteen."

<Damn…Harm better reimburse us; this is getting expensive, even for me.>

"Okay," the woman drew the word out as though she were convincing herself. "But I don't think that you'd do well as either of their standard openings. People like to talk to the mermaids and octowomen. Being pleasant and helpful in customer service situations while getting treated like crap by…well…people like you, Miss Claire, is a rare skill."

"What are you saying?" Tanis asked.

"Well, I'm going to pitch a new idea to them and see what they think."

* * * * *

When Tanis regained consciousness in the medcenter—

one that Darla had carefully selected and then bribed to do the work and hide the fact that Claire was far more augmented than she purported to be, not to mention that she had an AI—the first thing she did was blurt out, "How bad is it?"

<You know…all things considered…I think it turned out pretty well.>

" 'Pretty well' is far from encouraging, Darla."

Tanis's hearing seemed off, and her voice sounded strange. She opened her eyes, which also felt odd, as though her eyelids were far too heavy, and saw that she was in a recovery room with the lights dimmed and soft music playing.

<Well, the staff manager at the Blue Lagoon sent up some last minute alterations after you went under, so things aren't quite the same as they were going to be.>

"Darla…."

<You kinda look like a giant, silver squid.>

Tanis didn't wait any longer. She held up her hand—which was a tentacle—and flushed out a passel of nano to get a view of her body.

"Oh wow. I'm like…an *automaton* silver squid."

Her body was once again silver, but this time, she could tell it wasn't a mirrorsheath, but rather a new skin. Her torso was mostly unchanged, but from the hips down, her body was simply a mass of very long tentacles. Twelve, if she counted correctly. Likewise, her arms were gone, and sprouting from each shoulder were four tentacles. Her face was nearly featureless, barring large, round eyes and a thin mouth slit.

Atop her head were another dozen tentacles.

"OK.... One: they cut my arms and legs entirely off, and two: how do I move!? Who could ever manage this many limbs?!"

<*Good thing you've got me to lend you a* ***hand***.>

"Oh yeah, you're so funny, Darla. This is the last time I let you get me modded while I'm unconscious. Why all these extra changes, anyway?"

<*I think the Blue Lagoon's staff manager has a tentacle fetish, and you were a bit too eager to get the job.*>

Tanis switched to the Link. <*Next mission we go on, it needs to be one where I just have to shoot stuff. This is getting ridiculous.*>

<*Considering that you're about to spend the foreseeable future at the bottom of the ocean, it's not bad, though. I bet once you master all those limbs, you're going to be able to swim really quickly.*>

Lifting the same 'arm' she had the first time, Tanis pushed herself upright, the motion confirming that her hipbone was at least still present, and the two thickset tentacles below her waist were neurally mapped to her legs. She stretched one out to see if she could somehow walk on it, but managing the three-meter length proved difficult.

As she flopped the elongated limb on the floor, trying to curl it up beneath her, the door opened and the private clinic's lead doctor, a tall, dark-haired woman named Mauve, stepped in.

"Ah, Miss Claire, I saw that you were awake. I hope you and Darla are pleased with my work. You're quite the masterpiece, if I do say so myself."

Tanis glared at Mauve, but the woman seemed to be genuinely excited. "Yeah, I suppose this is impressive,"

Tanis almost gritted out.

"You have no idea! May I use images and sims of this work to show other clients? I think I may find myself doing a few similar jobs in the future."

"Umm…I don't know, Doctor Mauve…."

"I swear, I'll keep your identity a secret. No one will know you want to be a servant, Claire."

"One month," Tanis said, raising a tentacle. "No one knows about this for four weeks. I can't have someone showing up and ruining my fun."

"OK!" Mauve nodded rapidly. "I can do that."

<You think this will take a month?>

<No, I just want to be on the other side of the Sol System before anyone can even guess that this was me.>

IN THE WATER

STELLAR DATE: 03.05.4084 (Adjusted Years)
LOCATION: Chora Dive Tube, Europa
REGION: Jupiter, Jovian Combine, OuterSol

Tanis had to admit that once she was in the water, everything worked a lot better.

She spun her tail-tentacles in a clockwise rotation, the motion driving her body down through the water, while she used her arm-tentacles for stabilization.

Luckily for her, Darla had picked a good doctor, and Mauve knew her work. She'd connected all the new limbs to Tanis's existing neural network at the point where her natural body ended and the synthetic began.

Each limb was mapped to a preexisting part of Tanis's body, so she just had to remember what did what.

Controlling her tail-tentacles was easy because the two largest were mapped to her legs, while the other ten were mapped to her toes. Her arms were trickier because there two of the tentacles were mapped to two fingers each.

She hadn't managed to gain any meaningful control of the ones on her head, and had left those to Darla to deal with.

However, Tanis was barely even considering that as she propelled herself deeper and deeper into Europa's cool waters.

Granted, the water in the Chora Dive Tube was heated to a balmy twenty degrees, as opposed to the near-freezing water this close to the moon's ice-shell.

Anchored into the ice above were massive illumination

panels that lit the surrounding water for kilometers, as well as the dive tube, which contained hundreds of people—of all shapes and sizes—as well as small, personal submarines.

Outside the tube, larger craft plied the depths, travelling to and from the surface city of Chora's Station, built atop the moon's crust.

The lift ride down through twenty kilometers of ice had felt slightly unnerving, as she considered that much mass over her head, but as soon as she slipped into the water, Tanis couldn't help but feel perfectly at home.

The tube's first stop was Chora's Height, a platform city just four kilometers below the surface. The lights of the city filtered up through the water like it was a hazy dream, and Tanis wondered what it would be like to live in such a place, with what must feel like endless darkness below.

She knew there were deeper cities, but it was not possible to swim to such depths without a pressure suit. Even though Europa's gravitational pull was only one eighth that of Earth's, the pressure at the distant, hundred-kilometer-deep ocean's floor would crush all but the strongest hulls.

A group of women swam by, all with long tails and monofins. Most had an obvious mid-tail bend as they swam, belying legs and knee-joints beneath, but a few swam with their tails swishing sinuously side to side, meaning they'd had their legs altered—or removed.

Despite the fact that some of the women were still bipedal underneath, none wore any breathing apparatuses, as gills were evident on the sides of their necks.

Two turned and stared at Tanis as they drifted past, their wide eyes and smiles showing that they were clearly impressed with her level of modification. She waved, and the pair gave bubbly laughs before returning the gesture and swimming off to rejoin their friends.

Tanis did not have gills, thankfully; instead, her breathing apparatus was her skin, which, for all intents and purposes, functioned as a single lung, drawing oxygen out of the water all around her. In addition, once she'd hit the water, her lungs had filled with a gel to keep them from compressing under the pressure.

Doctor Mauve had said that Tanis had received one of the best diveskins money could buy. It was able to easily supply her with all her oxygen needs, and handle depths of to twenty kilometers.

The doctor had gone on to explain that her human eyes were still present beneath her large, ocular coverings, but it had been necessary to remove her ears and nose—as well as fill in her sinuses—to avoid pressure-related issues.

Though it appeared that Tanis had a thin, lipless mouth, it was really a facsimile that no longer connected to her throat, using vibrating chords to provide speech, both in air and under water.

<*You seem to be enjoying this a lot,*> Darla commented. <*Which relieves me to no end.*>

<*Were you worried I'd hate it and want to tear you out of my head?*>

<*Well…maybe nothing that extreme, but yeah. I'm riding along with your synthetic nervous system a bit, too. I'll admit, for all my talk of getting a body, I've never really seriously considered it until now. The thought of just walking around in two dimensions seems so limiting after this.*>

<*I don't disagree,*> Tanis replied as she twisted and twirled through the water.

As she flitted back and forth through the dive tube, starting to master fine motor control, she noticed a pod of bottlenose dolphins swimming along outside it. She spotted seven cows and five pups, plus one bull trailing behind to keep an eye on the pod.

She could see their mouths opening, signaling that they were talking, but she couldn't hear them. She attempted to sign to them, but couldn't manage any of the correct shapes with her four tentacles.

<I wish I could go out there, I'd love to talk to them. The vocalization system Doctor Mauve made is preloaded with their full sound library.>

<You sure?> Darla asked with a laugh. *<Dolphins eat squids.>*

<Seriously, Darla, I'm a bit bigger than a regular squid. Tentacle to tentacle, I'm almost five meters. Plus I look like I'm made of metal.>

<I see two orcas out there. I bet they'd be up for a good silver squid snack.>

<Most of these dolphins have the Link. Those orcas are probably noted philosophers or something.>

Tanis managed to make the hello symbol with her tentacles, and the dolphins responded with the standard up-side swipe in response.

She was about to signal goodbye and move back into the main flow of the dive tube when someone named 'Gerald' reached out to her.

<I've not seen you before, Silversquid, are you new to these waters?>

Beyond the dive tube's clear wall, the bull had swum closer, his eyes peering at her curiously.

<I am, yes. Though I've explored the depths of the Melas Chasma with your cousins on Mars before.>

Gerald gave a bob of his head. *<I should like to test the sounds of Mars's waters someday—thick though they may be.>*

<The echoes from the deep there are like the world thunder here on Europa,> Tanis replied. *<Though their timbre is not so sonorous.>*

<You're well versed for someone new to these waters,> Gerald replied. *<You do your people proud. Though with your shimmering skin and many tails, I do wonder if you really are a human. If I could smell you, I'd know.>*

<At present, there is not much human flesh in me—though this form is not my preference, it does feel delightful in your light and airy waters. I'm curious, Gerald, what brings you to Chora? I had been led to believe that your people find the dive tubes and areas beneath the surface cities to be too loud.>

Gerald's lips turned down in the half-grimace of his kind. *<You are not wrong about that, but the pups wanted to see the tube, as well as the surface. They dove through the air until they could barely swim.>*

Tanis always found it amusing how dolphins insisted on referring to moving through the air as 'diving'.

<Then you should definitely bring your pod to Mars someday. They could sail through the air for days on end, in open oceans with only the sky above and deep blue below.>

A chuckle from Gerald came across the Link. *<They were wary of the hole in the ice, even though the surface was far, far above. I don't know how well they'd handle sky.>*

<Have you seen it?>

<Once. I went to Venus many, many years ago. Though their waters were warm and soothing, I disliked the gravity. Here in

Europa, we fly through the deep.>

<*I understand,*> Tanis said while twirling around, nearly entangling herself in her arm-tentacles.

<*Silly Silversquid, you should not have changed your body so much. Though you do look beautiful, those orcas may mistake you for a snack.*>

<*Told you,*> Darla said privately.

<*Are they native?*> Tanis asked.

Gerald laughed again, his mouth jerking open in a wide smile. <*Oh, Silversquid, I'm playing with you. Sylanus and Jusari would never eat a human. You have too much metal in you.*> He gave her a slow wink and laughed again.

<*You never did say what actually brought you to the surface,*> Tanis prompted.

The bull's eyes narrowed, and his smile disappeared. <*I was lodging a protest in person with the SSF office of treaty enforcement. That the oligarch has been able to build his noxious den of foolishness in the midst of our home is unconscionable.*>

<*I was surprised as well to hear that there was a casino in the Sargasso Mountains,*> Tanis replied. <*It is to my shame that such is my destination.*>

Gerald jerked away from the far side of the dive tube, a suspicious eye narrowed and glaring. <*And at first it seemed as though you were a friend of the sea, Silversquid. I have found you on the sky-dweller's networks. You are quite wealthy; you are going there to hand over your money to the oligarch in exchange for time in his house of decadence.*>

For reasons she couldn't quite identify, Tanis didn't want Gerald to think ill of her.

<*I have a sand-covered reason for going, and I did not expect to travel there until even a few days ago. It saddens me that I must*

spend time in a place that intrudes on your home's peace and beauty.>

The dolphin continued to eye her for a few long moments before responding. *<I wish you calm waters, Silversquid, but I hope you are not surrounding me with your pod's breath. You are well-spoken for a skydweller, even one who takes on absurd shapes for pleasure.>*

<Calm waters and may the rossby waves carry you home safely,> Tanis said in farewell.

Gerald gave her another of his judging gazes, and then nodded. *<May they not uproot your pod.>*

With that, he swam off, rushing to catch up to his cows and pups, who had moved on ahead.

<You must have researched the Europan dolphins a lot to know their localized salutations,> Darla said as Tanis moved back into the main downward stream, the city below now only a kilometer away.

<It didn't take that long,> she replied as she increased the rotation of her tail-tentacles and picked up speed. *<I'm sure you could tell that most of their phrases are the same as on Mars—albeit with slight twists. Though I've never spoken to one over the Link before; it's always been through signs or their vocalizations. They sound less…foreign this way.>*

<Makes sense. He was using your language, not the other way around.>

<I suppose. I do wonder if it's because his people have the Link, and the dolphins of Mars are natural.>

<Well, natural-ish.>

<You know what I mean.>

* * * * *

Though the city of Chora's Height was well within the safe pressure range for even unmodified humans, its many sections were still covered in domes that—while not removing water—lowered the pressure to make it less onerous to decompress from.

Unlike the deep cities, which were entirely aired, platform cities like Chora's Height saw many of their buildings without air at all, the humans who lived within modified to spend their entire lives in water.

From what Tanis had learned, many ocean dwellers in Europa never even ventured to the surface. As much as she tried to appreciate the idea, the thought of spending an entire life never seeing the stars was one that saddened her. The light of the galaxy was a beautiful thing, one she didn't think she could ever do without.

She swam quickly through the streets of Chora's Height, making her way toward the tube that would lead her to the Sargasso Mountains and the Blue Lagoon casino.

<*Has the IC done anything suspicious?*> Tanis asked as she tucked in behind a personal submarine, allowing herself to be pulled along in its wake.

<*No, she's been spending her time at the casino—I'm still miffed that she got in as a patron. Anyway, she's gambling and going to shows.*>

<*Modded?*> Tanis asked.

<*No, she's using a breathing apparatus and a monofin tail. Nothing altered, from what I can see.*>

Tanis couldn't help a laugh, which came out of her vocalizers as a squeaky warble. <*Once again, the machine looks more human than me.*>

<Well, your IC's biological camouflage is quite good, but it certainly wouldn't stand up to mod surgery. She'd be outed for sure.>

<Well, she got in as a guest when you couldn't work around the wait list, so whoever is pulling her strings is well connected. I imagine they could have modded her however they wished.>

<True…you know what doesn't make sense, though?> Darla asked.

<There are so many things I could answer with. Which are you thinking of?>

<Well, I get why our nefarious puppetmaster used 'you' on Ceres. You were convenient, and 'Commander Richards' had a starship with a loyal crew, which is a definite asset.>

<Right.>

<Well,> Darla paused a moment. *<No offense, but you're not the best operative to hit the oligarch here in Europa.>*

<I should hope not. I think whoever is behind this has limited resources.>

<Or….> Darla drew out the word.

<Or?>

<Or they have it in for you personally.>

Tanis mentally berated herself for never considering that *she* could be as much the target as the oligarch. *<OK, so if someone does want to ruin my life because they don't like me, who could that be? I've—Deering? Could it be her?>*

<I don't know…they shuffled her off to the ass-end of nowhere…though I still haven't heard where that is. I don't know if she could have orchestrated this.>

<Unless she pulled some strings with people loyal to her in the division before she shipped out,> Tanis suggested.

<True, could be that….>

<Or?>

<Or it's the separatists in the Scattered Worlds Space Force. They've been trying to play Terra and Jove against one another for some time. You're probably also on their shit-list.>

If Tanis could have groaned aloud, she would have. Instead, she had to satisfy herself with a warbling burble sound.

<Great, so I'm either an unwitting pawn who is convenient, I'm on a corrupt admiral's shit-list and she's pulling strings to ruin me and my reputation, or the SWSF is doing roughly the same thing.>

<At least you're popular. No one even ***knows*** *that I'm in your head.>*

<Funny,> Tanis chuckled. *<OK, Darla, we need to make a grab for the IC at the first opportunity. I don't care if it runs the risk of alerting its controller, things can't keep going on like this. I need answers>*

<I agree. I think the risk is worth it. I can fully breach the IC's core, and when…well, if…it makes contact, there will be no way we can miss it.>

Tanis was surprised that Darla hadn't put up a fight on that front, but she wasn't about to question her acquiescence.

<OK, that's our plan, then.>

<Such as it is.>

THE BLUE LAGOON

STELLAR DATE: 03.05.4084 (Adjusted Years)
LOCATION: Sargasso Transport Tube, Europa
REGION: Jupiter, Jovian Combine, OuterSol

It was impossible not to gape at the Sargasso Mountains as they began to take shape in the distance.

While the Europan Ocean was a hundred kilometers deep, its floor was crisscrossed by massive ridges that stretched nearly to the ice crust, formed by the moon twisting for billions of years in Jupiter's gravity.

One of the tallest series of ridge series in Europa, the Sargasso Mountains were home to much of the ocean life beneath the ice. Brilliant lights were anchored to the crust above, and luminous globes hung down in the water, illuminating the deep valleys.

Despite what Tanis had told Kaebel about Vesta and Mars having the highest mountains, the fact was that the highest peaks in the Sol System were really beneath Europa's surface. From the ocean floor to the tops of the Sargasso Mountains, one could stack nearly five Olympus Monses.

Most people discounted Europa's sub-ocean ridges because they were technically within the planet, beneath its crust. The argument was made that there were taller formations within Earth's magma, and they were not counted as mountains.

But as Tanis approached the Sargasso Mountains, with their waving kelp forests growing up their slopes and schools of fish swimming throughout, she couldn't help but think they looked like surface mountains with flocks of birds flying overhead.

These definitely count as mountains.

Here and there, human settlements dotted the slopes, many of them grandfathered into the preserve centuries before, while others were cooperative facilities run by humans and the dolphins who lived in the mountains.

<*And here I thought Chora's Height was beautiful,*> Darla whispered as they drifted over the peaks, watching the sea life dart about.

<*Still is, just a different kind of beautiful.*>

When the Blue Lagoon finally came into view—situated in a shallow valley between two peaks—Tanis had to admit that the casino *did* look nice…if not for the fact that it shouldn't be there. Knowing that the peoples of the Sargasso Mountains hated the place ruined its appeal.

Why are people such jerks? Tanis wondered rhetorically.

She knew the answer. It stemmed from what people prioritized above all else: the individual, the family unit, or the state.

She wasn't sure where she fell in that spectrum—likely leaning toward the state, though she'd do anything for her crew, even if it meant going against the state.

People like Oligarch Alden clearly valued themselves above all others—which was especially disconcerting, since he oversaw the largest human population in existence.

An exit in the travel-tube appeared ahead, and Tanis twisted to the right, angling for the side-passage. The current moved her further over, keeping her from a collision with the divider, and then, with a sudden rush, she was out and into the warm waters over the mountaintops.

The first thing that Tanis noticed were the smells.

While the water in the tube had been pleasant, here it was *alive*. Her skin's olfactory senses fed the aromas into her mind; the forests below, sprinkled with the scents of the life that lived within them, hints of minerals in the water, and the microbes that flourished all around.

A bale of giant turtles swam by, several of their number turning their heads to gaze at the strange creature that was Tanis as she swam past them.

It occurred to her that, given her many-tentacled, gleaming, silver body, she would seem far stranger to the sea life around her than they to her.

I'm almost like an alien, come down from space.... Beautiful and very likely dangerous.

A shadow drifted up from the depths, and Tanis watched a blue whale—with a calf tucked in close— swim by. She'd never seen any living thing so large, and the sight left her awestruck for nearly a full minute.

<You do have to get down there on time,> Darla reminded her. *<You have a meeting with Damon, the staff manager, in thirty minutes.>*

<Right...yeah.... It's just amazing that something that large can get enough air from the water through gills alone.>

Darla highlighted a light blue ring above them. *<Those are air domes. The larger sea animals that can't absorb oxygen through their skin or enough through their gills take extra breaths there. Looks like that's where mama and her baby are going.>*

<Ahhh...makes sense,> Tanis said as she shook herself free of all the woolgathering and picked up the pace, falling in with a few people and personal submarines that were also headed to the casino.

What became apparent very quickly was that the majority of the visitors to the Blue Lagoon were modded for the trip. Mer-people were the most common, and some individuals looked almost normal, barring gills and webbed hands—which may or may not have been clothing or cosmetic mods. Others were more extreme, such as one…something…that appeared to be a diaphanous jellyfish.

The Link ident flagged the drifting blob as 'Sam' and indicated that it was a human citizen of the Jovian Combine, but Tanis couldn't even spot anything as small as a human brain in the mass.

<That has to be aided by some sort of clever holotech,> she commented to Darla. *<But even with my vision, I can't tell where the costume or mods end and the holo begins.>*

<Beats me. At first I thought it was a remote-controlled avatar, and someone was controlling it via full-immersion sim, but it's registered as a 'primary personage'.>

<Huh,> was all Tanis could think of to say.

<That about sums it up. Oh, you have to use the employee entrance. It's over there on the left.>

Tanis looked over the sprawling complex ahead. It was over two kilometers across, with towers, large buildings, and what appeared to be darker patches of water that were partially obscured by all the bubbles rising off the surrounding structures.

The employee entrance was around a small hillock and then down a gully, at the bottom of the shallow valley the casino rested in.

When Tanis reached the bottom, she could see a number of personal submarines attached to tethers near a shrouded set of doors.

An Auth & Auth arch stood in front of the door, flanked by a pair of guards who were rather unorthodox, which was to say that they looked like mako sharks with human-ish arms.

They floated next to the security arch, their mouths partially open, showing rows of teeth as they regarded Tanis.

*<That sort of thing **cannot** comfort the patrons,>* Darla commented.

<I guess they like the authentic experience.>

When she reached the arch, she paused—careful not to let her tentacles drift too closely to the guards' mouths—waiting until one of them gave a jerk of its head and waved her through.

<You know...> Darla commented as they passed under the arch and through the doors. *<Those weren't human.>*

<I saw that. Clever automatons, I suppose.>

*<I don't think so. I think those **were** sharks.>*

Tanis gave a low whistle of appreciation, *<Now **that** is dedication to authenticity. Though I bet that's part of what bothers the dolphins.>*

<Did you spot the group of orcas patrolling just outside the casino's property line?> Darla asked.

<Missed them. I guess they're not keen on a bunch of modded sharks in their back yard.>

<Seems not.>

Once inside, Tanis accessed the casino's public network and pulled up its layout, swimming down the halls to where she was to meet the staff manager.

She passed a wide variety of people in the back passages.

Everything from perfectly normal humans wearing divesuits and small rebreathers, to a wide array of merpeople, tentacled octohumans, and a few more sharks—which she steered clear of. She even saw a group that appeared to be otters with human-ish heads.

<*A real life choice to work here,*> Tanis said to Darla as they passed a man who had the spiny body of a pufferfish.

<*Says the Silversquid.*>

<*I'm a short-timer,*> Tanis laughed in response as they came to an office area.

A woman in a divesuit floated behind an array of holodisplays, speaking without looking up from her work as Tanis arrived.

<*Third door on the right. Damon is waiting for you.*>

<*Thanks,*> Tanis replied, getting no response from the woman.

She carefully drifted down the hall, noticing that most of the people in this section were unmodified. When she came to his door, she saw that Damon, however, was not.

The man's body was nearly jet black, and well-muscled from the waist up. From there down, he had long tentacles lined with octopus's suction cups. Gold and silver bands adorned both his tentacles and his arms, and a silver crown rested on his head.

"Oh ho!" he roared when his eyes settled upon Tanis, the sounds transmitting through the water in a low rumble that she was able to translate into audible sound. "Well, well, Claire. When I sent up the enhancements, and Doctor Mauve said you'd agreed, I couldn't believe it. But here you are…silver and beautiful."

"Why thank you," Tanis replied, dipping her head. "The

dolphins I met on the way down gave me the name 'Silversquid'."

Damon's expression darkened, and he muttered, "Dolphins." Then he shrugged and smiled—not a nice smile—and added, "Still, they have good names for things. I like 'Silversquid'. I'm changing your Blue Lagoon ident; that's who you'll be from here on out."

The words carried a note of finality, and Tanis found herself not liking the…man's…tone, nor the way he spoke in general. There was nothing in his words that was 'wrong'; it was the way that he said them, as though Tanis was a possession of his, something he would use as he saw fit.

She supposed that, in a way, he'd already proven that such was the case. He had sent up a rather extensive list of body modifications, and—so far as he knew—she had accepted them without complaint.

The realization made her feel like a layer of oil had settled on her skin. As Claire, she was all about trying new things and simply having a good time. Tanis had adopted that feeling, and to her, the form she wore was an extension of that free spirit.

Damon made it all feel dirty, like she had turned herself into a thing that was only good for one purpose: to be possessed and controlled.

However, she didn't feel an urge to tear herself free of the mods that were her body because he made them feel wrong. Rather, she contemplated what it would be like to slap Damon in the face with thirty-two tentacles. Repeatedly.

<Dude's a dick,> Darla commented a moment later,

summing up Tanis's thoughts.

<Yup. I'm more than motivated to find my doppelganger, get what I need from her mind, and get out of here.>

Tanis realized that Damon was staring at her, waiting for a response, and she nodded. "That's fine. I'm OK with being Silversquid."

The man's eyes narrowed. "OK, Silversquid. We need to get something straight. You may be a wealthy woman who owns a bunch of shit out in the Oort cloud, but you signed a contract. A very clear and ironclad contract. For the next year, you belong to the Blue Lagoon. So when I say that you *are* the Silversquid, I mean that I expect you to behave like an automaton squidwoman at all times. Do I make myself clear?"

Tanis quickly considered a scenario where she simply subdued Damon—with extreme prejudice—before searching the casino for her doppelganger.

<Don't even go there,> Darla cautioned. *<The network here makes the TSF's at Vesta look like swiss cheese. I haven't come close to getting past their staff-only subnets. If you take out Damon, you'll have sharks biting off your tentacles in five minutes.>*

Tanis nearly laughed aloud. *<I don't think I* ***ever*** *expected to hear someone say that—especially not about me.>*

<Deep breaths. Answer the man.>

"Of course," Tanis said without any emotion in her voice. "I am Silversquid."

A wide—and very unpleasant—smile broke out across Damon's face. "Excellent. Now. You're rather unique—both because we don't have anything in the tanks that looks like you, and also because you're a rich woman who wants to be an autonomous object." His smile grew toothy as he spoke. "Yes, I know what your type is into. You feel guilty about your wealth, so you want be punished for it—not so much that you're willing to give it up, though. So after everyone has gotten a good look at you, I'm going to have you perform. A friend of mine sent me logs of you low-*g* dancing on the *Whiskey Tango*, so I know you have the moves. Can you sing, as well?"

Tanis nodded. "I took lessons as a child, I'm passable."

Damon gave her a calculating look. "Well, I imagine Doctor Mauve gave you an underwater vocal system; it can simply be programmed to hit the right notes. We can give it the words, too."

"I speak orca." Tanis offered the information in an entirely bland tone, keeping to the character that Damon demanded she play.

"Oh? Well now, that will be fantastic. I'll send that information to Saniyah, our production manager. Expect her to pass you the song you'll be singing, and the dance moves. Ever since I told her what you'd agreed to, she's been quite excited to put together a routine for you.

<Well this sucks. Being put on display in 'the tank' and then giving a performance act won't give me a lot of mobility.>

<We'll think of something,> Darla said. *<Don't forget, you still have a ship overhead. If you call them, they'll cut a hole through the ice if they have to.>*

Tanis held back a grimace—not that her current facial structure could make one. *<One of my goals is to complete this mission without my crew seeing me like this—or at least knowing it's me.>*

"Well? What are you floating there for?" Damon

demanded. "Get moving, you stupid sea cow. Arnold is waiting for you at the tube to Tank 11."

He waved his hand in dismissal, and Tanis floated out of the room, reminding herself that *Claire* would probably enjoy all this—even if the man's treatment of her had *Tanis* at the edge of a blind rage.

As she drifted past the woman at the front desk, Tanis forced herself to accept that her current situation required the same mindset as the final night on the *Whiskey Tango,* when she had been fetching drinks.

She had to lose herself in the role and really *become* a gleaming, silver automaton squid. It was either that, or swim back into Damon's office and see how many tentacles she could wrap around his neck before his head popped off.

When she reached the entrance to Tank 11, a man in a divesuit was patiently waiting for her, an appreciative smile on his face.

<Wow, Silversquid, they weren't lying when they said you move through the water like a dream. I bet you're the most beautiful thing under the ice.>

<Thank you,> Tanis replied tonelessly, wondering if the man's casual manner was a test to see if she'd break character.

<Oh yeah, that's right, Damon said you want to always be in your 'persona'. I guess that's cool, but if you need to be regular for a bit, I won't tell. There's one mermaid who I let sneak into my room in the dry section every now and then. She just drinks coffee and stuffs her face with popcorn for an hour or two. Says it helps ground her.>

Tanis hadn't considered what life must be like for some of the people who worked in the casino because they had no other choice. They all seemed calm and serene in the hallways, but she supposed, with an overlord like Damon, they probably watched their behavior even in the staff areas.

<*What is required of me?*> she asked, trying to move the conversation along—still not certain it wasn't a test.

Arnold only shook his head before gesturing at the long, dark tube. <*Tank 11 sits overtop the main poker hall. Most of the time, you'll stay in the tubes, but every now and then, they open up, and you'll need to go swim around the patrons for a while. I'll warn you, though, they like to touch, and if you flinch...well, it makes Damon behave like even more of an ass than normal.*>

Tanis decided that if Arnold was playing her, he was doing an amazing job. The disdain with which he said Damon's name was almost palpable.

She nodded, floating serenely in front of the long tunnel.

<*You're a funny one, Silversquid. OK, go on in. At some point, Saniyah will call you out to get ready for your show, but for now, just enjoy yourself.*>

He gestured to the tunnel, and Tanis swam in, passing quickly through the shaft to emerge over a shadowy grotto.

The space was over a hundred meters across, and filled with poker tables nestled amongst stone outcroppings, coral reefs and carefully manicured kelp gardens. The floor of the room wasn't flat, instead rising and falling, with some of the tables near the roof, and others down in dark crevasses.

It was early in the day, and only a few dozen people were playing at the tables, each run by a merman or merwoman. A few merguards with gleaming tridents—not the exterior shark security, Tanis was glad to see—drifted over the area.

The waitstaff consisted of people who looked far more like seahorses than humans, but the patrons were a mix of individuals with very little in the way of mods—though their divesuits were quite garish—all the way to a person who made a very convincing hermit crab.

A dozen 'card up your shell' jokes ran through Tanis's mind as she began to swim through the transparent tubes that ran around the upper half of the grotto.

There were a few others in the tubes, one of the pufferfish people—gender entirely indeterminate—and a woman who was the long, eel version of a merwoman.

They gave her nods and smiles when they passed by, but none of them spoke, keeping to their characters.

She was glad for both Bella's meditation and Claire's penchant for remaining perfectly still, as they helped Tanis deal with what she found to be an utterly boring series of loops over the room.

Three hours later, she was wondering what would happen if she were to just float back down the tunnel and go searching for the Infiltrator Chameleon, when Saniyah reached out to her.

<Shoot, I forgot to send you your song, Silversquid! I'm passing it now. I need you to get to Tank 3 and rehearse before the amphitheater opens up in thirty minutes!>

<On my way,> Tanis replied dutifully, and picked up the pace, swimming through the tubes to the exit. She was nearly there, when a glance below revealed her doppelganger entering the room beneath her. At the same time, sections of the tubes slid open—the signal that the few performers drifting overhead were to swim down and mingle with the crowd.

The pufferfish person was the first one out, moving to the center of the room, where a crowd of patrons quickly gathered, running their hands along its spines.

<Well look at that, he's pumping out psychotropic drugs,> Tanis commented to Darla. *<I can smell them from here.>*

<Quite the crowd pleaser,> Darla replied. *<As is Miss Eel. She's already half-wrapped around that guy over there.>*

<I'm making my move,> Tanis announced suddenly, veering off and out of the tunnels, angling toward the table where the Infiltrator Chameleon sat.

Tanis caught a reflection of herself in a polished quartz pillar—sinuous, silver, many-tentacled—and then looked down at the Infiltrator Chameleon. Anger flared up in her that the IC had been 'Tanis' for weeks now, while *she* had been forced to go through a variety of covers until she'd become a *thing* all because of the machine below her.

She picked up speed, reaching the table where the IC and two other players sat with cards in hand. Letting out a low orca moan in greeting, Tanis began to swim around the table, brushing her tentacles across all the players, and depositing breach nano on the Infiltrator Chameleon.

<I'll need fifteen—make that twenty-five seconds,> Darla announced.

<What's the holdup?> Tanis asked as she wrapped a limb around one of the player's chests.

<I don't think this is the same IC that attacked you on Mars 1. Yeah, different model. Aha! I have a way in, get ready to grab her.>

Tanis moved behind her doppelganger, who turned to look up at her with mildly curious eyes—Tanis's eyes. Then the IC twitched and blinked rapidly.

<Do it.>

Tanis sank down, wrapping her tentacles around…herself.

She pushed the utter strangeness of what she was doing out of her mind and lifted the IC from her seat, pulling her back up to the tubes overhead.

The merman running the table looked up in surprise, but the Tanis-doppelganger only waved happily at the man, who shrugged and turned back to the remaining two players—one of which looked as though he wished *he'd* been chosen by the gleaming, many-tentacled creature now pulling 'Tanis' away.

<This feels icky,> Tanis muttered as she wrapped her tail-tentacles around the IC and pulled her through the tunnels and down the shaft leading to the back halls.

<She's not you, she's a machine.> Darla's voice was soothing.

<Tell that to my brain.>

<I am.>

Tanis almost laughed aloud as she turned the corner into the rear hall, glad to see that the always talkative Arnold was not in sight.

The map showed a storage room nearby, and she headed for it, praying that no one would look too closely and see that there was a person concealed within her appendages.

At the door, she passed another passel of nano into the locking mechanism and breached it quickly, darting into the interior while the passage behind was empty.

<OK…> Darla muttered. *<I have control of the IC's exterior, but her core locked down tight. It's going to take me a bit to work around its defenses and dig through its logs for clues.>*

Tanis nodded absently as she looked around the room,

which was filled with everything from chairs to chunks of grotto wall. Spotting a stack of wall pieces piled haphazardly, Tanis swam over and tucked the IC inside.

<Do you need a physical connection?>

<No, I've got her Link properly locked down. I can do this remotely, though I'm curious why it's a different IC.>

<Hopefully that will be in the logs.>

Tanis set down a piece of grotto wall over where the IC lay, pleased with herself for managing to move the cumbersome object with her tentacles.

Darla seemed to notice, too. *<You're surprisingly good at managing twenty limbs. Far better than I'd've expected.>*

<Still can't move the ones on my head for the life of me,> Tanis replied as she swam back to the door.

She attempted to use the nano she'd left in the corridor to check for any passersby, but the currents in the hall had swept them away.

<Silversquid!> Saniyah's voice thundered in her head before she'd opened the door. *<Where* **are** *you? We need to get going!>*

<Nearly there,> Tanis replied. *<I was interacting with patrons.>*

<Fine, fine, just get your tails in gear.>

Tanis sent an affirmative and then opened the door only to find Arnold staring at her.

<Silversquid?> he asked with a look of puzzlement on his face. *<I got an alert that this door had malfunctioned.>*

<I, uh…it wasn't closed all the way,> Tanis said.

<Oh…the real woman in silver skin comes to the surface,> Arnold said with a conspiratorial smile. *<I knew there was more to you than a cold automaton.>*

<It's harder than I thought it would be.> Tanis put all the emotion she could into her voice, unable as she was to make much in the way of facial expressions.

<You're not the first newbie to say that.> Arnold placed a hand on her shoulder. *<Look, here are the tokens to get into the air-breathers' living quarters and my room. You can hide in there later for a bit if you need to.>*

Tanis couldn't tell if the man was coming on to her, or if he was genuinely concerned for her well-being. While she wanted to believe he was sincere, the idea of someone behaving altruistically in a place like the Blue Lagoon was an incongruous one.

Takes all kinds, she thought, deciding to take him at face value—with a side-helping of skepticism—and accepted his access codes.

<Thanks,> she said softly. *<I'd better go, Saniyah is going to string me up by my tentacles if I don't get to Tank 3.>*

<Off with you, then,> Arnold said, lifting his hand from her shoulder.

Tanis half-expected him to slap her on her rear—such as it was—but he didn't, only giving her a smile and a nod before he firmly closed the door to the storage room.

GOING UNDER

STELLAR DATE: 03.03.4084 (Adjusted Years)
LOCATION: TSS *Kirby Jones*, orbiting Europa
REGION: Jupiter, Jovian Combine, OuterSol

Two days earlier…

"Smythe," Connie said as she walked onto the *Kirby Jones*'s bridge. "I need to get down to Europa. The H3 cap is leaking again. I've shunted the fuel off to a secondary tank, but we can't top off until it's fixed."

The lieutenant turned to look at her. "You heard what the commander said; no one is to leave the ship 'til she gets back."

Connie held in a frustrated sigh. So far, only she and Cassie knew that the 'Tanis' who had been aboard the *Kirby Jones* for the last week was not the genuine article.

While the faux commander had behaved well enough through the trip, she'd gotten a bit odd at the end, insisting that the *Jones* remain in a parking orbit around Europa—not docked with a station—and then ordering everyone to stay aboard.

It wasn't that the any of them were likely to run off, anyway, which made the order sit strangely with the rest of the crew.

"Can't you just order a new cap and have it couriered up?" Smythe asked.

"Already did that." Connie shook her head. "The new one leaks too; turns out the whole housing is a bit torqued. Fixing it will require changing the whole tank."

"Shit," Smythe muttered. "The commander'll be pissed.

That'll put us in refit for a day."

Connie nodded. "Yeah, but I checked the housing. It's solid—just a few microfractures that I can repair with nanowelds. I took detailed scans of the cap-mount, and if I go down to the local manufacturer, I can get them to make a custom one."

"Why not just send them the specs?"

"No can do," Connie replied. "Since it's a custom order, they want me down there to verify that it meets my requirements. They said otherwise they're not going to make a 'broken part'."

"Dammit," Smythe rubbed his hands against his face. "How long will it take?"

"Day, tops. I'm going to take Cassie, too. We can grab a few other things and fix up some of the stuff Tanis was pestering me about on the way over here."

Smythe sighed. "She's been in a hell of a mood, hasn't she?"

"Yeah, I think she's just pissed that she barely got to see Peter."

Smythe ran his hands through his hair. "These orders have been weird. First we go to Ceres for no real reason, and now Tanis is down on Europa doing stars know what."

"Yeah, but she's not due up for three days. Let me do this, and then we'll be fueled up and ready for the patrol before she gets back."

"I—" Smythe said, then stopped himself.

"Remember what I said about you and Jeannie?"

"Yeah, that you'd make sure Tanis didn't find out."

Connie nodded. "Right, well, the amount of effort I put into that is dependent on you scratching my back a bit, too."

Smythe groaned. "*Fine.*"

"Excellent!" Connie said brightly as she turned and walked off the bridge. *<Cassie? We're good to go.>*

<I was going anyway. I'm already in the skiff. Get here on the double.>

*****

A day later, the pair were in one of Chora Station's underwater departure bays checking over their private, two-person submarine.

Connie looked down at herself as she waited for Cassie to get into the small craft, casually brushing a hand against the divesuit she wore. It was covered in coral, textured in such a way that it looked as though her entire body was constructed of the calcium carbonate, but that was just a clever illusion.

Luckily, unlike natural coral, it was soft to the touch.

"So let me get this straight," Connie said. "Our fake Tanis has gone to this Blue Lagoon casino, where you believe Oligarch Alden is, with the intent of finishing the job?"

"Hole in one," Cassie said as she settled into the small submarine. "We have to head in there and get the lay of the land. Then we'll ferret out whoever is behind this."

"Shouldn't we just stop the bad Tanis before she kills Alden?"

Cassie glanced at Connie. "I went over this already. Stopping one attack doesn't keep Alden safe. We need to find out who is pulling the strings."

"Well, if we keep someone from killing him, that seems to be the sort of thing that ups his safety quotient."

"Only temporarily. Besides, that's what his security is for."

Connie could tell that there would be no convincing Cassie to change her mind. "Well, then why did you bring me along?"

The spy shot Connie a dark look. "So that I can feed you to the sharks they use for security down there during my getaway."

"Jeez, no need to get pissy about it," Connie muttered.

"Sorry." Cassie pursed her lips in frustration as the submarine dropped into the water, and they began to drift down the dive tube that led to the city of Chora's Height. "I'm just annoyed that this whole business is still so opaque. I brought you along because you're quick on your feet. We have no AI with us, so I need backup."

"OK, then as backup, what plan am I backing up?"

"Well, I'd like to see if we can find the real Tanis when we get down there—stars, I wish I'd set her up with emergency data dead drops before she went off to see Peter. She and Darla are *ridiculously* good at hiding. Granted, it would be easier if they were using a cover I made."

"Why would they not be using one of your covers, anyway?" Connie wondered.

Cassie shook her head. "Pretty sure it's due to Darla's penchant for playing dress-up. She kept pressuring me to make a rich heiress type of cover for Tanis, but those aren't as effective as one would think. Plus they're expensive, and the Division does not like paying for the sorts of places those people like to stay."

"Places like this casino?"

"Yes. Places exactly like this casino."

Connie pulled up the public information on the Blue Lagoon to review a second time, once again impressed by its amenities. Not to mention awed by how much staying at the place cost.

"I can see why the Division doesn't want to foot this bill. Plus side, if Tanis is masquerading as a wealthy woman, her cover should be able to get into a place like this."

"Maybe. I had to pull some serious strings for us to get in. Even with Darla, I'm not sure how Tanis will manage."

"Well, Evil-Tanis obviously got in."

Cassie laughed. "Evil-Tanis, eh?"

"Seemed to fit."

"Yeah, well, it's us versus Evil-Tanis in one of the most secure casinos in the Sol System."

"Good thing you brought me along."

TORFIN AND AMEONIA

STELLAR DATE: 03.05.4084 (Adjusted Years)
LOCATION: Blue Lagoon Casino, Sargasso Mountains, Europa
REGION: Jupiter, Jovian Combine, OuterSol

<How long do you think it's going to take you to breach the IC's core?> Tanis asked Darla as she followed the directions to Tank 3.

<Umm…this thing has some pretty tight protocols. It will also wipe itself if I brute-force my way in.>

<So you're saying I'm singing for my supper tonight, eh?>

<Yeah. I hate giving estimates on things like this, but I'd say that unless I stumble upon something, it's going to take me a few hours.>

Tanis nodded silently as she reached the entrance to Tank 3. She swam up through a long tube and found herself entering an amphitheater-like space through an opening in the stage.

The room was shaped like a large conch shell, and the rows of seats all had holodisplays in front of them. She guessed it was so that the viewers could gamble in a variety of ways while watching the show.

A seashell-encrusted woman drifted nearby, glaring at Tanis as she emerged.

"About time," she said, vocalizing the same way Damon had. "This parlor opens up in fifteen minutes, so we need to get you singing! Did you get the song?"

Tanis nodded. "I received it."

"Good. Let's hear it."

The expression on Saniyah's face led Tanis to believe that the woman did not have high hopes, so she decided that she'd knock the glittery woman off her high horse.

Pushing herself off the amphitheater's stage, she splayed her arm and tail-tentacles wide, calmed her mind, and brought up the song's lyrics over her vision.

When she had told Damon that she'd taken singing lessons as a child, she wasn't lying. Her father had constantly pushed her to do *something* that would lead her to greatness—specifically, *his* idea of greatness.

One of the avenues he'd pushed her down was performance arts. Though she'd had some skill, standing on a stage had never been something she enjoyed, and she'd fought against her father until he finally acquiesced.

By that time, she'd been singing for several years, so her instructor was rather displeased when one of her star pupils completely dropped out.

Summoning all her memories of the skill she'd once had, Tanis began the song with a single, sonorous, orca-like moan. The sound filled the amphitheater, reverberating along the ridged, conch-shell-like walls.

She paused, letting the note fall away to silence, and then launched into the song.

It was a tale of two orcas named Torfin and Ameonia. They lived long ago in the seas of Earth, near a place called Aleutia. It was a beautiful sea, and fish were plentiful. The pair met one night under the starlight and fell deeply in love, forming a life-bond. When they announced it, their pod celebrated their union with days of frolicking in the waves and hunting the largest tuna the ocean provided.

On the fifth day, after a particularly long hunt, Torfin

realized that Ameonia was nowhere to be found. He searched for her until he found one of the other bulls in the pod, bloodied and bruised. The injured dolphin told of a great monster that had risen up out of a dark crevasse and taken Ameonia.

Torfin rallied the bulls of his pod, telling them to prepare for battle. Then he sent the cows of his pod to other groups to tell them of the beast that had taken Ameonia. When they were assembled, he led fifty bulls to the crevasse, and they scouted it carefully, searching for the monster below.

There were no bubbles coming from the dark depths, and he feared for Ameonia's life. He resolved that, if she had perished, her loss would not go unanswered.

After much searching, the bulls left two watchers below while the rest surfaced for fresh air. When they dove back beneath the waves, Torfin and his bulls saw the very face of horror itself crawling out of the gash in the ocean floor.

It was an octopus so large that Torfin believed it would dwarf even the greatest of the blue mothers. Its coarse hide had allowed it to blend in with the crevasse's deep shadows, but now it shifted from grey to red in color as its massive tentacles lashed out at the two orcas left behind to keep watch.

One dodged the attack, but the other was bowled over, slamming into a rock outcropping and going limp.

"It is the Worldrender!" one of the bulls called out in fear, but Torfin would not be cowed by the beast, so great was his love for Ameonia.

He directed two of his bulls to bring the injured orca to

the surface, while the rest dove toward the great beast, dodging its ponderous limbs and biting where they could.

One of the bulls was caught by the beast's tentacles, which began to crush the fighter, but the rest of the bulls rallied and tore at the monster's flesh until it let go.

Another bull began to convulse, and Torfin's fear that the beast was venomous came true.

Torfin knew that unless he did something decisive, he would lose many of his kin that day. Confronting the danger head-on, he dove through the monster's writhing limbs and tore at its face, biting one of the fiend's eyes.

The taste was sickening, but he ignored the bile that spilled out and went for the other eye as well.

Emboldened by his attack, the rest of the bulls pressed forward and, though the writhing beast fought mightily, the orcas were triumphant, ultimately tearing off the Worldrender's very limbs, and leaving the carcass to drain its lifeblood out for the creatures of the deep to feast upon.

Torfin cared nothing for the beast's remains or why it had attacked the pod. He dove into the crevasse, searching for Ameonia. He raced along the sandy bottom, praying to the earth thunder that he would find her, when suddenly he did.

Ameonia's beautiful white and black body had been pushed under an overhang, not moving, but seemingly unscarred. Calling for help, Torfin began to push at her tail, trying futilely to get his love free.

Hearing his call, a dozen bulls came down to his aid, and together they nudged Ameonia's body clear of the overhang and lifted it to the surface. Holding her blowhole above water, they nudged at her chest, trying to make her breathe.

But Ameonia did not draw breath, and one by one, the other bulls drifted away in sorrow until only Torfin remained, holding his love's blowhole above the waves.

All through the night and into the next day, he held her aloft. The bulls and cows of his pod came to him, trying to tell him to let her body fall and return to the sea, but Torfin could not bear the thought and continued his vigil, though his strength was greatly flagging.

As the night grew deep around him, a luminous presence appeared in the waters below.

At first, Torfin thought he was seeing things, but the light grew and grew, until an eye larger than Torfin himself surfaced next to him.

It was the greatest and oldest of the blue mothers, Usuria.

Torfin quaked with fear, knowing she could swallow him whole should she choose.

But she only said, "Why do you still hold Ameonia above the waters, Torfin?"

Torfin did not know how to express the great sadness that was balled up within himself, and he could only shake his head, even as Ameonia began to slip from his grasp.

"Let her fall, Torfin," Usuria urged. "Let her fall so she can swim forever in the oceans above."

"I cannot leave her," he finally managed to say.

"Your love is strong," the blue mother whispered with a thunderous rumble that vibrated through the waters. "But Ameonia is already in the sky ocean. She is that light you see rising above the sea even now. She waits for you."

The sorrow that cut through Torfin's body was so great that he could only keen his pain, the very nature of anguish pouring from his throat.

Pods far and wide heard his cry and wondered at what great tragedy had befallen one of their kind.

"I have a gift I can offer you," Usuria continued to whisper, her voice pushing away the clouds on the western horizon. "You have killed the Worldrender, he who sought to break apart the seabed so the deep fires would swallow all life. Because of this, I can give you a gift. I can send you to be with Ameonia now. You can swim together in the sky ocean.

Torfin could only muster one word: "Please."

Across the northern ocean, pods looked into the sky and saw a blinding light flash through the heavens and stop next to one of the evening stars.

Rumors spread of the battle of Torfin's pod against the Worldrender, and the blue mothers told of his reward, reminding the pods that through his great love and bravery, Torfin saved the oceans from the Worldrender. They told the pods to remember his sacrifice whenever they saw the two intertwined stars.

As the final notes of Tanis's song died out, she turned to see Saniyah sitting on the floor of the amphitheater, mouth agape.

"Wow, Silversquid. That was…that was amazing," the shell-encrusted woman finally said.

"Then it was sufficient for the audience?" Tanis asked, forcibly suppressing the emotion that the song had brought out in her.

Saniyah nodded vigorously. "Oh hell yeah. Who would have thought a silly debutante like you could sing like that—even if that is one of Mauve's voxboxes…it was masterful."

"I'm pleased to hear it," Tanis replied.

Five minutes later, the amphitheater's doors opened, and the crowds that had heard of this new performer began to file in. Tanis stayed below the stage, waiting for Saniyah to give her the signal to begin her performance.

When it came, she rose up once more, spreading her limbs, and began to sing of Torfin and Ameonia's love for one another. Looking across the crowd, she saw that the oligarch himself was down in the front row, his face turned up toward her in rapture.

She'd just reached the part of the story where the bulls attacked the Worldrender, when something caught her attention. A quick glance to the right revealed a series of small darts, slicing through the water toward the stage.

Ducking out of the way, Tanis avoided almost all of them, except two that hit her arm-tentacles.

<Crap! They're loaded with breach nano!>

Tanis scoured the seats as her song faltered, looking for the attacker, when more darts streaked toward her. She avoided them deftly, only to realize that she wasn't the only target. Some were streaking toward the oligarch as well.

His guards had already moved in to shield him, their light armor deflecting the incoming shots with ease.

Tanis was moving toward the tunnel's cover—which was a little difficult, with two of her right arms spasming from the breach nano—when she saw one of the oligarch's guards holding a fistful of the darts, driving them toward the Jovian leader.

Demetri!

She surged forward toward the man, stretching out a limb to wrap around his arm, but it was too late.

He plunged the darts into Oligarch Alden's side, just as Tanis got a tentacle around his wrist. Demetri's eyes grew wide and he turned to Tanis, gesturing wildly at her.

Half a dozen of the oligarch's guards turned to Tanis and began firing flechette pistols at her as their leader fell, spasming and clutching at his chest.

Twisting away, she made for the hole in the stage, her artificial limbs registering impacts, but luckily, her frantic swimming managed to keep her body and head obscured.

Once in the tunnel, she picked up speed, reaching the staff halls as a general alert began to sound. She heard a voice calmly telling all patrons that there was a security issue, but to remain in place.

<I guess you were right about whoever wanted to assassinate Alden having someone on the inside,> Darla said, as Tanis rushed through the back halls, pushing through a group of mermaids and knocking a divesuited man into a wall. *<What's our plan, now?>*

Though her voice wasn't panicked, Tanis could tell that the AI was more than a little worried.

<We have to get out of here.> Her voice carried far more worry than the AI's. *<But I don't know* ***where*** *to go. How close are you to breaching the IC?>*

<Nearly there, but I'm being distracted by the breach nano that is making its way up those two tentacles.>

Tanis didn't hesitate. She pushed one of her 'arms' into

a pocket tucked in where her tentacles emerged and drew out her lightwand. She set it for underwater use—causing it to fire a charged gas out of the hilt as the blade activated—and then deftly cut off the two twitching tentacles.

<Problem solved,> she replied, turning the lightwand off and noting that the underwater use had bled away almost a quarter of the weapon's electron reserve. *<Now what?>*

<You need to stay in range of their network so I can keep working on the IC. No leaving the casino.>

Tanis pulled up the Blue Lagoon's map and saw that the entrance to the air-breathers' quarters was nearby. She swam as quickly as she could toward the moon pool that led up into the aired-up section.

Not even slowing, she surged out of the water, landing heavily on the floor of the room above.

There were three people in the room, all pulling on their divesuits; one cried out in surprise at Tanis's explosive entrance, tripping over an air tank as he backpedaled.

"What the hell?" another yelled.

"There's shooting down there!" Tanis exclaimed, surprised that her identity hadn't been plastered all over the staff or public network yet.

"Seriously?" the man asked as he pulled himself back to his feet. "No way I'm going down there, then. Damon can kiss my ass."

"We have to at least take a look," one of the women said.

While the trio argued, Tanis slithered as best she could across the room and out into the hall beyond. Pulling herself along the deck by grasping anything within reach, she made her way to Arnold's room and opened the door, flopping inside on her back.

"Shit! Who are you?" a woman's voice asked, and Tanis twisted around to see a mermaid laying on the sofa with a large bowl of popcorn on her lap and a mug of coffee in her hands.

<*Wow…he really wasn't lying,*> Darla commented.

"There's shooting out there," Tanis gasped, doing her best to sound terrified.

"Up here?" the mermaid asked, her eyes growing round.

"No…down in the water," Tanis spoke as breathlessly as her voxbox could manage while shaking her head. "At least, I didn't see any, once I got up here. Arnold gave me his codes, said I could come here if I needed to…."

The mermaid nodded. "He's good like that. Gets that we're still people. Shit gets weird under Europa's ice—easy to forget what's real."

Tanis wiggled a few of her tentacles in the air. "I can't imagine why. I'm Claire, by the way."

"I know," the mermaid said with a wink. "I saw something on the net about you being a rich woman who gets off on being a servant automaton. I didn't buy it, though. Smelled like Damon's usual bullshit. Oh, I'm Alice. Welcome to Wonderland—little joke of mine."

Tanis laughed more at Alice's quirky smile and the fact that there were popcorn bits all over her seashell breast coverings than the joke. "That seems to apply. Out in the ocean, things are juuust normal enough, but this place seems to have tipped over into the surreal."

"Not sure where you're from, but even out in the oceans, it can get pretty weird. I think that's why the dolphins like to keep us at arm's length." Alice finished off the statement by shoving a fistful of popcorn into her mouth.

"I wonder how long it'll take for them to secure things out there?" Tanis asked

"Hmmph." Alice shrugged, giving an exaggerated 'I don't know' expression as she munched on her food.

<Tanis! I'm in!>

<The IC?>

<No…the casino's water bill records. ***Yes*** *the IC. Trying to sort through everything in here—oh, look at that!>*

Darla sent over a data packet, and Tanis opened it up. It contained communication log entries noting messages that had been passed back and forth to the Infiltrator Chameleon.

<OK, so this IC wasn't the one on Mars 1 or Ceres. Wonder why they switched them out?>

<Maybe they couldn't get the other one off Ceres in time to head for Europa?> Darla mused. *<Damn, but look at that token on the inbound orders.>*

Tanis pulled up the long string of characters, wondering what she was looking for. *<Oh shit! I know where I've seen that!>*

<Me too. Some of the messages that the SWSF officers were using back on Vesta used these tokens. I never traced it to anyone doing anything illegal, so they were never flagged for monitoring, but I always suspected that these were Colonel Urdon's.>

Tanis shook her head, sending her top tentacles

flopping around her face. <*And he got off free and clear, too. Said he had no idea what the rest of his people and Deering had been up to.*>

<*Well, I guess he was in on it—and has it in for you, as well.*>

A sickening feeling settled in the pit of Tanis's stomach. <*Was the other IC the one shooting the darts?*>

Darla didn't respond for a second. <*Not sure, I don't have access to all the feeds yet, but so far, the only person they're looking for is you. Well…Claire-you, not Tanis-you.*>

Just as Darla said those words, Alice squealed in surprise, spraying bits of popcorn everywhere. "You! You're the murderer! You killed Oligarch Alden!"

<*Annnnd they've put Claire's ID on the public nets. Do you realize that you've burned three really good covers in one mission?*>

Alice began screaming, and Tanis snapped a tentacle across the room, wrapping it around her neck and squeezing gently.

"Go to sleep, Alice."

The mermaid thrashed on the sofa for a moment, and then passed out. A quick check showed that she was breathing easily, and her bloodflow was fine.

<*Time to get moving,*> Tanis said, pulling open the room's door only to find a pink-haired woman standing in the entrance.

"You really know how to cock shit up," the woman growled, then ducked as Tanis slashed at her with a tentacle.

"Tanis!" another voice called out, and if Tanis's jaw could have dropped, it would.

"Connie?"

TURNING THE TABLES

STELLAR DATE: 03.04.4084 (Adjusted Years)
LOCATION: Blue Lagoon Casino, Sargasso Mountains, Europa
REGION: Jupiter, Jovian Combine, OuterSol

One day earlier...

After checking in to their room, Connie followed Cassie out through the halls toward one of the air-breather restaurants.

As Connie watched the woman ahead of her—who still had bright pink hair and now wore a bright pink divesuit to match—she worried that she'd do something to mess up her new cover.

Cassie—who was now 'Amari', which made her/him at least four covers deep now—had set Connie up with a cover named 'Prudence'. Both of them only had slight modifications made to their faces for their new identities, though Connie was certain that Cassie had also plumped her hips even further.

At least it sure seems like it from back here.

They reached the aired-up section of the casino by passing through a moon pool, which was a hole in the overhead that led up to a pressurized section of the casino.

Once through, Connie happily removed her breathing apparatus and let it hang from her neck.

"You know, despite all this, I'm actually *starved,*" she said to Cassie as they joined in with the crowds heading to the restaurants.

"Same here. I sure hope you like seafood."

"Think they have swordfish?" Connie asked, her

mouth watering.

"I'll fall on one if they don't," Cassie said with a laugh as she looked over her shoulder. *<Shit! Don't look back, but Tanis is right behind you.>*

<Shit!> Connie said, suddenly feeling like she was in the academy, and the commandant was following on her heels. *<You sure?>*

<Well, it's Evil-Tanis, not the real one.>

<Oh…well that's less exciting, she—>

<I think we should hack her.>

Connie almost tripped as they stopped at the maître d's podium. *<Pardon? If that was an option, why didn't we do that back on the* Jones*?>*

<I've been over this, Connie. I didn't want to do anything that would ruin our chances of catching whoever is behind this. If they checked her over and found evidence of a hack, it would have clued them in that we're in the know.>

<Why does it not ruin our chances now?>

<Because,> Cassie said while informing the man at the podium that they were a party of two. *<This is where shit's going to go down. I'll bet that whoever is orchestrating this whole thing is onsite, and if we nab their assassin, they'll do something drastic so that they can still achieve their goal.>*

<Or they'll bail,> Connie countered.

<Yeah, that could happen, but I'm betting that after missing their opportunity on Ceres, and especially considering how much of a PITA it is to get into a place like this, they're not going to back down.>

<So what's the plan?>

* * * * *

Twenty-three minutes later, Connie was just cutting into her swordfish when Evil-Tanis rose from her chair and walked toward the restrooms.

Cassie's plan seemed light on details, but Connie trusted that the spy knew what she…he…whatever was doing. Due to the fact that many of the casino's guests were highly modified, the restrooms were individual rooms that gave people enough privacy to deal with whatever elaborate getups they were in.

Cassie believed—and Connie hoped—that this would make a great location to take out the Infiltrator Chameleon.

<*Wish me luck,*> Cassie said as she rose and followed after Evil-Tanis.

Connie nodded before replying aloud, "Let me know if you need any help peeling yourself out of that pink monstrosity."

Cassie laughed aloud. "I'll send an S.O.S. if I need you for that…or anything else." She added a wink before sashaying away.

Connie looked down at her swordfish. *Well, I better take care of you before things go off the rails.*

She'd only taken her first bite when Cassie called out, <*Holy* ***crap*** *she fights just like Tanis. I need a hand!*>

Trying to act as though nothing was the matter, Connie rose and made her way down the hall toward the room where Cassie was fighting 'Tanis'. Other than a few muted thuds, no sounds were coming from it, and she drew in a deep breath before opening the door.

I've seen Tanis fight. I really don't want to be on the

receiving end—even if it is a bot.

Screwing up her courage, Connie opened the door and slipped inside, only to narrowly avoid an elbow to the head from Evil-Tanis. She ducked to the side and saw that Cassie had a cut on her lip and was holding her hands up defensively, while Tanis threw a punch at her before attempting to kick Connie.

"Crap!" Connie blurted out, barely avoiding the attack—mostly because Cassie jumped in front and took the punch in the chest, grunting as she pushed off the wall and slammed into the Infiltrator Chameleon, knocking her to the ground.

They struggled in a rather undignified fashion up against the san, while Connie stood in muted shock, wondering what she should do.

"The breach kit!" Cassie said, jerking her chin toward a small hard-Link plug that was laying on the floor.

"Right!" She knelt down and tried to get a hand on the IC's hard-Link port behind her ear, taking a knee to the head in the process. Her shoulder slammed into the san, and she nearly lost the breach kit down the drain, but managed to maintain her grasp and slotted it into the IC's hard-Link port.

The bot continued to thrash, knocking Cassie free, and then slammed a right hook into Connie's jaw. The blow stunned Connie, and she worried that the breach kit hadn't seated correctly until the machine suddenly froze.

"Faaaawk," Cassie whispered, touching her forehead where a deep cut was bleeding profusely. "That bitch is hardcore."

Connie rose on shaky legs. "So, what now?"

"I'm setting up a privacy shield so no one will realize there are three people in here."

"Good call," Connie said breathlessly, wishing her limbs would stop feeling so wobbly.

Cassie rose and looked her over. "OK, privacy shield is up. You're not bleeding, so clean up and get back out to the table. I'll—"

As Cassie spoke, the door clicked open a hair, and they heard a voice on the other side saying, "OK, guys, I get it. It's risky business, being here in my casino, but can I at least shit in peace?"

A muttered response came back, and then none other than Oligarch Alden stepped into the room.

TEETH

STELLAR DATE: 03.05.4084 (Adjusted Years)
LOCATION: Blue Lagoon Casino, Sargasso Mountains, Europa
REGION: Jupiter, Jovian Combine, OuterSol

"Hold up," Tanis said, raising a hand in the air. "Are you telling me that you stumbled onto the *perfect* opportunity to take out the Infiltrator Chameleon, and then the damn oligarch walks into the same san?"

Harm, who she was still having trouble reconciling as Cassie—or Amari, depending on which level of cover one was thinking of at the time—nodded. "Yeah, I couldn't have planned it that well if I'd tried. I—"

"I hate you," Tanis muttered.

"Why?"

"Because I've been traipsing about the Sol System for weeks trying to get to the bottom of this, I nearly die in the Insi Ring ruins, spend half my time with wheels on my feet, and then get turned into the Silversquid, and you…you just walk into a fucking san, and everything falls into your lap?"

Connie snorted. " 'Silversquid'. I like it."

"Well, we did travel to all the same places you did," Cassie said. "Wasn't all peaches. I spent a week putting panels and deck plate in place on the *Kirby Jones* while you were sipping drinks by the pool on a cruiseliner."

Another snort came from Connie. "You *supervised* while Liam and Seamus spent a week putting the ship back together."

"You get my point, though; we've all been working

this thing from our angles. That is, 'til you went and screwed it up, Tanis. What were you thinking?"

"What are you talking about?" she asked. "Someone was shooting at the oligarch, and *me*!"

Harm-Cassie-Amari nodded. "Yeah, that was whoever we were trying to flush out. Would have been handy to know you were the Silversquid…or that you can sing that well. Seems like you were doing just fine down here."

"But our poor IC isn't, Tanis," Connie added. "You jammed a bunch of darts into it before we could get a bead on the shooter."

Tanis shook her head, trying to keep her tentacle-hair from flopping around. "*I* didn't. That was Demetri. I was trying to stop him."

"Demetri who works for Alden?" Harm asked, and Tanis nodded.

"Yeah, he seemed fishy to me back when I met him on Ceres. I suspected that Alden's team would have a turncoat in it—though Darla didn't—"

<Hey…I never said that. I agreed that it was possible.>

"You were suspicious of my suspicion."

<Yeah…which seems totally reasonable.>

"Wait," Tanis's gaze slid from Connie to Cassie. "So if Demetri killed the first Infiltrator Chameleon and not the oligarch, where's the real Alden?"

The two exchanged a sheepish look, then Connie spoke up.

"Uhhh…the orcas have him as their prisoner."

"What?"

"Easy, Tanis," Cassie said in a calming voice. "We were trying to get him offsite to a sub I'd called down, when we almost ran into a shark patrol. Which is nuts…who uses augmented sharks for security? One fried control chip, and everyone in this place is chum."

"You were saying?" Tanis prompted.

"Well…we managed to avoid the sharks, but had to leave the casino grounds to get clear. That's when we ran into one of the dolphin protest groups. They spotted who we had right away, and were…"

"Incensed," Connie supplied.

"Yeah, in a nutshell. Some of them were ready to kill him, but luckily, these two orcas showed up and managed to calm the bottlenose dolphins down."

"And this all happened right out in the open?" Tanis asked skeptically.

"No, we were skulking down one of the gullies at the bottom of the valley. We were almost free and clear when they found us, too."

"OK, so let me get this straight," Tanis said, glancing over at Alice the mermaid, who had let out a moan in her sleep. "You nabbed Alden, replaced him with my reprogrammed doppelganger IC, then whisked him off in the hopes that whoever was behind this would show their hand?"

"Pretty much," Cassie said.

"But because they hate *me* so much, they sent in a second IC to do the job, but I grabbed that one, and so they just went ahead with the hit themselves?"

Cassie slapped her knee. "So *that's* what happened to the second one. We were looking for it in the amphitheater when the attack happened. Problem is…now we don't know who was doing this."

A smile grew on Tanis's lips. "Well, that second IC was only operating down here for a day. And it was getting its orders directly from someone we all know. My money is on him being the one who took the shot at Alden."

"Oh?" Cassie's eyes grew wide. "Do tell!"

"Colonel Urdon of the SWSF."

* * * * *

Once Tanis had shared all the evidence they had on Urdon, Cassie sat back on her heels. "OK, Tanis. We need to do two things. One is grab that IC you stuffed in that storage closet, and the other is get you the hell out of here. We're not equipped to hunt down Demetri and Urdon right now. We get the evidence to safety and get them later."

"Weird that they haven't called off the hunt for you, yet," Connie said. "Alden's people have to realize that it was an Infiltrator Chameleon that died in the amphitheater."

"Yeah," Tanis nodded. "But the real Alden is missing, and I ran off. That's mighty suspicious. Also, they have the whole place on lockdown, how are we getting out?"

"Well, Connie and I aren't wanted," Cassie said. "So we'll go get the IC. Since no one is suspecting 'Tanis', we should be able to get it out without too much trouble.

<*Except for the part where Colonel Urdon—wherever he is—and Demetri will both have an eye out for one of their chameleons,*> Darla added.

Cassie tapped her chin and nodded. "You're right. In fact, what I *should* do is make the IC masquerade as

Connie.... Walk it and all its logs out to our submarine."

"What about me?" Connie asked. "If the IC is 'me', how do *I* get out of here?"

Cassie glanced at Tanis and then at Alice, who was still passed out on the couch with popcorn strewn around her. "Give me a second, I'll think of something."

Just then, the door opened, and Arnold rushed in.

"Alice? You OK? This lockdown is—hey, what are you all doing in here?"

* * * * *

<Harm really wanted to figure out how to work Alice into some sort of disguise, didn't he?> Darla asked as Tanis and Connie crept down the passageway.

<Seemed like it. I think he was just hoping that her tail was cosmetic, but with Arnold's 'help' we got squared away,> Tanis replied. *<I feel a bit bad for him. Maybe we can make it up to him and Alice later.>*

Darla let out a long laugh in Tanis's mind. *<You're the most conscientious spy ever. You feel bad for Kaebel, Sawyer, Alice, and now Arnold. What about that dickhead you laid out with your rollers on the* Whiskey Tango*?>*

<No, he can suck it.>

<This all sounds fascinating, but can we hurry up? Swimming in this thing is hard!> Connie said from where she wiggled along next to Tanis.

In the end, the disguises they opted for were rather simple. Connie was wearing a mermaid's tail, her personal ident changed to that of Alice. Tanis's mass of tentacles were crammed into a monofin divesuit.

It was a bit lumpy here and there, but considering how half the people in the casino looked, a slightly lumpy divesuit didn't even begin to rate any special attention.

Over her head, she wore a helmet with a semi-opaque visor, and for the first time in weeks, anyone checking her ident on the Link would find that she was indeed Tanis Richards.

They'd debated her taking on Arnold's ident, but Tanis rather *wanted* Urdon and Demetri to come looking for her.

While she was relieved to be wearing her own name again—if not her own skin—the one thing she was a little worried about was the prospect that somehow her helmet would come off, and Silversquid would be linked to Tanis Richards.

That was the sort of thing that could never be scrubbed from the nets.

Even so, she squared her shoulders and swam down the submerged passageways that led toward the staff entrance with Connie at her side, as though she had every right to be there.

They had just turned a corner and were in sight of the exit when a voice called out from behind them.

"Alice! Where the hell do you think you're going?"

<*Who's that?*> Connie asked, as the pair slowed and turned.

<Dammit. That's Damon, king of assholes.>

Connie snorted, blowing bubbles around herself as she turned, careful to keep her hair over her face. <*He kinda looks like what comes out of one,*> she noted, then called out a reply, speaking through a voxbox that Arnold had supplied them with while 'helping' with their disguises.

"I'm going for a swim with my friend Tanis, here."

"We're in fucking lockdown, Alice," Damon snarled as he approached. "And I need you entertaining guests, not *entertaining* guests."

Tanis made a move to get between Connie and Damon, but the engineer swam forward.

<I've got this, Tanis. I get the feeling that this guy needs to be put in his place.>

<Sure, yeah, but that's not our goal right now. We just need to get out of here.>

"Look, Damon. I know you think you're something special, but do you know what we all call you behind your back?" Connie asked.

"What the hell are you talking about?" Damon demanded, surprise registering on his face at being backtalked by one of the staff.

Connie chuckled. "Well, I suppose that I spoke a bit out of turn. There's nothing that we *all* call you, because we can't decide between 'barnaclehead', 'whale diarrhea', or just 'shitstainsforbrains'. Honestly, I think all your octolegs are making up for something."

<That's a bit weak, Connie,> Darla interjected.

<I'm improvising.>

<Well, next time let me help you with your improv,> Darla replied. *<Snappy insults are kinda my thing.>*

Damon's mouth hung open, but once he recovered from his shock, he began sputtering with rage, bubbles floating from his mouth. Finally, he composed himself enough to shout, "You'll be scrubbing algae off the tanks with your tail for the rest of your life, Alice!" He stopped abruptly, and his eyes grew wide as he peered at Connie.

"Wait a second...you're not—"

Tanis couldn't help but smile as Connie punched Damon in the gills. Seven times. He'd gone limp, but Connie drew back a fist to hit him again.

<OK, Connie, you've defended everyone's honor, now let's go.>

"The pair turned and raced toward the door, knowing that the moment anyone saw Damon drifting in the hall, things would get hairy.

They reached the door and were passing under the Auth & Auth arch when someone behind them cried out, "What the *hell*?"

For a second, Tanis forgot to keep swimming, but then she saw the sharks turn toward them, baleful eyes focusing on the two people swimming by.

<*Halt!*> a voice said, and Darla laughed.

<Look at that, they do have an NSAI watching the exits. I guess that's better than just sharks.>

<But it'll send the sharks. Go!> Tanis said to Connie as she pushed the engineer ahead, glancing back at the toothy carnivores.

Shit! Those things are fast, she thought, as nature's favorite eating machines raced toward her and Connie.

Tanis knew that if she weren't stuffed into the divesuit, she could outswim the beasts, but that wasn't an option, especially with Connie struggling to maintain a good clip with her regular legs inside the mermaid's tail.

The stretch of seabed between them and the edge of the casino's property was devoid of any cover. Tanis gauged the distance that she and Connie still had to swim, and knew they wouldn't come close to making it—assuming the sharks would even stop at the property line.

As Connie swam on, Tanis slowed and turned, reaching into her divesuit to pull her lightwand free, grasping it clumsily in her gloved tentacle.

She knew that, in the water, the electrons would bleed off in under a minute, which meant she had to wait until the sharks were upon them to activate the weapon.

It didn't take long for the sleek makos to close, and seconds later, the blade was glowing brightly in the water as she slashed at the first beast.

The blow caught it in the side of the nose, cutting through to the bone, and the shark veered away just as the other one closed in, angling to take a bite of Tanis's monofin-encased 'legs'.

She jerked them out of the way just in time, slashing at the second shark and managing to cut its dorsal fin half off.

The first shark was already circling back around, its tail slashing through the water as it picked up speed. Tanis managed to cut its face again, nearly losing her arm in the process.

As the fight with the makos continued, the water began to turn red, obscuring her vision. The sharks became indistinct blobs, and Tanis was wondering what it was going to take to defeat them when one of the creatures came up from below. She twitched her 'legs' out of the way, but the beast managed to get its teeth around her arm, taking a sizeable chunk out of it.

Tanis was grateful that the limb was nothing more than tentacles stuffed into the divesuit, but her relief was short-lived as her lightwand flickered and shut off.

<*Tanis!*> Connie cried out from somewhere behind her.

<*Keep moving,*> Tanis sent back as she punched one of the sharks in a cut she'd made.

<*Incoming,*> Darla warned, and Tanis saw four more of the makos closing in. <*I'm trying to hack the staff submarines over there, see if I can smash them into the bastards.*>

Tanis didn't reply as she frantically scrambled backward, slapping her monofin at the first two attackers, desperate for some amount of cover.

Then, just as the other sharks arrived, a series of grey shapes shot past Tanis, and the water bloomed red with blood as a dozen shrouded forms thrashed in the underwater mist.

Tanis stared in wonder, eventually able to make out at least twenty bottlenose bulls, all swimming around their hated enemies, sharp teeth tearing the makos to shreds.

Even so, the casino's defenders were managing to hold their own, getting bites in on several of the dolphins. Tanis worried that the bulls were going to suffer losses, when a pair of orcas arrived, one biting the tail off a mako in its first pass.

Less than ten seconds later, the sharks were all dead.

<*Come,*> a voice said in Tanis's mind. <*We will get you to safety.*>

<*Gerald?*> Tanis asked as she recognized the speaker's ident, and then cursed at herself. *I'm Tanis, and Tanis does not know who Gerald is.*

A dolphin's wide smile and curious eye came within centimeters of her head, peering through her faceshield. <*Silversquid! What are you doing squished into that divesuit?*>

<*No time, and no one can know that I'm Silversquid.*>

The corner of Gerald's lips turned up in a curious smile, and he bobbed his head. <*Of course...Tanis...what a strange name you have. The ancient god of a great, seafaring nation. Our ancestors always liked the Carthaginians, you know.*>

<*That's great, Gerald, but we need to—*>

<*Go, yes. There are more of those vile creatures coming.*>

Tanis was suddenly surrounded by warm bodies that began to push her forward.

<*Connie, are you OK?*> Tanis called out.

<*OK? I'm fantastic! I'm riding a dolphin! Well...sorta, you get the idea.*>

The dolphins carried Tanis and Connie down the long valley, out of Link range from the casino, and then led them through a series of caves that seemed to go on forever. Eventually, they came out the other side of the ridge, and Tanis could see the lights of Chora's Height in the distance.

<*We lost them in the caves,*> Gerald said, as the group led Tanis and Connie at a much slower pace to a spherical structure nestled amidst tall strands of kelp.

Connie looked back, a worried expression on her face. <*I didn't know we were still being chased.*>

<*I can't tell you how much I appreciate this,*> Tanis said to the bull.

Gerald ducked his head. <*We would have done it for anyone. Even if you are a supporter of the oligarch, we would not leave you for those abominations to consume.*>

"*Wait!*" one of the orcas said in a keening bellow as they approached the spherical building—which Tanis saw bore the name 'Waystation 281'.

The orca who had spoken was circling Connie.

"You smell like the coral woman. Yes, you ***are*** *the coral woman. You brought us the oligarch."*

At that, the dolphins all began speaking at once, circling around the two women. She had trouble making out all the words, but they seemed happy.

<*Gerald,*> Tanis said. <*What's happening?*>

<*Oh, you probably haven't heard. Right before the sharks attacked you, the pod that has the oligarch announced that they were holding him hostage until the casino is removed.*>

If Tanis were able, she was certain she would have choked. <*Hostage?*>

<*Yes, they claim that he was found trespassing on ceremonial breeding grounds. They are places no human is allowed to enter. Under the original treaties forged over a thousand years ago, trespassing is even punishable by death.*>

<*Really?*> she asked aghast. <*I had no idea.*>

<*It's never been enforced,*> Gerald replied. <*It was to remind humans of how many of our kind have died at their hands, and that some things are sacred to us.*>

<*Will the orcas that have the oligarch actually follow through?*> Tanis asked as they reached the waystation, and her Link connected to Europa's public network once more.

<*I don't know.*> Gerald regarded her with somber eyes. <*Do you think they'll have to?*>

She shook her head. <*I doubt it. If the Jovians attack and kill your people, the Federation will come down on them like a meteor shower. I'd bet that the Blue Lagoon's days are numbered.*>

CLEANUP

STELLAR DATE: 03.06.4084 (Adjusted Years)
LOCATION: Chora's Height, Europa
REGION: Jupiter, Jovian Combine, OuterSol

Tanis sat across from Harm and Connie in an aired room deep within a secret Division 99 facility in the city of Chora's Height.

"So no sign of Colonel Urdon," Tanis said with a shake of her head. "I can't believe he got away twice!"

"Well," Harm said, still a pink-haired woman with hips the size of Tanis's and Connie's together…and then some. "He technically didn't 'get away' on Vesta. He wasn't under direct suspicion then."

<Sure, not 'direct',> Darla said sardonically. *<But I bet the Division sure would have liked to speak with him. A lot. With pointy objects in hand.>*

Harm laughed—a tittering, squeaky sound.

"Stars, Harm, you need to turn back into a guy. Girl doesn't suit you."

"What?" Connie slapped her palms on the table. "You know he was originally a guy? I couldn't get it out of him for the life of me!"

Tanis shrugged. "Sure, Connie. Think of it. 'Harm Ellis'. Harmellis. Harmless…. That's guy humor, if anything ever was."

"Shiiiiit," she muttered. "How did I miss that?"

Harm gave an innocent shrug, which actually managed to look rather convincing. "Or that's all part of my cover, to add in layers like that to trip you up."

Tanis shook her head. "No, you think you're far too clever and it shows. You're totally a guy, Harm."

"Unless I wanted you to think that, Tanis. The layers can go on forever."

"Nope." She shook her head. "I've got a nose for this sort of thing. You're totally a dude."

No one spoke for a few minutes, and then Connie glanced at Tanis. "OK, so now that that's settled, are you looking forward to getting topside and having that mad doctor turn you back into a real woman again?"

Tanis lifted a few tentacles in the air around herself. "You know? I'm kinda getting used to this. Think you can modify my captain's chair into a tank? Better yet, let's fill the whole bridge with water. It'll be like a big inertial dampener."

Connie raised a hand. "Don't make me slap you silly, Silversquid."

Tanis laughed and gave Connie as much of a smile as she could manage. "Yeah, I'm more than ready to just be Tanis again. If for no other reason than a burning desire to eat something with meat in it. It's been *weeks*."

"I bet you're pretty glad that pigs aren't sentient," Harm said with a wink.

Tanis let out a long sigh. "You have no idea."

*<They're **pretty** smart, Tanis.>*

"Darla…" Tanis began, then turned to Harm. "Actually, Harm, this is *your* fault. Why did you make all my covers vegetarian? And why did you make Claire so weird?"

Harm held up his hands defensively. "I only made Bella a Vegan. Sasha ate meat, and I didn't have anything to do with your 'Claire' cover."

"Darla!"

<Shit…I really wish I had legs right about now.>

"We'll talk about this later," Tanis growled at her AI. "Maybe when we finally get some shore leave."

"Back to Mars?" Connie asked. "Plus…the rest of us would really appreciate some time off, as well."

"Yeah," Tanis nodded. "Though I wouldn't mind taking a swim with Gerald and his pod before we go."

Harm cleared his—her—throat, causing both Tanis and Connie to turn to him.

"What?" Tanis asked, her voice carrying an almost threatening note.

"Well, there's still Urdon…and—"

<You'd better stop there, Harm,> Darla chuckled in their minds. *<Or you're gonna find out whether or not you can outrun Tanis's tentacles.>*

"Umm…yeah, maybe a little bit of shore leave is in order."

Connie snorted. "I've heard this tune before."

THE END

* * * * *

Although Tanis, Connie, and Harm all know that there are still subversive elements at work within the Scattered World's Space Force, they have no leads other than the missing Colonel Urdon.

What's more, there is still the strong likelihood that someone within Division 99 is working in concert with the Scattered Worlds.

Find out where Tanis and the crew of the Kirby Jones end up next in ***Tanis Richards: Blackest Night***.

THE BOOKS OF AEON 14

Keep up to date with what is releasing in Aeon 14 with the free Aeon 14 Reading Guide.

Origins of Destiny (The Age of Terra)
- Prequel: Storming the Norse Wind
- Book 1: Shore Leave (in Galactic Genesis until Sept 2018)
- Book 2: Masquerade (Summer 2018)
- Book 3: Blackest Night (Summer 2018)

The Intrepid Saga (The Age of Terra)
- Book 1: Outsystem
- Book 2: A Path in the Darkness
- Book 3: Building Victoria

- The Intrepid Saga Omnibus – *Also contains Destiny Lost, book 1 of the Orion War series*

- Destiny Rising – *Special Author's Extended Edition comprised of both Outsystem and A Path in the Darkness with over 100 pages of new content.*

The Orion War
- Book 1: Destiny Lost
- Book 2: New Canaan
- Book 3: Orion Rising
- Book 4: The Scipio Alliance
- Book 5: Attack on Thebes
- Book 6: War on a Thousand Fronts
- Book 7: Precipice of Darkness
- Book 8: Airtha Ascendancy (Nov 2018)
- Book 9: The Orion Front (2019)

- Book 10: Starfire (2019)
- Book 11: Race Across Time (2019)
- Book 12: Return to Sol (2019)

Tales of the Orion War
- Book 1: Set the Galaxy on Fire
- Book 2: Ignite the Stars
- Book 3: Burn the Galaxy to Ash (2018)

Perilous Alliance (Age of the Orion War – w/Chris J. Pike)
- Book 1: Close Proximity
- Book 2: Strike Vector
- Book 3: Collision Course
- Book 4: Impact Imminent
- Book 5: Critical Inertia (Sept 2018)

Rika's Marauders (Age of the Orion War)
- Prequel: Rika Mechanized
- Book 1: Rika Outcast
- Book 2: Rika Redeemed
- Book 3: Rika Triumphant
- Book 4: Rika Commander
- Book 5: Rika Infiltrator
- Book 6: Rika Unleashed (2018)
- Book 7: Rika Conqueror (2019)

Perseus Gate (Age of the Orion War)
Season 1: Orion Space
- Episode 1: The Gate at the Grey Wolf Star
- Episode 2: The World at the Edge of Space
- Episode 3: The Dance on the Moons of Serenity
- Episode 4: The Last Bastion of Star City
- Episode 5: The Toll Road Between the Stars
- Episode 6: The Final Stroll on Perseus's Arm

- Eps 1-3 Omnibus: The Trail Through the Stars
- Eps 4-6 Omnibus: The Path Amongst the Clouds

Season 2: Inner Stars
- Episode 1: A Meeting of Bodies and Minds
- Episode 3: A Deception and a Promise Kept
- Episode 3: A Surreptitious Rescue of Friends and Foes (2018)
- Episode 4: A Trial and the Tribulations (2018)
- Episode 5: A Deal and a True Story Told (2018)
- Episode 6: A New Empire and An Old Ally (2018)

Season 3: AI Empire
- Episode 1: Restitution and Recompense (2019)
- Five more episodes following...

The Warlord (Before the Age of the Orion War)
- Book 1: The Woman Without a World
- Book 2: The Woman Who Seized an Empire
- Book 3: The Woman Who Lost Everything

The Sentience Wars: Origins (Age of the Sentience Wars – w/James S. Aaron)
- Book 1: Lyssa's Dream
- Book 2: Lyssa's Run
- Book 3: Lyssa's Flight
- Book 4: Lyssa's Call
- Book 5: Lyssa's Flame

Legends of the Sentience Wars (Age of the Sentience Wars – w/James S. Aaron)
- Volume 1: The Proteus Bridge
- Volume 2: Vesta Burning (Fall 2018)

Enfield Genesis (Age of the Sentience Wars – w/Lisa Richman)

- Book 1: Alpha Centauri
- Book 2: Proxima Centauri
- Book 3: Tau Ceti (November 2018)
- Book 4: Epsilon Eridani (2019)

Hand's Assassin (Age of the Orion War – w/T.G. Ayer)
- Book 1: Death Dealer
- Book 2: Death Mark (Fall 2018)

Machete System Bounty Hunter (Age of the Orion War – w/Zen DiPietro)
- Book 1: Hired Gun
- Book 2: Gunning for Trouble
- Book 3: With Guns Blazing

Vexa Legacy (Age of the FTL Wars – w/Andrew Gates)
- Book 1: Seas of the Red Star

Building New Canaan (Age of the Orion War – w/J.J. Green)
- Book 1: Carthage
- Book 2: Tyre (2018)
- Book 3: Troy (2019)
- Book 4: Athens (2019)

Fennington Station Murder Mysteries (Age of the Orion War)
- Book 1: Whole Latte Death (w/Chris J. Pike)
- Book 2: Cocoa Crush (w/Chris J. Pike)

The Empire (Age of the Orion War)
- The Empress and the Ambassador (2018)
- Consort of the Scorpion Empress (2018)
- By the Empress's Command (2019)

The Sol Dissolution (The Age of Terra)

- Book 1: Venusian Uprising (2018)
- Book 2: Scattered Disk (2018)
- Book 3: Jovian Offensive (2019)
- Book 4: Fall of Terra (2019)

ABOUT THE AUTHOR

Michael Cooper likes to think of himself as a jack of all trades (and hopes to become master of a few). When not writing, he can be found writing software, working in his shop at his latest carpentry project, or likely reading a book.

He shares his home with a precocious young girl, his wonderful wife (who also writes), two cats, a never-ending list of things he would like to build, and ideas...

Find out what's coming next at www.aeon14.com

Made in the
USA
Columbia, SC